س

THE KNIGHT'S RIDDLE: WHAT WOMEN WANT MOST

A MERLIN MYSTERY

THE KNIGHT'S RIDDLE: WHAT WOMEN WANT MOST

JAY RUUD

FIVE STAR
A part of Gale, Cengage Learning

GALE
CENGAGE Learning·

Farmington Hills, Mich • San Francisco • New York • Waterville, Maine
Meriden, Conn • Mason, Ohio • Chicago

GALE
CENGAGE Learning

LIBRARY OF CONGRESS CATALOGING-IN-PUBLICATION DATA

Names: Ruud, Jay, author.
Title: The knight's riddle : what women want most / by Jay Ruud.
Description: First Edition. | Waterville, Maine : Five Star, a part of Gale, Cengage Learning, 2016. | Series: A Merlin mystery
Identifiers: LCCN 2016001558| ISBN 9781432832032 (hardback) | ISBN 1432832034 (hardcover) | ISBN 9781432831981 (ebook) | ISBN 1432831984 (ebook)
Subjects: LCSH: Merlin (Legendary character)—Fiction. | Guenevere, Queen (Legendary character)—Fiction. | Knights and knighthood—Great Britain—Fiction. | Great Britain—History—Medieval period, 1066–1485—Fiction.| BISAC: FICTION / Mystery & Detective / Historical. | FICTION / Mystery & Detective / General. | GSAFD: Mystery fiction. | Historical fiction.
Classification: LCC PS3618.U88 K57 2016 | DDC 813/.6—dc23
LC record available at http://lccn.loc.gov/2016001558

First Edition. First Printing: June 2016
Find us on Facebook– https://www.facebook.com/FiveStarCengage
Visit our website– http://www.gale.cengage.com/fivestar/
Contact Five Star™ Publishing at FiveStar@cengage.com

Printed in the United States of America
1 2 3 4 5 6 7 20 19 18 17 16

For Wesley and Samantha Jane

CAST OF CHARACTERS

Agravain of Orkney: Sir Agravain is a nephew of King Arthur, a brother of Gawain and Gareth. He is red-haired and fiery tempered, like his brother Gawain, but without Gawain's warm humanity. Agravain is a cold and bitter knight who has little good to say of anyone.

Anne: Lady Anne is the oldest and wisest of Queen Guinevere's ladies-in-waiting. She tends to take charge in the queen's absence, and the other ladies let her. She has fair hair and enjoys embroidery.

Arthur: King of Logres, holding sovereignty as well over Ireland, Scandinavia, Scotland, Wales, and Cornwall, Brittany, Normandy, and all of Gaul. And he is claimant to the emperor's throne in Rome. He is the son of Uther Pendragon and Ygraine, former Countess of Cornwall.

Baldwin: Squire to Sir Agravain, Baldwin is as surly and aloof as his master. He and Gildas have never been close.

Bertrand of Toledo: A Spanish Moor, converted to Christianity, serving as squire to Sir Palomides. Skilled at the hunt and at the harp, Bertrand acts as his master's jongleur, singing the troubadour-style lyrics that Sir Palomides composes.

Bess of Caerleon: Daughter of a carpenter in Caerleon, Bess is an ambitious young woman who works as a tavern maid and dreams of a better life.

Bleoberis: Sir Bleoberis is not known for any of his individual feats of arms, but is a reliable knight of the Round Table and a member of the group of knights that forms Sir Lancelot's usual entourage.

Brandiles: Sir Brandiles has been a member of the Round Table for many years, but has never distinguished himself. He is a close ally of Sir Lancelot, and his squire is Gildas's good friend Colgrevaunce.

Colgrevaunce: Colgrevaunce is squire to Sir Brandiles. He is tall and thin, and shows little promise of excelling in the skills of knighthood. He is a close friend of Gildas.

Dinadan: Sir Dinadan is Sir Tristram's closest companion. He is a skilled knight but better known for his sharp tongue than his prowess.

Elaine of Ireland: Lady-in-waiting to Queen Guinevere, Elaine is the daughter of a landed Irish lord and close kin to King Angwish of Ireland. She was betrothed to Sir Sagramore as a young girl.

Florent of Orkney: Eldest son of Sir Gawain, knighted by King Arthur early in this book. Florent is the knight accused of rape in the novel, and his innocence must be proved.

Gaheris of Orkney: Sir Gaheris is son of King Lot of Orkney and Queen Margause—whom he is known to have beheaded when he found her in bed with Sir Lamorak. Gaheris resembles his younger brother Sir Gareth in coloring, but not in temperament.

Gareth of Orkney: Knight of the Round Table and younger brother to Sir Gawain, Sir Gaheris, and Sir Agravain, and half-brother to Mordred. He is son of King Lot of Orkney and Margause, the daughter of Ygraine and Duke Gorlois of Cornwall and so Arthur's half-sister, which makes him King Arthur's nephew.

Gawain of Orkney: Sir Gawain is Arthur's nephew and heir apparent. He is the eldest son of King Lot of Orkney and Arthur's half-sister Margause, and the older brother of Sir

Gareth, Sir Gaheris, Sir Agravain, and Mordred. His son Florent becomes a knight in this book.

Gildas of Cornwall: Son of a Cornish armor-maker, squire to Sir Gareth, former page to Queen Guinevere. Gildas narrates the story and is Merlin's assistant in his investigations.

Guinevere: Queen of Logres, and married to King Arthur. Gildas was formerly a page in her household. She is the daughter of Leodegrance, king of Cameliard, an early ally of Arthur's. Her long-standing affair with Sir Lancelot, Arthur's chief knight, is a perilous secret in the court.

Hoel: Duke of Brittany, and Arthur's vassal and close ally from the beginning of his reign. He is the father of Lady Rosemounde.

Ironside: Sir Ironside, also known as the Red Knight of the Red Lands, is a powerful but discourteous knight who killed forty knights before Sir Gareth defeated him and made a name for himself. In compensation, Sir Ironside was forced to pledge fealty to Arthur, and became a knight of the Round Table.

Isolde: La Belle Isolde is the daughter of the king and queen of Ireland, and is queen of Cornwall, married to King Mark. She is the secret lover of Sir Tristram.

Isolde of the White Hands: Isolde of the White Hands is Sir Tristram's wife in Brittany. He married her essentially because she had the same name as his beloved, but he has never consummated the marriage.

Kay: Sir Kay is King Arthur's seneschal, which means he is in charge of the king's household. He was Arthur's foster-brother when they were boys, and Arthur promised Kay's father Sir Ector that there would always be a place for Kay in his court.

Lady of the Lake: Queen of Faerie, a being of great mystical power. She is responsible for giving the sword Excalibur to

King Arthur. She lives in an enchanted palace north of Camelot on a lake named for her.

Lamorak de Galis: Sir Lamorak is one of the three great knights of Arthur's table. He was the son of King Pelinore, who killed King Lot and thus began a feud with the house of Orkney. Sir Gaheris caught Sir Lamorak in bed with his mother Margause and let him escape, but Gawain, Gaheris, and Agravain killed Sir Lamorak later in ambush.

Lancelot: Sir Lancelot is the greatest knight of Arthur's table, and is the secret lover of Queen Guinevere. He is the son of King Ban of Benwick, and his close kinsmen—Sir Bors, Sir Hector, and Sir Lionel—form a powerful bloc of Round Table knights.

Lot: King Lot of Orkney was an enemy of Arthur's who would not accept the fifteen-year-old boy as king of Logres. With an alliance of other kings, he made war on Arthur to get him off the throne, but was ultimately defeated and killed. He was married to Arthur's half-sister Margause, and was the father of Gawain, Gaheris, Agravain, and Gareth.

Margause: Mother of Gawain and his brothers, Margause was the wife of King Lot of Orkney and was one of Arthur's half-sisters, daughter of his mother Ygraine and Duke Gorlois of Cornwall. Not known for her high moral standards, Margause was killed by her own son Sir Gaheris when he caught her in bed with Sir Lamorak.

Mark: Mark is King of Cornwall, married to La Belle Isolde. He is the uncle of Sir Tristram, who is his wife's lover.

Merlin: Arthur's chief adviser in his early days, Merlin helped Arthur solidify his realm, and win the war against King Lot and his allies and the war with Ireland. Rumored to have magical powers and to be able to see the future, Merlin is essentially just a more logical and scientific thinker than most of his contemporaries. His hopeless love for Nimue, the damsel of the lake, regularly sends him into fits of depression.

Mordred: Mordred is the youngest brother of Sir Gawain and Sir Gareth, the youngest child of Arthur's half-sister Margause. He is an unpleasant lad, likely to grow into an even more unpleasant man.

Morgan le Fay: Queen of Gore, wife of King Uriens and mother of Sir Ywain, Morgan is King Arthur's half-sister, the daughter of his mother Ygraine and Gorlois, Duke of Cornwall. Though she has a reputation as a troublemaker, Morgan is sometimes on good terms with her brother, and early in his reign was mistress of Camelot, before Arthur's marriage to Guinevere.

Nimue: Lady-in-waiting to the Lady of the Lake, Nimue lives in the Lady's mystical palace and never ages. Her beauty enchanted Merlin, who remains in love with her though she has definitively rejected him.

Palomides: Sir Palomides is a Moorish knight who has joined the Round Table and become a Christian. He is Sir Tristram's great rival for the love of Isolde, and is known as a composer of love poems. He is also fascinated by cooking with the spices of his native lands.

Robin Kempe: Captain of the King's Guard and of the Royal Archers, Robin spends a good deal of time on guard in the barbican of Camelot, when he isn't training his archers. One of Robin's favorite pastimes is goading Gildas of Cornwall, for whom he has a good deal of affection.

Roger: Roger is the chief cook of Camelot.

Rosemounde of Brittany: Lady Rosemounde is the sixteen-year-old lady-in-waiting to Queen Guinevere who is the object of Gildas's deepest affections. She is daughter of Duke Hoel of Brittany, and therefore is obligated to make a politically advantageous marriage.

Safer: Sir Safer, a Moorish knight, is brother to Sir Palomides and his closest companion and confidante.

Sagramore: Sir Sagramore is a nephew to the Emperor of Constantinople. He is second son of a duke, and so does not stand to inherit. He travels regularly between Camelot and Cornwall taking messages between Tristram and Isolde.

Thomas: Young sandy-haired squire to Sir Ywain, Thomas is one of Gildas of Cornwall's closer friends.

Tristram: Sir Tristram is nephew to King Mark of Cornwall, and in love with his uncle's queen, La Belle Isolde. He is married to Isolde of the White Hands, a noblewoman of Brittany. He is well known as one of the three greatest knights of the Round Table.

Vivien: Lady Vivien is one of Queen Guinevere's ladies-in-waiting. She is French by birth, has green eyes, and enjoys romances, poetry, and gossip.

Ywain: Sir Ywain, known as the "Knight of the Lion" because he often goes on adventures with his pet lion, is another nephew of King Arthur, the son of King Uriens and Morgan le Fay, Arthur's half-sister through his mother Ygraine. Sir Ywain is devoted to his cousins Sir Gawain and Sir Gareth.

CHAPTER ONE:
THE OTHER SHOE DROPS

She stumbled into the throne room, barefoot and bare-legged, dressed only in a light brown linen smock that was torn away from her body along her shoulders, forcing her to hold it in place with her left arm for decency's sake. The smock was caked with mud in the back, and in front was spattered with blood from her knees down. Her long dark hair flared out from her head like tangled branches, and as if to underscore the similarity several dead leaves clung to it like lonely, frightened children. Her dirt-smudged face was blank and dazed, her brown eyes glassy and unseeing.

The press of the crowd parted for her as she made her way forward, to the high dais on which the greatest king in Christendom sat in an elaborately carved, gilded throne. On this love-day, when anyone in the kingdom of Logres could bring before the king legal questions to decide, Arthur had opted to wear his heavy, ceremonial crown—silver encrusted with rubies and a huge star-sapphire over his forehead. Its weight very likely contributed to the strained expression on the king's face as he gazed imperiously down at the young woman standing directly below his throne.

"My lord," came the hoarse call from her bruised mouth. "I demand the king's justice!"

"What is it, my child?" asked the king, his voice not without pity.

"My lord, I have been brutally assaulted and raped. And by

one of your knights."

I don't have to tell you pandemonium broke forth in the throne room at that. Standing in clusters around the room in attendance on the king, many of the knights were indignant. I saw Sir Kay, Arthur's fat and blustering seneschal, turn angrily to Sir Tristram standing next to him and mutter, "We have to listen to accusations like these from peasant girls now? What's next, lessons in courtesy from highwaymen?"

My master Sir Gareth turned his fair head to his brother Gawain, prince of Logres and Arthur's oldest nephew and heir apparent, with a more sympathetic view. "The lady has most certainly been through hell," he said. "She needs help."

Sir Gawain, always the paragon of courtesy in a court that looked to him to take the lead in such matters, stepped forward. He bowed his crimson head toward the king and offered his service in the matter.

"My lord king," he began. "I pledge here before you and these present, that I will be the lady's protector, and if she wishes will ride with her to find the culprit guilty of these deeds and challenge him to the utterance."

Never mind that the plaintiff was clearly no lady but a woman of lower class, either a peasant from one of the villages around Camelot, or a shopgirl of some sort from the nearby city of Caerleon. In Gawain's extreme version of courtesy, all women were entitled to the respect and consideration due the highest-born dame in the kingdom.

And personally, I won't say he was wrong about that. I looked across the room to where the queen's ladies-in-waiting stood, serving as the eyes and ears of the absent Guinevere. There were the fair-haired Lady Anne, saucy-tongued Lady Elaine with her hint of an Irish brogue, and green-eyed Lady Vivien— and standing slightly apart in her own world of transcendent beauty, the dark-featured Lady Rosemounde, flower of the world. Her dark eyes caught mine and the right side of her mouth twisted up slightly in a little smirk. She knew what I was thinking—that for her sake I would have done the same thing as Sir Gawain had for the suppliant girl, if I had actually been a knight, instead of merely a squire, and at sixteen still one of the least accomplished squires in Camelot.

"That won't be necessary, nephew," the king answered Gawain, "though we thank you for your courtesy. The young lady is under our own protection, and we promise that the knight responsible for this assault will be found and will hang. We will see to it. The outrage he has committed within the bounds of our kingdom cannot be allowed to stand, nor can we deign to allow him the honor of a trial by combat as you suggest. This is the deed of a villain, and does not merit punishment under a knightly code."

I could tell how angry the king was by the way he kept using the royal "we," something he generally reserved for dealing with unruly stable hands or with surrendering enemy kings. He stood now to his full height, framed by the scarlet banner and three rampant golden dragons that had served as the coat of arms of his father, Uther Pendragon. The power of those symbols of sovereignty made him seem twice his actual stature, and his voice boomed out so that everyone in the throne room could hear him clearly.

"What is your name, my girl?" he asked, his tone authoritative but not without sympathy.

"Bess, my lord. They call me Bess."

"And you are from Caerleon, or one of the neighboring villages?"

"From Caerleon, my lord. My father is a carpenter there . . ." her voice, strained and tired, trailed off. Sir Gawain, standing close by her, reached out a hand and steadied her with a touch on her arm.

"Can you tell us anything more about what happened to you, Mistress Bess? Anything about who it was that committed this outrage?"

"I . . . I was on the path through the woods . . . the ones north of the castle. My father had done some work for the Lady of the Lake, and he had sent me to . . . to collect . . ." She spoke more and more slowly as she went on, and began to weave with exhaustion, so that her voice faded completely at the end. Finally, with a gasp, she threw her head back and collapsed.

Sir Gawain moved quickly to catch the young girl before she hit the ground. With a befuddled look he picked her up and pulled her torn smock up to cover her breast. His calm demeanor was broken for only that brief moment before he turned to the king and, with a slight bow of his head, reported as one who had the situation well in hand: "My liege, she has fainted. No doubt the shock of the situation finally catching up with her. Shall we have some of the ladies attend to her?"

Arthur nodded toward the four ladies-in-waiting, and my Lady Rosemounde, though youngest of the four still the most courteous, responded immediately. "Have her brought to the inner chamber of the queen's rooms," she told Gawain. "We shall attend to her there, and will call a physician if we are not able to revive her soon. But she will be well taken care of, and we will have her whole story out of her in a place more private than this." With that she raised her eyebrow at me, as if she were chiding the king himself for forcing Bess to relive her trauma before the entire court and visiting suppliants. She turned and swept out of the throne room, to prepare the way for the young girl to be brought to the queen. Gawain trailed Rosemounde out the door with his unconscious burden, and the ladies Elaine and Vivien quickly followed. The Lady Anne stayed behind, the only remaining representative of the queen at the session.

"Little tart probably enticed the young knight to it." The nasal voice of Sir Kay rose above the buzz of the crowd, addressed to anyone who happened to be listening. His flabby lips stretched into an ugly grimace, revealing a set of teeth any horse would have been proud of. "These young peasant sluts are all the same—lead you on and then cry 'rape' if the knight drops them. I've seen it a hundred times." He shook his fat face until his greasy black hair swung to and fro. I had a sudden urge (and not for the first time) to put my fist through his yellow teeth, but I felt a firm hand from Sir Gareth on my shoulder to steady and dissuade me.

"Kay is a great fool, but no one pays any attention to his blusterings. Don't let him goad you out of moderation and courtesy, especially before the king." I looked into Sir Gareth's deep blue eyes and honest face, and nodded. I certainly wasn't going to embarrass him before the court by any brash display, or forget my place as his squire, just as things were going well for me. He had taught me more about the ideals of knighthood over the past six months since I had become his squire than I had ever hoped to learn. And between him and his nephew Florent, I had made great strides in learning the martial skills of the armored knight. Someday soon, I had every right to believe, I would be ready to take part in the knighting ceremony myself—as Florent had just done—and then I would be of sufficient rank to take as my wife the lovely Lady Rosemounde, daughter of the Duke of Brittany. That was the one thing I was truly aiming for.

The girl had interrupted the orderly progress of cases for the day, a process to which the court now returned. Sir Bedivere, Arthur's most experienced knight and oldest friend and advisor, acted as herald for the session and had a list of cases that he had promised the king would hear. The untidy business of the girl having been dispensed with for the moment, he returned to his list, and called out the next case from a scroll of parchment that he held onto like an emblem of his office: "William Bailey, innkeeper, come forward."

A large rustic-looking fellow, some sixteen stone if he weighed an ounce, ambled forward to stand before the dais where sat the king on his throne. He was dressed in a simple dark brown chemise that came down to his thighs and was belted in the middle by a band of leather. His green hose were threadbare but clean, and he held a blue hood in his hands for his courtesy. Hanging his close-cropped head in deference, he spoke in low tones that I could hear only because Sir Gareth and I stood close to the king's right hand.

"My lord," William Bailey began, "I ain't one to complain, God knows, but I feel like I've got to this time. I'm an innkeeper, your highness, in Caerleon. I run a good and honest hostelry, and at night folk from the town and from the castle will come in and wet their whistle a bit, if you take my meaning, sir."

"We understand," Sir Bedivere said, the impatience in his voice barely noticeable. "But what does this have to do with your king? Understand that we have many cases to hear today, some of grave importance . . ."

"Enough, Bedivere," Arthur interrupted. "This man is as much my subject as the greatest baron in the kingdom, and today he has the right to be heard." It was a civil chiding, but a chiding nonetheless, and Bedivere was suitably reproved. He stepped back, bowed his head, mumbled, "Yes, Your Grace," and let it go.

"Well, sir, I . . . I was getting to it . . ." William Bailey stammered on. "You see, sir, last night a pretty good group of young men from the castle came into my inn, and they wanted drink, the strongest stuff I had. Well, I've got some pretty potent ale, sir, and that's what they wanted. Six or seven of 'em I think there was, my lord, and they set up to drink around vespers and kept drinking until well past compline, my lord. I swear they drank half a barrel of my best ale between 'em. But after they were all, well, pretty much drunk, if you don't mind me saying so, Your Highness, they got into some kind of big row, yelling and screaming at one another and calling each other 'dunce' and 'villain' and I don't know what all, so that a couple of them like to come to blows. But then they all split up, and some went one way and some the other, and so what I'm trying to say, your honor, I mean Your Highness, I mean my lord, is that I never did get paid for my half a barrel of ale."

"I see," the king said. "And would you know these men if you saw them again?"

William Bailey shrugged his huge, round shoulders and answered truthfully, "I don't know that I ever had seen 'em before, so it ain't like I actually knew any of 'em. And I didn't look at 'em real close—my wife, you see, and our hired barmaid, did the serving of 'em. Maybe they could recognize their faces better than what I could. All I know is, they was from Camelot. Squires mainly, I think, and maybe a couple of young knights. Not regulars in my hostelry, anyway, and not travelers neither."

"All right." The king sighed. "It's somewhat disheartening to me to hear that some of my knights, or their squires, behaved in public in such a vulgar manner. But present your bill to Sir Kay there." Arthur gestured toward his former foster-brother, the fat seneschal, to whom he had entrusted the overseeing of the royal exchequer. Sir Kay bowed to the king and motioned for William Bailey to follow him out of the throne room. "Sir Kay will see to it that you are paid, if you'll go with him."

"Thank you, my lord, you are wise and just," William said, bowing his head as he backed out of the room in Sir Kay's wake.

"And now, Sir Bedivere," Arthur said, his voice betraying a

slight edge of weariness—he had been at this since the hour of terce, and it was now well past none. "How many cases do we have yet to hear?"

"We have but two left," Sir Bedivere told him. Then in a formal voice he called the next case: "Harry Stabler, plaintiff, versus John Potter, defendant. Stabler accuses Potter of stealing a horse."

A tall, thin fellow with long brown hair stepped forward, followed more slowly by a shorter fellow with a shiny bald pate and a full red beard—I remember thinking that the fellow's hair had fallen through his head and then grabbed hold suddenly when it reached his chin. Both were dressed almost identically to the last petitioner, though the second man's clothes were far more worn and threadbare than the others'. Like Bailey, they both held their hoods in their hands as they bowed slightly before their sovereign lord.

"Now then," Arthur began, apparently glad to have a case of substance that he might be able to solve today. "Which of you is Stabler?"

"That'd be me, sir." The tall man stepped forward. "This bloke 'ere, I caught 'im snoopin' around me barn last night, an' I shooed 'im out right then. But when I come out this mornin', I sees there ain't no sign of my 'orse what I 'ad there last night. 'E's the only one coulda taken 'er."

"I see your point," the king replied. "And where is your barn, Stabler?"

"Just northeast of the castle, yer 'Ighness. Mine's the first farm that borders on the royal lands. It's not 'alf a mile from where we're standin' now."

"Yes, all right," the king responded. "Now you," he spoke to the second man. "What have you to say to these charges? Were you indeed loitering at Stabler's barn last night? What was your intent? Did you mean to steal this horse of his?"

"Yes sir. But, I mean, no sir," the bald fellow babbled. "I mean, sir, that it's true I was on this man's property. I was trying to find a way into the barn, but not to steal anything—only to find a sheltered place to sleep for the night. I've been traveling awhile and I had no money for lodgings at an inn . . ."

"And thought you might make a quick profit by stealing an 'orse that weren't your own and sellin' it in town, ain't that the way of it?" Stabler interrupted.

"No, I ain't never done a dishonest thing my whole life! I got a good trade, I'm a journeyman baker, but I fell out with my master in Monmouth and been traveling to get here . . . mostly to be in your demesne, my lord. Besides," he turned to Stabler, "if I stole the horse, where is it now?"

"Sold, I'll wager and the money pocketed!"

"When would I have had time to sell it between last night and the time you had me arrested to be brought here before the king? And if I sold it, where's the money? You can all see for yourselves that I haven't got a farthing on me." With that John of Monmouth held up his arms and turned about, demonstrating that he had no purse and no place on his person where he could be hiding any ready cash.

"Probably traded it for drink and 'ores last night in Caerleon, for all I know. My lord, I demand 'e gimme my 'orse back or else 'e 'ave 'is right 'and cut off as a warnin' to other thieves!"

"That will be quite enough, both of you," the king finally intervened. "There will be no lopping off of limbs in my kingdom. The law does order you to make restitution for Mr. Stabler's loss, or face some kind of public ordeal if you are in fact guilty of this crime, John Potter of Monmouth. But I see that you have no means to make restitution. Nor am I convinced there is evidence to prove that you did in fact take the horse. You are certainly guilty of trespassing, but that may be all we can lay at your door.

"Therefore hear my judgment: John of Monmouth, journey-man baker, you are hereby sentenced to employment in the kitchens of Camelot, where you will ply your trade under our chief cook, Roger. If the horse is not found, we will pay Harry Stabler out of your salary the price of his horse. Meantime, Stabler, you are to give our Captain of the Guard, Robin Kempe, a clear description of your horse, and he is to have his men search the city of Caerleon for the beast until it is found, or until they are certain it is not in the city. If we do find it there, we will take further action when we have determined how it got there. That is my decision. You are dismissed."

Stabler and Monmouth looked at each other, apparently astonished at the king's generosity that seemed to give justice to both sides of the dispute. Then like William Bailey before them, they backed out of the throne room bowing, Stabler to report to Master Kempe his horse's description, and Monmouth to report to his new job in the kitchen with Roger.

That left one more case.

Sir Bedivere looked at the scroll, paused for a moment with a lift of his right eyebrow, cleared his throat, and announced, "Sir Gawain of Orkney, please come forward to present your case before the king."

Well, you could have knocked me over with one of Rose-mounde's hair ribbons when I heard that one. What was Gawain up to? This was a session for anyone to bring cases before the king, it's true, but the knights usually brought their complaints in private, if they had any legitimate grievances, and Arthur took care of them discreetly. Airing out the dirty linen in public like this was simply not done. And to have the king's own eldest nephew bringing something up before the court— well, it was unprecedented, that's all. I looked over at Gareth, but if he had any notion of what his brother was up to, I couldn't read it in his face. Though he seemed to be deliberately avoiding my eyes.

But hadn't Gawain taken the young girl to the queen's chambers when she fainted? I hadn't seen him come back in. Looking across the room through the crowd, I spotted him. He must have made his way back in silently during the last case. He stood against the far wall with his son Sir Florent, beneath the large tapestry depicting his own father, King Lot, on his knees surrendering to Arthur and acknowledging his kingship after the first war of Arthur's reign. Now, twenty-five years later, Lot's son and grandson stood together before that tapestry, suing for the favor of the man that had bested him.

You could see the red hair and the determined, stubborn chin portrayed in the tapestry reborn in the faces of Gawain and Florent as they stood shoulder to shoulder. Gawain, a replica of his own father, had produced a son that resembled him just as much physically. Less so emotionally—where Sir Gawain was fiery and occasionally explosive, though a paragon of courtesy when his passions were in check, Sir Florent was as calm and steady as his uncle Gareth, sometimes even a bit too intent on following the rules and keeping an even keel.

Sir Florent. I had to admit that galled me a bit. He'd been through the knighting ceremony just the day before. Not that I begrudged him his moment—oh, damn it, I did too. There was no doubting that he was ready for knighthood: he was far and away the most accomplished squire in Camelot, on horseback, with the lance or sword. And he was a paragon of courtesy; that, he'd learned from his father. It wasn't even fair of me to envy him. He'd spent not a few hours with me over the past six months helping me catch up on my training for knighthood, a training I'd come to pretty late. But I begrudged him his promotion because I was the one that really needed to be made knight, and quickly too. The Lady Rosemounde was my goal, and she couldn't be made to wait. If I didn't become a knight soon, her father would marry her off and I'd be lost.

"My lord," Sir Gawain spoke, stepping forward and pulling Sir Florent after him, and pulling me from the maelstrom of my thoughts. "My case is a simple one, and I hope a pleasant one. I have only to ask your blessing, your permission, and your approval of a contract I have just negotiated with your ally, Duke Hoel of Brittany."

Duke Hoel? My ears pricked up at that. Duke Hoel was the father of my beloved, the Lady Rosemounde.

"As is your right as my liege lord as well as the patriarch of my own family, I ask you to approve the marriage contract that I have recently concluded between my son and heir, the newly knighted Sir Florent . . ." At that, Florent, as he had no doubt been coached all day long, bowed reverently to the king. "The marriage, I say, between Sir Florent and the Duke of Brittany's youngest daughter, the Lady Rosemounde, attendant upon your own Queen Guinevere."

Whatever else was being said was lost to me as my knees buckled. I could no longer stand or catch my breath, and my head was spinning as I sank to the floor. If others around me marked my behavior, I was unaware of it, except for Sir Gareth, who pulled on my arm and whispered hoarsely, "Gildas! This is not seemly!"

The king was saying, "And is the lady willing to agree to this arrangement?"

I heard a rushing wind in my ears as Gawain answered, "Like an obedient daughter, she has assented to her father's will."

"Get up!" Gareth hissed to me through his teeth. "You must present a courteous posture in court."

"Don't care," I murmured. "My life is over."

"Then this match has my blessing," the king acquiesced. "And now, I pronounce this session ended."

CHAPTER TWO:
ORDINATION

"Leave me alone, will you? Just let me die right here."

"Keep it up and I'll make you wish you were dead!" Gareth threatened.

I was in bed, though just how I got there I really didn't remember. I think Sir Gareth dragged me to the spot where I usually slept in the lesser hall and left me there. I don't mean to say he was unkind, but he didn't know what to do with me. Tears had been streaming down my face since Gawain's announcement that my Lady Rosemounde was betrothed to his son, and Gareth had no idea how to stop them.

"Pull yourself together, lad," I remember he said to me before he left. "There's other fish in the sea, you know. They say one woman's pretty much the same as another once the lights are out."

"God, is *that* your advice? Get me a new master, quick!"

I knew he was just making one of his coarser jokes, trying to jest me out of my mood, but it did me no good. "If that's true," I asked him managing only with the greatest strain to talk without sobbing, "then why didn't you marry Lynette instead of her sister Lyonesse?"

Sir Gareth had told me, during the first night I spent in his company, of his initial adventure as a knight—one in which he had saved the beautiful Lady Lyonesse from the siege of the infamous Red Knight of the Red Lands. The essence of his story was how he had fallen in love with Lyonesse at first sight

25

when he saw her on the battlements of her castle. But he also had told of the rude and ungrateful nagging of her sister Lynnette, whom Gareth had finally married off to his brother Gaheris.

"If Lyonesse had been betrothed to Sir Gaheris, would you have thought Lynnette just as fine a catch and married her?"

Any note of playfulness left Sir Gareth's blue eyes and he looked at me solemnly, saying, "Your point is taken, young Gildas of Cornwall. Some pains are beyond a physician's healing, and some sorrows beyond jest. I leave you to your thoughts, and pray that you find a way to accept the things you cannot change." And with that he left the hall.

I lay on my pallet tossing and turning, knowing that other squires, pages, and even a few knights would soon make their way into this hall to sleep. I longed for the privacy I'd had as the queen's page, when I slept in her outer chamber, usually by myself since she seldom had other pages in her household. But here, if I was going to weep it would have to be in a large room full of other men. All I could think of at that moment was trying to get through the night. Rosemounde's face kept haunting me: her brown hair and deep brown eyes. The upturned corner of her mouth when she poked fun at me. Her courtesy and pure manners and devotion to her queen. The giggling whenever I entered a room that had made me first take notice of her. The kiss she had given me when she pressed upon me the blue ribbon from her hair that I kept next to my heart. All of it was there, all of it racing through my brain in a ceaseless whirl, none of it ever to be mine.

How could she do this to me? But no, she had warned me. *Make me yours,* she had told me, *before my father marries me off to a knighted lord with property.* But it seems I was too late. Noble women—particularly the daughters of dukes, as my Rosemounde was—had less say in the choice of husband than the poorest peasant on the land. And why should not the daughter of a duke marry the son of a prince? It made perfect sense dynastically. Why should Duke Hoel and Prince Gawain let a little thing like love interfere with their fiscal plans?

And why should anybody give a second thought to the feelings—or the life—of an expendable young squire from Cornwall?

I thought seriously about leaving Camelot and returning to my village, to apprentice myself to my father and become an armor-maker. I thought even more seriously of throwing myself from the walls of Tintagel Castle on the Cornish coast, to dash myself to pieces on the indifferent rocks and put myself out of my misery. Mostly I thought about Sir Florent, and how yesterday I had been excited and envious over his promotion to knighthood, and daydreamed of myself in his shoes. His shoes! How I wished I were in them now!

I rolled about in a vain attempt to get comfortable. I forced my eyes closed and thought if I could only will them to stay closed, I could finally drift off into unconsciousness, beyond the reach of biting sorrow.

But it was to no avail. As I lay there trying to sleep, I couldn't get the memory of Sir Florent's knighthood ceremony out of my head. How I had envied him that ceremony! Throughout the rites, I kept putting myself in his place, wishing it was *me* going through them, wishing the Lady Rosemounde could see *me* enter the solemn and holy order of the Knights of the Round Table.

I rehearsed those rituals in my mind, step by step as the night wore on. I knew, first, that Florent had gone to confession the night before the ceremony, and had taken the holy rite of the Eucharist. I had seen him enter the castle's private chapel to be confessed by Father Ambrose. From there he had gone into Sir Gawain's chambers in the castle where a bath had been prepared for him. He would have emerged from the bath a new man, in body and in spirit—pure and chaste as a child, for the order of knighthood could abide no sin or impurity.

After the bath, he would have lain down on a bed with pure, clean sheets, never before slept on. In his bed, Florent was supposed to feel at ease and reconciled to his Maker, so that he would enter the ceremony the next morning confident in his new position as a soldier of God.

When the bells of Saint Mary Magdalene's convent rang matins, Sir Gawain would have awakened him and with the help of my master, Sir Gareth, and Florent's other favorite uncle, Sir Gaheris, Florent would have been attired for the ceremony. They'd have begun by dressing him in new white linen, never worn before, to remind him to keep himself pure, now that he had been reborn the evening before. Gareth and Gaheris next would have placed a blood-red tunic over his white linen, to remind him that it may be necessary to shed blood— his own or that of his enemies—in defense of his king, his God, and his Church.

Gareth and Gaheris would next have brought a pair of black shoes to place upon Florent's feet: black to remind Florent of his mortality. The knight's life was a warrior's life, and a warrior must be ready at any moment to lay down his life for a cause. As a knight of Arthur's table, that cause should only be the cause of right, but it might come as the defender of his king's realm or of a lady's virtue, and these were of equal value in King Arthur's ideals of chivalry.

His father Sir Gawain then would have brought forward the white girdle to tie around Florent's waist. White again for purity; Sir Florent should surround himself with purity and chastity, for knighthood was the secular equivalent of holy orders.

Finally, Sir Gawain and Sir Gaheris would have placed on Florent's shoulders a fur-lined red mantle, to symbolize humility. The weight of the mantle was to remind him of the necessity that he remain humble, in spite of his elevation into the noblest of classes. Despite his prominent station, he was still a servant—of his God, of his king, and in Arthur's kingdom, of anyone else in need or distress.

Once appropriately attired, Florent was led to the chapel where he was to keep vigil until morning, praying for God's help and the grace to perform valiantly in His service all his life.

That, at least, was what I imagined. As I say, all of these things would have happened in Gawain's private quarters. At the time this was going on, two nights ago, I had been here in this very spot, tossing and turning and thinking about it just as I was now, and envying Florent then even as I was at this moment.

But that morning, like almost everyone else in Camelot, I had been present in the castle chapel, ready to witness the formal knighting ceremony. At the altar stood William of Glastonbury, Archbishop of Caerleon, and at his right hand stood the king himself, dressed in royal blue and wearing his crown of state. Before them at the altar, where he had been since matins, knelt Florent. The chapel was filled with knights, ladies, and squires. Pages and servants congregated around the door looking in. The chapel had been unseasonably warm, what with all the body heat, on that sunny April Sunday, and we all sat through the archbishop's chanting of the mass in perfect bookish Latin.

At the conclusion of the mass came the ceremony all of us had come there to witness. It began as the king called Sir Gareth and Sir Gaheris forward, and handed each of them a golden spur. Florent remained on his knees, while Gareth and Gaheris attached the spurs to his black shoes.

The king then took a newly forged sword and held it high, its silver blade glinting in the morning light that streamed through the stained glass of the chapel windows. The archbishop made the sign of the Cross over the sword, and then spoke the words of a blessing in English:

"Almighty and all merciful Father, grant, we pray, Thy blessing on this sword, which Thy servant Florent desires to gird about him. May he use it with skill in the defense of Your holy Church, and of widows, orphans, or others in need, and may he always be faithful in striking with this sword in the cause of right. Amen."

And the congregation echoed the archbishop's prayer with a loud "amen" of their own. At that point the king lowered the sword, and Sir Gawain, Sir Gareth, and Sir Gaheris filed past the still-kneeling Florent, each embracing him and placing a kiss on his cheek, to demonstrate the love and loyalty that pertained to the brotherhood of Knights of the Round Table that he was about to join.

Arthur raised the sword again, and delivered the *colée*, striking Florent hard on the right shoulder with the flat of the blade. It was a blow he would forever remember, and would always put him in mind of the one who had made him a knight—the king himself, his liege lord—and the expectations and duties of the order of chivalry that he had just received.

Handing the sword to Sir Gawain to be girded around Florent's waist, Arthur pronounced the words all of us in that chapel had come there to hear: "As King of Logres and head of the order of chivalry known as the Knights of the Round Table, I hereby accept you into the order, and dub you Sir Florent. Rise, Sir Florent, and go in peace to serve your lord and your God."

Sir Florent rose, and his father embraced him again, then helped Florent gird on his sword. Smiling, they went off together to the cheers of the assembled crowd, ready to fill the day with celebration that was to last far into the night.

And I sat in the chapel, all the time wishing it were me up

there receiving the order of chivalry, and vowing to redouble my efforts from that moment on to achieve knighthood soon and to finally become worthy to claim the hand of my Lady Rosemounde.

A hand, I acknowledged bitterly, that now belonged not to me but to that same Sir Florent. That prating, priggish, smarmy son of a bloody murderer. Oh, I swallowed all that stuff about the purity of knighthood all right, and I believed it in theory. I believed in the ideal and saw myself in a romantic light saving widows and orphans and damsels in distress and all that. But anybody who knew me knew I wouldn't have got as far as I had in life if the queen hadn't been won over by my cynicism. I mean, really—I knew Gawain had led his brothers in an ambush of the Welsh knight Sir Lamorak not long ago. I knew Gaheris had beheaded his own mother when he found her sleeping with that same knight. I knew that even Sir Lancelot, held up to all as the paragon of knightly skill and virtue, had for years been engaged in an adulterous affair with that same queen I had served so faithfully. So don't tell me I wasn't aware of the irony in all the holy ritual pertaining to that knightly ceremony.

But what is irony other than the failure of reality to live up to our dreams? And what is a cynic but an idealist who won't let go in the face of real-life disappointments? I was the best cynic in Camelot. Except maybe for the queen herself.

By now some of the other squires and younger knights were making their way into the lesser hall, lying down on their pallets or sleeping on benches. They conversed in low tones and joked with one another a bit, but for the most part they were tired and ready to rest. I turned my face to the wall and feigned sleep so as not to have to talk with any of them. Before long things quieted down and I could hear gentle snoring coming from some of the bodies lying throughout the hall. But still I couldn't sleep. I felt flushed and restless. Lady Rosemounde at her

embroidery, Lady Rosemounde reading a romance, Rosemounde walking in the bailey, Rosemounde giggling at me with
her hands in front of her mouth, Rosemounde leaning over to
kiss me and running away—all these images flashed continually
through my mind's eye. I rolled over and sighed. Two minutes
later I rolled the other way and sighed again. Five minutes after
that, I sat up, adjusted my bedding, grunted and, yes, sighed,
and lay back down in what was beginning to feel more like the
rack than a bed.

Finally Thomas, Sir Ywain's squire, couldn't take any more.
"Gildas! Will you stop rolling around like a dog on an anthill?
Some of us are actually tired and want to go to sleep."

"I know, I just can't sleep for some reason."

"Well, take it somewhere else, then," came the voice of Sir
Agravain's squire, Baldwin. "Give the rest of us some peace and
go someplace else!"

"All right, all right, you've made your point," I grumbled, sitting up and rubbing my face with my hands. I stretched and
grabbed my purse before stumbling out of the room. If I was
going to sit up, I was going to sit up with something to pass the
time.

I let the door to the lesser hall close, and once outside I
snatched a candelabrum from a niche in the wall and sat down
in the corridor next to the door, resting my back against the
wall and setting the candelabrum at my right hand. I reached
into my bag and pulled out a few folded scraps of parchment
and a stick of sharpened charcoal. I carried these with me to
practice my writing without committing anything permanently
to an expensive sheet of parchment or vellum with ink. With the
mood I was in, the best way to purge my feelings might be to
get them out, to set them down in the form of a poem—a
complaint to my lady that spoke ardently of my passion and
sense of loss. Maybe I'd even show it to her sometime. But

probably not.

I spread a piece of parchment out on the floor before me. Then I put my chin in my hand and thought. *Let's see.* "You're *promised to another man. Without you I will die." Die . . . sigh . . . cry . . . or how about man? Plan? "This wasn't in my plan . . ."? Ban? Uncan . . . ny? Began? "It happened just as our love began . . ."? Uh . . . let's see . . .*

Finally I began writing a verse. It went like this:

> *Without your love, dear Lady, I must die.*
> *Another man is now vouchsafed your hand,*
> *And all that I can do is watch and sigh.*
> *Oh Lady, please, help me to understand*
> *Why have you forsaken your love? Why?*

All right, I asked myself, *is that any good? Does it say what I want? Could I say it any better? Maybe if I changed the last line to "What you have done to make my poor heart cry . . ." Or wait, maybe "What you have done will only make me cry." No, I liked it better the way it was.*

Because that was exactly the thing, wasn't it? She'd promised herself to Sir Florent, even when she said she loved me. I felt betrayed. I felt angry. Maybe that needed to go in the poem, too. "Lady, you've betrayed me . . ."? Too short a line. "I'm angry with you, Lady, for your betrayal . . ."? No, too long a line. Well how about this—I wrote another verse:

> *I feel betrayed, my Love—your marriage day*
> *Will send me into throes of grief and pain*
> *And if I live to see you wed, I pray*
> *That God does not let me become insane—*
> *Though if He bids me die, I shan't say "nay."*

Maybe. Or maybe change the second line to "pangs of grief and pain"? *No, no, "pangs of pain" really doesn't sound right. Keep it the way I've got it. That's good, that's good,* I thought. I mean, I didn't know whether it was decent poetry—perhaps I'd show it to Sir Palomides when I was done. He was the castle troubadour of sorts, I had found. Maybe he could give me some pointers. *But really,* I thought, *this says it all.* How could Rosemounde resist? Maybe I would show it to her after all. All right, I didn't really believe she'd break her engagement to Sir Florent—that was up to her father and Sir Gawain anyway, wasn't it? But at least she'd know what it was doing to me. And then if I did perish, she'd never be able to let go of the poem I'd given her before dying for her love.

Dying for her love—that plunge off of the castle walls at Tintagel was looking more and more inviting. What was the point of my whole life without her? Everything I was doing—the training for knighthood, my efforts as squire to Sir Gareth—it was all for her and only for her. I really had nothing else I cared about without my Lady Rosemounde.

Amid pleasant thoughts like these I finally drifted off to sleep that night, my unfinished poem on the floor in front of me and the candles burning down to nothing at my right hand. For several hours, oblivion was kind enough to overcome me and give me peace.

And that's pretty much the position I was in when a commotion inside the hall woke me. At first I didn't know where I was or what had happened. I could barely move my head because my neck was stiff from sleeping with my head twisted forward, and my back was sore from leaning against the stone wall all night. There were pools of dried wax next to me from the candles that had melted down to nothing, and of course a half-finished complaint lay on the floor before me.

Coming quickly to my senses, I realized something of moment was going on inside the lesser hall, something that caused all the knights and squires to be up and about much earlier than usual, and noisily too. I gathered my scraps of parchment and stick of charcoal and stuffed them into my purse (where, sadly, they were not forced to share space with anything that resembled actual money) and bounded up to find out what the furor was all about. When I opened the door, I saw fifteen or twenty fellows pulling on tunics or hoods, girding on belts and pulling on shoes or new hose, all in what seemed uncommon haste.

"What is it? What's everybody in such a big hurry for?" I grabbed the arm of Colgrevaunce, Sir Brandiles's squire, who was fully dressed and heading for the door.

"You didn't hear?" He looked at me quizzically. "Oh, right, you left in the middle of the night, didn't you? Well, a herald just came in from the king. He's requiring all knights and their squires to report to the throne room right away, and the knights are to bring their shields with their coats of arms."

It was an odd request, to say the least. "Why? What's going on?"

"That . . . peasant wench," Colgrevaunce mumbled at me as he rushed nervously out the door. "The one what claims she was raped."

Lord, I'd forgotten all about that particular case in the midst of my grief over Rosemounde's betrothal. But the king had promised to get to the bottom of her accusations, and now I remembered my near-quarrel with Sir Kay and the strong feelings I had about the case. "What about her?"

"She says she's ready to make an identification." Colgrevaunce's face had turned a bright shade of crimson.

"Identification?"

Colgrevaunce was off down the hall. He yelled back, "She's going to tell"—here he stopped and swallowed hard—"who it is what raped her!"

CHAPTER THREE:
THE QUEST

By the time I entered the throne room, it was crowded. Every knight in residence at Camelot had appeared at the king's command. Most of them were accompanied by their squires, and all of them, as ordered, held their shields on which were emblazoned their coats of arms. In a circle around the large room I saw the golden lion rampant of Sir Ywain, the green pentangle of Sir Gawain, the eagle gules on a field sable of Sir Palomides, and there, in a corner at the rear of the hall, was the silver unicorn on its field of gold, the blazon of my lord Sir Gareth.

I rushed to Gareth's side and stood behind his right shoulder. "What the blazes is going on?" I whispered to him. "Why are all the shields out?"

"I'm as much in the dark as you are, young Gildas," Gareth answered with a shrug. Then he added, "At least about this." He looked over his shoulder at me and smiled. I was still not in the mood for jesting, but gave him a half-smile in response. I appreciated him trying, anyway.

Gareth was looking beyond me over his shoulder now, and whispered, "Looks like you're in demand, Gildas of Cornwall. You'd better go." I looked in the direction he was nodding, and saw the queen.

On a small dais built against the back wall just for this occasion, a smaller and more modest throne had been set up directly opposite and facing that of the king in the front of the hall. The queen must have slipped in while I found my way to Gareth's side, and she was beckoning to her former page, yours truly. I swallowed hard—I did not relish the encounter, knowing how much Guinevere knew of my personal life and my feelings for her youngest lady-in-waiting. But one doesn't turn down a royal summons, so I nodded to Gareth and slipped away: "With your leave, my lord."

I climbed onto the dais and took a position, as I had with Gareth, directly behind the queen's right shoulder. She was dressed simply, for her: a light blue satin gown, with sleeves that hung to the floor as she rested her arms on the throne. Girdling her waist was a leather belt whose tongue hung down as far as the sleeves did. For this particular occasion, the queen wore a crown of her own: a tiara-like circlet encrusted with diamonds mounted in silver, simpler and more elegant than the king's great crown of state.

"My lady," I began, "we have not spoken for some time."

"Well, you've been a stranger, young Gildas," she answered. "No doubt your knighthood training has kept you far too busy to visit a lonely old woman," and she pouted in what she knew was a particularly attractive manner designed to elicit stumbling adoration from any male within eyeshot.

But I wasn't in the mood to play. Instead, I went in an entirely different direction. "Kept me busy, yes. But all my work has apparently been for nothing."

"Never say so," the queen chided me. "Your mood is sour this morning."

"My lady knows the reason as well as I do."

She looked up at me with a sudden glimmer of recognition. "Ah. Lady Rosemounde. You had not anticipated this, though I warned you of the probability."

"Yes. You told me so. Congratulations, my Queen. May I now have permission to return to Sir Gareth?"

She glared at me with icy blue eyes and then let me have it.

"Stop acting like a spoiled child. You're sixteen. What do you know about life? What do you know about sacrifice? So your poor heart's broken? Grow up! There are bigger things to worry about. There are more important things than your personal happiness."

"Not to me." She had always spoken to me frankly, more frankly than anyone else did. More frankly than I cared to hear sometimes. This was one of those times. And besides, she was wrong.

She sighed and lowered her tone somewhat. "A woman has to make sacrifices, sometimes—for the good of her family, for the good of her people."

"I thought we were talking about the Lady Rosemounde, not her queen."

"We're talking about both, damn it, Gildas—shut up and listen. A woman marries because she has to. There is no place in our society for an unmarried woman outside the Church. Widows, perhaps, but not young unmarried women. And among our class, a woman makes virtue of necessity by using marriage to cement relationships. You know this. What surprises you about the situation?"

"I'm not surprised. Bitter, angry, disappointed, heartbroken, suicidal, lots of things, but surprised isn't one of them."

"Then you tell me what the alternative is. This is an ideal wedding. If and when Gawain inherits the kingdom, Florent will be his heir, and Rosemounde is sole heir to Duke Hoel's lands. Therefore Florent and Rosemounde will rule over Brittany as well. And their son will inherit and unite both realms. Would you deny her that? Would you deny her family? Would you deny Logres?"

"Logres and her family can go to hell. And if you think this will bring her happiness, you're all wrong."

"Oh, and is it you who will bring her happiness? How many

realms do you stand to inherit? How many castles can you make her mistress of?"

"You think happiness consists of realms and castles?"

"I think happiness consists of doing one's duty. To family. To country. To God, who blesses marriages and who places us in the positions He has but gives us the responsibility, too, to rule in peace and in prosperity. The people of Logres and of Brittany are better off because of this bargain. They will know peace because they will live in a stronger realm with strong allies."

"The people? They will live as they always have. One noble marriage more or less means nothing to them. Who is it you're trying to convince, my Queen? What happened to the queen who told me she was only truly happy before she was married? That her life seemed pointless without the kind of love she needed?"

The queen's face grew red. Perhaps she had forgotten that conversation. But she had an answer. "I continue to do my duty. There are ways to satisfy the demands of duty and of love."

"Well, perhaps my Lady Rosemounde will not choose to satisfy the demands of love in the same manner as her queen."

With that even I realized I had taken one step too far. Queen's favorite or not, there were some things that had damn well better be left unsaid. I looked down and cleared my throat, unable to stand long in the glare of those wide, piercing eyes. It was some time before she spoke, and when she did it was in very quiet tones.

"I see you have forgotten the lessons in courtesy you learned in my tutelage. Perhaps I had better speak with Sir Gareth about this egregious gap in your training."

Now my face was glowing bright crimson. I stammered, "My lady, I have offended you. My presence must displease you. By your leave, I will go now and rejoin Sir Gareth."

"Stay right where you are, Gildas of Cornwall. When I'm done with you, I'll let you know." The queen continued to speak in that same low voice, and she looked straight ahead as she spoke.

At the moment she was looking ahead at the king himself, who had entered without fanfare from a small door behind his throne that led directly from the outside into the throne room. He mounted his own dais to sit on his own throne. Robed in royal purple this morning, the sleeves of his surcoat and the borders of his cloak trimmed in sable fur, Arthur once again wore his imperial crown of state, and in his left hand he held a golden scepter as tall as a man, an emblem of power he carried only on days that he expected to make major decisions affecting his reign. Clearly the king considered the rape of this peasant girl a case worthy of his closest attention.

In from the corridor walked the plaintiff. Bess of Caerleon had been washed and given a new plain brown linen dress since yesterday. Someone had taken the time to brush out her long brown hair and set a circlet of flowers in it. She looked almost like a different person, though her lower lip was swollen and the bruises were still visible on her face, and she was still clearly weak and devastated by her experience. As she walked toward the center of the room to stand before the king, she was supported on either side by the Lady Elaine and the Lady Anne, and when they faced the king three abreast it was Anne who spoke, apparently by previous arrangement, as Bess hung her head.

"My Lord King," the Lady Anne began, bowing her head reverentially toward him and curtsying low. "We have gently questioned young Bess until we have been able to put together the complete story of what happened to her the night before last. I can relate the story for her if it is your will; Bess finds it too difficult to speak out among so many nobles, and besides, it pains her to speak in her present condition."

The king rose from his throne and stood to his full height, holding the scepter beside him, which stood even taller. His brows were lowered in anger when he spoke, but the anger was not addressed to the ladies. "That is our will," he said imperially. "And when we have found out the culprit from among these present, we will punish him to the utmost. For know this: we will not tolerate this behavior in our court, from one of our own. The order of chivalry demands purity and virtue. The Order of the Round Table demands that we protect the innocent, the weak, and the oppressed. To become the oppressor is a crime we refuse to tolerate. Speak on, Lady Anne."

She bowed again and then began the poor girl's story. "It was after lauds had rung at the convent, Bess says, well before prime and while the woods were still dark, that she set out for the house of the Lady of the Lake and her followers. As she mentioned yesterday, it was a matter of collecting payment for work that her father had done for the Lady.

"She had not gone far through the woods north of the castle when she heard the sound of hooves on the path behind her, approaching rapidly. She turned to see a knight on a white destrier, and the horse reared up as the rider pulled back on its reins so as not to run her down.

"She says at that point she was not afraid, since any knight riding through the woods of Camelot must be a knight of the Round Table, whose sole purpose was to protect the weak and distressed. She told the knight he had startled her, but then, thinking that one of Arthur's knights would probably escort her to the Lady's house, she began to explain where she was going and why she was up and about so early."

"May I ask," the king interrupted, "how she can be so sure the mounted figure was indeed a knight?"

The Lady Anne bowed slightly in acknowledgment of the

king's question. "Bess says she knew first, by the horse, which was indeed a warhorse that only a landed knight could afford, and second by the clothing he wore, a fine velvet surcoat and hose of a color and texture far beyond the means of any but the noble class. He also wore a dark woolen outer coat and a hood pulled down well over his face. In addition to all those things, the knight carried his shield, on which was blazoned a noble coat of arms."

"I see," the king replied softly. "Am I to understand that the hood hid the fellow's face from view, so Bess did not get a good look at him? Is that so, young lady?" The king addressed this last remark to Bess herself, who shook her head but did not speak. King Arthur followed with an observation that was almost a refutation: "If he was close enough to rape her, even in that dark night, would she not have seen his face?"

At this, Bess looked toward Lady Anne with a face twisted in frustration and anxiety, her panicked eyes pleading for help.

"My lord," the Lady Anne continued, drawing in a deep breath as if to steel herself. "I hesitate to speak a discourteous word in this illustrious court, but for the sake of justice I must do so. Mistress Bess could not see the knight's face because he was holding her face down in the dust. That is how her mouth and face were bruised. He forced her into the dirt and raped her in the manner of a dog. Therefore she never saw his face unshrouded by the hood. Forgive me, my lord, for speaking so frankly."

The king sat on his throne again, blowing out as if someone had struck him in the stomach. He opened his mouth twice, but each time closed it without speaking. His knit brows looked like threatening storm clouds lowered over his flashing eyes. When he finally spoke, he was clear and concise: "Mistress Bess of Caerleon, tell me—nod if you have difficulty speaking. You say the knight carried a shield bearing his coat of arms. Can you tell us what was on that shield?"

Again, Bess looked perplexed at Lady Anne. Anne leaned toward the girl, and Bess whispered something in her ear. The lady turned back to the king. "Bess is not familiar with terms of heraldry, my lord, and so cannot describe the device. But the knights of the Round Table have here assembled with their shields, as we requested. Mistress Bess will recognize the right one when she sees it."

A buzz traveled through the assembled knights as they turned to one another in surprise and curiosity. Who was it that was about to be betrayed by his own arms?

The king rose to his feet again. "Very well," he said. "The assembled knights are to remain standing as they are, and allow Mistress Bess and the Lady Anne to examine your shields closely. If Mistress Bess recognizes the shield of the knight guilty of this heinous crime, that man's life stands forfeit to the king's law, and let no person here utter a word in plea for mercy if once we establish that knight's guilt."

At that the buzzing stopped. This was no longer a curiosity. This was a grim case of life and death, and one of the knights was likely to leave this room a condemned man.

Bess bowed to the king in thanks, and then she and Lady Anne, with Lady Elaine on her other side, began examining the shields. They began with the triple golden fleur-de-lys on a blue background, held by the tallest and proudest of the knights, standing closest to the king on the left. Sir Lancelot's rugged face was stoic as he looked straight ahead, with no worry in his countenance. Bess glanced at his shield and moved on.

She passed by the golden oxen on blue that denoted Sir Bleoberis, the swan argent on a field purpure of Sir Sagramore, the white ram on gold that decorated Sir Safer's shield, all without so much as a backward glance. She stopped and looked thoughtfully at the green tree on its white background that was the shield of Sir Tristram, and passed on from there with her eyebrows knit together. She eyed the sun in splendor gules, on a field azure, that bedecked the shield of Sir Ironside, the Red Knight of the Red Lands, and though it would not have surprised me, given Ironside's reputation, to have her identify that shield as the one she had seen at her ravishing, she passed it by without a word as well. The lion rampant or on a field azure held by Sir Ywain, the Knight of the Lion, she glanced at with some interest and passed on, as she did with my own master's unicorn sejant regardant argent on a field or.

For a moment she stopped to stare at the portcullis argent on a field sable that decorated the shield of Sir Kay. Kay was visibly sweating as Bess examined his shield for what seemed like far too long. His thick lips were curled back over his yellow teeth in a kind of grimace—everyone knew he had been the most vocal in his dismissal of the girl's accusations, and now he was afraid some of the other knights would suspect his motives for that outburst if it looked as if she was contemplating naming him. But Bess finally moved on without a word, and Sir Kay tried very hard not to look like he was breathing a sigh of relief.

Mistress Bess passed by several more shields without showing any sign of recognition. Suddenly, at a place near the right of the king, she stopped dead. A pained screech sprang from her mouth and froze me where I stood. Bess held one hand over her mouth while the other clutched at her heart, and the ladies Anne and Elaine had to prop her up, one on each arm.

"There!" The cry issued loud and clear, as Bess lifted her hand from her lips and pointed accusingly at a fresh-looking shield that bore a black tree on a field argent. I saw the Lady Elaine's face turn a ghastly white. Holding the shield, his face frozen in shock and disbelief, and glowing as red as his flowing hair, was the newly knighted Sir Florent.

★ ★ ★ ★ ★

My own heart was pounding and the blood in my temples throbbed so loudly I couldn't hear what happened next. Or maybe it was because I felt faint and the dizziness made it hard to concentrate. I held on to the queen's throne to avoid collapsing onto the dais then and there.

Sir Florent? Hadn't he just sworn on all he held holy that he would uphold the right and protect the weak? That he would champion damsels in distress and defend holiness? Wasn't he supposed to be reborn pure and spotless, to be worthy of the revered order of knighthood he had just had the grace and good fortune to enter?

So how exactly did raping a defenseless peasant girl fit into this picture?

By the time my head stopped spinning and the blood stopped roaring in my ears, I realized the king had called Sir Florent to stand before him to defend the charges, and Sir Florent had stumbled forward as if in a daze. From the corner of my eye, I could see Sir Gawain, standing as first of knights directly to the right of the king. I saw in his eyes the anguished need to do or say something to defend his son against these outrageous charges, but I recalled, and Sir Gawain doubtless did as well, that the king had demanded no word be raised to defend the culprit found guilty in this case. Glancing down, I noticed that the queen's eyes were riveted on the proceedings, her jaw so tense I could see the muscles bulge in her cheeks. Her hands clenched the arms of her throne so tightly the fingers were turning white. I had never before seen her so passionately interested in a case before the king's court.

"Sir Florent," the king began in a voice ready to condemn but holding out a slim promise of mercy if things proved otherwise than they now appeared. "How do you answer this charge brought against you? Your shield was unequivocally

identified as bearing the coat of arms of the man that raped
Bess of Caerleon the night before last in the wood north of
Camelot. Do you have any defense against this accusation? Can
you prove you were not in the woods at that time? That you
were in the presence of someone else who can vouch for your
innocence?" The king was coming close to putting words in
Florent's mouth. He did not want to condemn his nephew's
son to the gallows any more than Sir Gawain wanted him to—if
only Florent could give some evidence to cast doubt on his
guilt.

Certainly a part of me hoped Florent had no defense against
the charges. I couldn't help thinking that his removal would
make it possible once again for me to at least hope to achieve
the Lady Rosemounde for my wife. And if Florent was guilty,
why then, he really should pay for his crime, shouldn't he?

But I had a hard time convincing myself that Sir Florent
really had done this wicked deed. Unfortunately for him,
though, he couldn't come up with an alibi.

"My lord," Sir Florent began, his head hanging low. "The
truth is, I cannot remember what happened that night."

The king looked incredulous. "Your memory had better
improve, Sir Florent. You are facing capital charges. How can
you fail to remember something that took place not two days
ago?" Anger and frustration made Arthur's voice grow louder as
he spoke, until he nearly shouted this last at the hapless Sir Florent, who stammered weakly and turned even redder for shame.

"Your majesty, I . . . I . . . it was the evening after my knighting ceremony. I had been celebrating all day. It seemed
everywhere I turned someone else wanted to congratulate me
and drink a glass in my honor. At the end of the day a group of
my peers—squires and some young knights—decided they
should take me into Caerleon, to celebrate at a tavern they
knew there. Even by the time we arrived, I was not thinking

clearly. Most of what happened there I don't remember distinctly. I do remember getting up to leave, but after that I recall nothing that happened until I woke up some hours later."

"And where exactly were you when you awoke?" the king demanded.

"I was in the woods, just inside the trees bordering the fields north of the castle. The birds were singing; the sky in the east was just beginning to brighten. I suppose it was just before prime. My head ached and I still felt groggy. I was alone."

The king gave him one more chance. "Then no one can vouch for your whereabouts before you awoke?"

"N . . . no your highness," Florent stammered. He glanced around, as if to see whether any of his companions from that evening could answer the king's question. I made a quick sweep of the crowd and noticed Colgrevaunce avert his eyes, and Thomas look around the throne room as if to say *he* knew nothing of the matter, and was curious whether anyone else did. No one spoke up for Florent. "It appears I had wandered off by myself." He paused for a moment, hung his head again, and said quietly, "My shield was leaning against the tree near my feet."

At that the room exploded. Every knight and squire there exclaimed something to his neighbor. Most were shocked, many were saddened, a few seemed relieved, as if finding the culprit had restored their image of the Round Table. But at a word from the king, all talk ceased and they looked toward the throne again.

"Sir Florent of Orkney," King Arthur began formally, drawing himself up to his full height and grasping the golden scepter. "Son of Sir Gawain, grandson of King Lot, this court finds you guilty of the ravishing of Bess of Caerleon."

At that a small cry of pain issued from the king's right, and I saw Sir Gawain fall to his knees with his face in his hands. I glanced over to where my master Sir Gareth stood. His face had gone pale in sympathy, and then he saw Gawain and fell to his knees himself.

The king had forbidden anyone to speak a word asking leniency for Sir Florent once he was found guilty, but Gawain had found a way to plead eloquently without words. He looked toward the king and held out his folded hands in an attitude of prayer. On my right, Sir Gareth did the same in silent plea for his nephew.

The king, his hand shaking as it held the scepter, blinked several times before he spoke, and even from across the hall I could see the glint of tears in his eyes. When he pronounced his judgment, his voice was hoarse. "As king, we cannot allow personal sentiments to interfere with the application of the law in all cases that come before us. We are king, we are impartial, and we are just. And we find that Sir Florent's actions in this case have merited the penalty of death."

Sir Gawain slumped on the floor, sobbing. The king continued: "Because of the nature of this crime, flagrantly disregarding the very essence of courtesy as we know it and undermining all the most sacred ideals of knighthood, we find it inappropriate that Sir Florent should die in an honorable manner. We therefore sentence him to be hanged by the neck until dead, in the manner of a common criminal, and we hereby decree that the execution shall take place tomorrow at the hour of prime. This case is concluded." King Arthur struck the dais with his scepter, with a note of finality.

The queen had taken in all this in the same posture: eyes riveted ahead, jaw set, clutching the arms of her throne. She spoke now through clenched teeth in a low, steady tone intended only for my ears. "So, Gildas of Cornwall. What say you? Shall we allow this travesty to continue? Shall we make your precious Lady

Rosemounde a widow before she is ever a wife?"

I had no idea how to answer that. I would do anything to win the Lady Rosemounde. This trial and the sudden calamitous fall of the golden Sir Florent was like an answer to my prayers. But I also thanked God Rosemounde was not in the room to witness this. If she had any feelings for Sir Florent at all, the pain and shame of this moment must devastate her. Looking again at Sir Gawain, inconsolable in his grief, I swallowed hard and tried not to think of Rosemounde in the same posture.

But what was it the queen was asking me? I certainly had no control over this situation. What did she expect from me? "My lady," I finally answered her. "The king has pronounced the sentence. Sir Florent has been found guilty."

"Sir Florent is no more guilty of this crime than you are, young squire," the queen answered in the same clenched tone. "I'd stake my crown on it. And furthermore, you know it. Do you not?"

So shocked had I been by the swift accusation and conviction of my beloved's betrothed that I truly had not had a chance to consider the question. Bess had identified the shield. Florent had the shield when he awoke alone in the woods near the very scene of the crime. He had no alibi and could not remember what had happened. All of this pointed to his guilt.

But this was Sir Florent, after all. Sure, I had always been jealous of him, but I was jealous because of his skill at the knightly arts, at which he had worked unceasingly from the time he could lift a sword. As he had worked on his courtesy, his father being the paragon of courtesy at the court, Florent wanted desperately to follow in Sir Gawain's footsteps. He had never done anything even remotely against the code of chivalry, and in fact made me and other pages feel guilty if we stepped even a toe over the line. Add to that the fact that he had generously helped me in my belated efforts to learn the martial skills, and it added up to someone who, in my mind, was as incapable of committing this crime as anyone in Camelot.

"No," I finally answered the queen. "Sir Florent cannot have done this."

Guinevere's jaw relaxed and she looked relieved to have heard me say so. Then, with a look of grim determination, she set her face toward Arthur's throne. Robin Kempe, captain of the castle garrison, and two of his archers were holding Sir Florent by the arms, preparing to lead him away to the castle dungeon to await tomorrow's gallows. Only one person in that throne room could possibly stop this execution.

The queen rose from her throne to do just that.

"My lord Arthur!" She spoke over the hum of the crowd in a voice loud enough to arrest Sir Florent and his captors well before they reached the door to the hall. Like everyone else in the room, they turned to stare at the source of this unexpected outcry. The king, halted in midstep as he made his way off the dais, turned back to face Guinevere with a puzzled expression. There may have been a hint of annoyance in his voice as he answered her, but it was well suppressed. The queen had never before interfered in any court decision of the king's, so her willingness to do so now was not something the king felt inclined to begrudge her. In fact, he seemed curious, if only because of the novelty of the situation.

"My lady?" he answered her. "You wish to address the court? But I must remind you," he added, as if suddenly remembering himself, "that I have forbidden anyone to ask for mercy in this case."

"The culprit responsible for this vile crime must indeed face the severest punishment." Guinevere chose her words carefully. "And I do not ask for mercy for Sir Florent. But I do ask, my lord, that you grant me the boon I shall ask." As if taking a cue from Sir Gawain, Guinevere got down on one knee and held her hands out toward the king. He rolled his eyes in response. He knew, better than anyone, that it would be discourteous to refuse to grant a boon requested by a lady, and more discourteous still when that lady was the queen, and most discourteous of all when one was the king and so the model for behavior in the court.

Where justice and courtesy were in conflict, though, should not the king, as arbiter of the law, opt in favor of justice? But of all men, Arthur knew true courtesy embraced justice, as it embraced truth, beauty, and virtue. Taking the chance that the queen actually meant what she said about mercy and Sir Florent, and realizing that, as she had never asked him for such a thing before, there must be significant reason for her request, Arthur relented.

"We recognize your interest in this case and grant you the boon you request. What is it you desire, my Lady?" There was genuine curiosity in the king's voice as he looked across the room at Guinevere. All eyes were now on her, most eagerly the not-disinterested eyes of Bess of Caerleon and of Sir Florent himself. Proceeding cautiously, the queen began to make her case, pacing slowly across the dais.

"My lord, Sir Florent's crime is not simply the violation of an individual woman, this poor young girl. I suggest, and believe, that his crime is truly a sin against the idea of woman."

A few eyes glazed over as the queen began to speak in the abstract. With no prospect of any sparks flying between the king and queen, some people had lost interest. Arthur's gaze simply showed a little more impatience. "A sin that perhaps God will need to deal with. This court deals with crimes against individuals," he reminded her.

"But also with sins against the idea of chivalry—that, you said yourself! The courtly ideal involves respect for all women, and the protection of those in need. That is what has here been violated."

"Bess is what has here been violated," the king shot back. "Let us not forget that."

"Not for a moment, my lord," Guinevere continued. "But through her every woman has been violated. This is an act that says 'You are an object and I will use you as such. You are of no consequence as a human being but only as an object with which to slake my lust. I have value as a person, you do not.' That is what this act says. And that is why my request to you is that I, as chief representative of woman in this court, be allowed to make the final determination in the sentencing of this felon."

She nodded to Florent, who seemed to see no hope in anything she said and merely hung his head again for shame. Even Bess seemed to trust in the queen's words, as she nodded in agreement.

King Arthur bowed slightly in the queen's direction. "I have granted your boon. I take you at your word. The case, my lady, is yours. As is," he added with some emphasis, "the responsibility to do justice."

"And justice, my lord, I swear to uphold," the queen stressed again. Then she called out, "Sir Florent, convicted rapist, step forward."

With some hesitation, flanked by the two archers of the king's guard, Sir Florent came across the hall to stand before the queen's throne.

"Sir Florent," the queen began thoughtfully, "you have been condemned for a heinous crime. But I would not have you die in ignorance and without any opportunity for atonement. Your death sentence stands for now. But I am postponing it for one week. For the duration of this week's respite I have granted you, I send you out on a quest. As you are a true knight, you must not fail to return to this hall in one week's time with the quest achieved and ready to meet your fate as I decide it."

Now it was Florent's turn to go down on his knees. "Oh, lady," he said in gratitude, in part for the week's reprieve but in part, too, for the implication that some mitigation of his sentence might be possible if this quest was achieved. "Command me, and I will show the world that I am a true knight of Arthur's court. What is the quest? Is there an enemy I must fight? A damsel I must save? A monster I must destroy?"

"More difficult than any of those," Guinevere said, the corner of her mouth twisting up in the ironic smirk I was so familiar with. "Here is your quest: in a week's time, you must do all you can to learn what it is that women desire most. Come back to me with that question answered, and find a way to make that desire come true for Bess of Caerleon, who has been so wronged, and at that point I will reexamine your case. That is my judgment. That is my command. Now go."

Sir Florent, set free by the guard, bowed in some bewilderment to the queen and left the room, scratching his head. The other knights shared astonished looks. The king stood on his dais across the way, hands on his hips, gazing at the queen as if she had somehow undermined him. Sir Gawain had stopped sobbing and stood at attention again, a look of new hope on his ravaged face.

The king left without another word and the court broke up in some confusion. They, and I, seemed to understand only one thing: for now, Florent was free, and that was the topic of discussion as knights and squires thronged out of the room. Only Bess of Caerleon did not move, but stood staring at the queen with hatred in her eyes.

Chapter Four:
Merlin

I had no appetite for breakfast that day, and no ambition to join in any of the swordplay or tilts at the quintain that most of the other squires were scheduled to engage in that morning as part of their training for knighthood. I'd lost interest, frankly.

I hadn't even bothered to ask Sir Gareth whether he would need me for anything today, but went straight back to the lesser hall and sat up on my pallet, my back against the wall, to meditate on my future. Now I was alone in the room again, everyone else having gone about the day's business. The problem was, no matter how many ways I looked at it, I didn't seem to have one. A future, I mean. My goal of knighthood had lost any meaning for me. The happiness I knew I could have only with the Lady Rosemounde had been denied me. If Florent lived, she would be his. If Florent died—but that would be a monstrous injustice and the queen would not let it happen. I couldn't return to Cornwall to be apprenticed to my father. He had sent me here to rise in the world, to make myself one of the aristocracy. It had cost him every penny he had and the use of every influential person he had ever worked for to have me set up as the queen's page, and abandoning that plan now would devastate the old man's hopes and dreams for his only child.

How long I sat there immobile I couldn't say. Lost in my reveries, I hadn't noticed that the sunbeam from the window high on the wall had moved a good way across the stone floor. From where I sat, the sunlight streaked down between me and the door to the hall, so that when *she* opened the door and began to walk toward me, she looked like an angel, surrounded by light and so dazzling to my eyes that for a moment I could not be sure she was real.

She wore a white samite gown of simple but elegant cut, the sleeves hanging low. The long-tongued belt augmented her waist, and her brown hair was held in place by a golden wire net that hung from a gold circlet around her brow. She would not have worn this rich a gown and accessories for her normal day, and I would have been forced to realize, if I'd been able to think at all, that she had dressed in this manner for the sole purpose of coming to see me.

She walked toward me with a determined step, passed through the sunbeam and glowed momentarily like a goddess, then came to stand before me where I could focus on her incomparable brown eyes and coral lips—pursed in concentration, and perhaps some uncertainty.

"My Lady Rosemounde," I said, rising clumsily and with exaggerated courtesy, after swallowing hard to force my stomach back down out of my throat. But my joy at seeing her was quickly losing the battle with bitterness and the feeling of betrayal, and I couldn't keep the sarcasm out of my tone when I added, "Or should I call you Mistress Rosemounde of Orkney?"

I wanted to reach out and grab back the words as soon as I said them. And I had to fight the urge to reach for her and take her in my arms once, just this once. I could do nothing except watch the flush of blood travel from her alabaster neck into her fair cheeks. She shrugged off my insolence and forged ahead into her purpose for visiting me.

"The queen warned me your courtesy was likely to be in a serious state of neglect if I came to see you, and so I find it to be. But that is not so surprising. You were always quick with a cynical remark—a trait I once thought mildly amusing, though of late it seems to have lost its charm." She was not smiling now.

What I wouldn't give to have her smirking at me, or giggling as she used to do behind her hands in the queen's chambers when I'd blunder into the room. It was painfully apparent that I had ceased to amuse her.

Or perhaps she just wasn't in the mood to be amused.

"My lady . . ." I bowed to her, trying to avoid too much self-conscious irony behind the courtesy—for I did indeed feel sorry for her position the more I considered it, and I was happy she had come to see me, whatever her motive. And by the way, what *was* her motive? "I beg your pardon for my rudeness. I beg, if it please you, that you tell me to what I owe the unexpected pleasure of this visit?"

"Can't you ever speak without your tongue in your cheek, Gildas? This is not the time for frivolity. I've come to you about a serious matter."

"Believe me, my Lady Rosemounde, my mood is as serious as it has ever been. And sometimes all we've got is frivolity. But lest you think me discourteous . . ." I went down on one knee and looked up at her ethereal beauty—and couldn't help smiling. How could I be in the presence of that masterpiece of Nature's handiwork and not feel joy? "My lady, I am yours to command. Tell me your will. As for my tongue, I shall endeavor to keep it away from my cheek, though what else I can do with it I cannot now imagine."

There it was—in spite of everything, there was Rosemounde's smirk, coupled with the raising of her left eyebrow. In spite of everything, and even in the face of the swirl of events that had recently betrothed her to a convicted rapist, she had enough left to give me that gift. I knew then, as I know now, that I would forever treasure that moment when her lip twisted upward.

"If what you say is true," she continued, the sober look

returning to her face, "then there is a great deal you can do to serve me. I wouldn't ask it but . . . truly, I have no one else to turn to."

That declaration, coming as it did in that situation, sobered me as well, and when I responded, my voice had lost all irony. If I could help this young woman I loved more than my life, then there was nothing she could ask me that I would balk at. "Command me, my lady," I said, without rising from my knees. "Your will is my will, this I swear to you."

Lady Rosemounde's brows knit together and tears formed in her eyes as profound gratitude gazed out at me from those deep brown orbs.

"Oh, my own Gildas," she said, and my heart almost melted. "What am I to do?" The tears began falling down her cheeks. "I am to be married to him—my father and his have concluded the arrangements and we cannot now break the pact." I hung my head. "It was not my choice!" she insisted, rather loudly, I thought. But I certainly didn't mind hearing it. "We have no real choice, it seems. But that is not why I'm here." She shook her tears away and steadied herself to begin again. "He cannot be guilty," she said decisively.

"I do not believe he is, my lady," I told her truthfully.

"That is not enough! The woman has called him guilty. The king has found him guilty. The court believes—no, knows—that he is guilty. But he cannot be. I cannot be betrothed to a guilty man."

I wasn't completely sure where she was going with this. "But Lady Rosemounde, as you say, he is convicted. I am certain the queen will not let him hang, though. This quest she has sent him on—he will acquit himself well and come back with some surprising accomplishment, mark my words. Just wait and see . . ."

"You're not hearing me, Gildas! Whether the queen spares

him or not—and I truly hope she does—I am shamed, and shamed forever. Whether or not the marriage takes place, my name will be forever linked with his. A rapist. A convicted renegade against the code of chivalry. Do I then live a life of shame as his wife, unable to show my face in court? Or do I live a life of shame as his widow, going off to hide in a convent the moment his renegade, rapist body is cold after the hangman cuts him down?" Her imagination flowing freely, her tears followed suit, and she sobbed out, "Oh Gildas, I can't stand the thought of it. I can't stand to think of him dead, or hanged, or suffering."

"My lady . . ." I rose, finally, from my knees. She was nearly hysterical. I didn't know what else to do, and followed my instinct—to reach out and hold this confused, suffering creature in my arms.

At the touch of her, I realized what I was doing. And though it made me tremble with excitement and bliss, I could not release her from my tender grip. And then she said, finally, what it was she wanted from me. "You have to prove him innocent."

Well, that threw a bit of cold water on my mounting ardor. I froze, released her, and stepped back. Clearly her thoughts were with Florent, not with me. I was for her a useful servant who might serve her purpose of clearing her lover's name and, by extension, her own.

But what else did I expect? I had lost her; that was clear. Whatever happened, she would never be mine. If Florent lived, she would go through with the marriage. If he died, hadn't she just said she would enter a convent? If I meant to serve her, as I'd promised to do, it couldn't be for *my* benefit, could it? I mean, then it wouldn't exactly be *service*, now would it? If I loved her . . . if I really loved her with the love of a courtly gentleman, then I needed to remember love was selfless and that, in this new world of woe I had come to know over the past

few days, the only reward I could expect was another of Rosemounde's smiles.

That and the satisfaction of serving her, of doing something
for her nobody else could do.

With that thought in the forefront of my mind, I cleared my
throat. "My lady," I said with a slight bow, "I will do everything
I can."

"Oh, Gildas," she said, sounding almost chatty now that she
had laid much of her burden on my shoulders. "I know you can
do it! You and Merlin were so clever the way you proved the
queen's innocence in the case of the poisoned apple, when Sir
Mador de la Porte accused her of murder and treason. This is a
much simpler case, isn't it? I mean, there can't be more than a
few suspects, and they all have to be young knights or squires
from here in Camelot, don't they? Only you must find out who
did this within the week, before Sir Florent returns from his
quest, because you may have to prove his innocence to save his
life . . ."

"The queen will not let that happen, my lady."

"Even if she doesn't, everyone will still think he's guilty if
you don't speak up at that hearing. Thank you, Gildas. You will
bring Merlin into this as well, won't you? I knew you would."
And with that, for the second time in my life, the Lady Rosemounde leaned over and kissed my cheek. Then she turned and
walked rapidly out of the lesser hall. I stood looking after her
for a few moments, my hand resting on the spot warmed by her
kiss, pondering whether it would make my life worthwhile to
have Rosemounde kiss my cheek once every six months, when
her last words finally sank in. I repeated, with a sinking feeling,
"Merlin?"

So it was that, sometime around sext when everybody else was
sitting down to a nice midday meal, I was tramping through the

woods north of the castle on my way to a hidden cave on the banks of Lady Lake, the domain of the mysterious Lady of the Lake whose devotee Nimue was Merlin's unrequiting beloved. He'd been so besotted with the young nymph that she'd placed him in an enchanted cave several years ago, one from which the old necromancer was unable to escape.

Or so the popular story went. The truth of the matter was, Merlin suffered from a profound melancholia, made more severe by Nimue's rejection, and his imprisonment in the cave was self-inflicted. He preferred to avoid the company of others as much as he could when the dark mood was upon him. And it was usually upon him.

So I had to wonder whether he'd even agree to help me— whether finding a rapist and saving young Florent's skin was enough of a challenge to lift him out of his private hell long enough to make himself useful to somebody else. Oh, don't get me wrong, I was fond of Merlin. He could be cranky, insensitive, pontificating, overbearing, insulting, and downright rude, but he was the cleverest man I knew (the cleverest man anybody in Camelot had ever known), and he was somebody you could count on in a pinch. On top of all that he did have a terrific sense of humor when he wasn't suicidal, and sometimes that was the most important trait to possess.

Still, the last time I sought Merlin's help in the sleuthing vein, I had a mandate from the king himself, and that was something even Merlin had difficulty ignoring. This time, I thought as I tiptoed across the cool running water of the brook that separated Merlin's cave from the path I had followed, which split off in the other direction toward the Lady of the Lake's environs, this time all I had was the dilemma of young Florent, the grief of his father Sir Gawain, and the shame of his bride-to-be, none of which was all that likely to rouse Merlin if he was mired in his darkness.

I hadn't been to the cave in the six months since I'd helped Merlin find the murderer of the Irish knight Sir Patrise and cleared the queen's name, and as dozens of caves honeycombed the cliffs on the lakeshore, I shielded my eyes from the glare of the bright April sun and counted four holes in from the closest cave to the stream. That ought to be his.

I approached gingerly, hoping to find the old man in good spirits. But as I peeked slowly into the gloom of that grotto, I was disappointed.

Merlin lay on his cot, his left hand flung across his brow. He was dressed, as always, in the gray, threadbare robe he wore everywhere, and by the heavy breathing that issued from his open mouth, I realized he must be asleep, though it was the middle of the day. The only good sign was that he lay on his back, not curled up in a ball, which was his usual position in the deepest darkness of his mood.

I crept noiselessly into the cave, past the small table with the candles, past the smaller table with the chessboard set up and ready to play, until I stood directly over the cot. I looked down at the craggy face with its prominent nose, the long gray-streaked hair and beard, and the huge tangled garden of his eyebrows. I stared down at those brows for a few moments until I had the nagging feeling of something quite wrong. Then I realized what it was. Under the right eyebrow one eye was wide open, staring straight back up at me.

I jumped back with a small yelp, and then I heard the rasping voice, musty from long disuse, issuing from the old man's mouth. "Gildas of Cornwall, you great lunkhead, don't you ever knock before you come blundering into a fellow's house uninvited?"

Did I mention the part about "downright rude"?

"You're awake!" was all I said.

"Time has not dulled your amazing powers of observation, I

see," the old man grumbled as he sat up in bed.

"I only say so because I was afraid you were in one of your dark moods . . ."

"Not today," Merlin replied. He sounded almost chipper. "Needed some sleep because I was up all night reading," and he pointed to a vellum manuscript on the floor near the head of his bed. "It's a Latin treatise on Aristotle, something about poetics. Nimue brought it to me from the Lady of the Lake's library, which they say is massive—some fifty or sixty books, I'm told."

I let that pass. The stories told of the Lady's house were usually wildly exaggerated, and I assumed this must be as well. The queen herself had only a dozen manuscripts at the castle, one of which was usually being read aloud among the ladies-in-waiting. At the thought of them, I quickly returned to my purpose in being here. "My lord Merlin, I do apologize for disturbing you, but my business is urgent."

He gave me that half-ironic gaze with which he loved to transfix people, from beneath his shaggy brows, and said, "Urgent for you doesn't necessarily mean urgent for me. Does the king require my assistance again so soon? In that case, I might be interested; otherwise, you should probably head back where you came from and leave me in peace."

I swallowed and tried to see where this dance was leading. "The king himself does not request your assistance, my lord. But the prince, Sir Gawain, is in dire need. His son, Sir Florent—"

"Is a prissy little goody-goody who needs a dose of the real world to smack him on the side of the head."

"Right," I agreed. I'd expected nothing less from Merlin. "But he seems to have gotten that smack. Florent has been convicted of raping a maiden from the town, Bess of Caerleon. She says the man who raped her bore Florent's shield, though she didn't see his face."

"And the king has found Florent guilty?"

"Yes, my lord. And condemned him to hang."

Merlin gave a dismissive gesture, stood up, and wandered toward his chessboard. "Then the matter is concluded. There's certainly nothing I can do if the king has pronounced sentence. So why do you bother me? Leave me to my solitude and go tell Gawain to raise a better son next time."

"My lord Merlin," I continued. "I know you would prefer me to leave, and I promise to do so after I have told you the whole of Florent's story." Actually, I knew he didn't want me to leave, because I could tell he was interested in the case. He wouldn't have got up and begun fingering his chess pieces if he weren't. I didn't call his bluff because I knew he was enjoying the game.

"The queen has delayed the execution," I continued. At that, Merlin looked up with interest. He knew as well as anyone how extremely unusual it was—one might say unheard of—for the queen to take such an active interest in matters of law. I knew he was intrigued. "She has given Sir Florent a quest. He is to search diligently for the next week, to find the answer to the question 'What do women want most?' When he reports back to Guinevere next week, she will decide his fate."

Merlin snorted. "A question without an answer. Or rather, as many answers as there are women. He can't possibly find an indisputably true solution. Or from another view, he can say anything, and the odds are it will be true for some woman somewhere. An odd quest for our gracious queen to have bestowed on him. But I'm sure it really doesn't matter—the point of the queen's task was to give the poor young bloke something to do while she delayed his execution and tried to prove him innocent of the crime he's been convicted of."

I shrugged. "You may be right, Merlin."

"Of course I'm right, numbskull. So the queen has sent my

old partner to work with me again, eh?" At that he raised his heavy eyebrows and the hint of a smile cracked his wrinkled visage. I knew he was being ironic, but only slightly so. There was a compliment in there somewhere.

"Well, I did learn a lot by assisting you last time," I began. "And perhaps I can be of some help in this case, too. But Merlin, I haven't told you everything."

The eyebrows went farther up in a look of surprise. I continued: "Before the criminal charge was laid, Sir Florent was betrothed to the Lady Rosemounde. They are to be married at the earliest convenient time. Both Sir Gawain and Duke Hoel of Brittany, Rosemounde's father, wish it, and the king approved of their union."

Merlin nodded with a grim look on his face. I was sure he knew as well as anyone my feelings for Lady Rosemounde—he was with me as I tried to calm her when we rescued her from the murderous Sir Pinel. But he did not speak, and I went on: "It was in fact the Lady Rosemounde who asked for my assistance, asked me to convince you to help prove the innocence of her future husband."

I hoped the wise old man would have some words to help me to make sense of the whole situation. Instead, he merely nodded. When he was sure I'd finished speaking, he finally answered me.

"And you are willing to do this? To prove the innocence of young Rosemounde's betrothed? You yourself ask me to do this of your own will?"

I swallowed hard and gave the simplest answer I could. "It just seems like the right thing to do."

More nodding. More silence. Then he cleared his throat. "It seems, young Gildas, that you and I are to be partners again."

Not a word about my dilemma. Not a word about what he thought of Rosemounde and Sir Florent's betrothal. Only his agreement to help with the investigation. At the time I felt bewildered—I thought perhaps he didn't understand or, more likely, he just didn't care. But when I thought about it later, I wasn't so sure. What could he have said? Wise or not, he'd lost his own love. He could sympathize, but what was there to say? I later realized that his agreeing to look for the rapist was for me—not for Sir Florent or Sir Gawain or the queen, and certainly not for Rosemounde. He said he'd do it because I had promised, and he knew what it was like to agree to do anything for the person you love, without any hope of personal benefit.

"God's shinbones," Merlin exclaimed, rubbing his hands together. "This is going to be a knotty puzzle to solve! Let's get started."

"All right!" I agreed. "I thought we'd go talk to Florent to begin with—you know, find out exactly what he remembers, and then go from there to—"

"White or black?" Merlin asked, sitting down at the chessboard.

Chapter Five:
The Game's Afoot

"Pawn to king four," I said half-heartedly. I always picked white, or Merlin always let me have white, since I didn't have a prayer of even making it a game with black.

With Florent's life in the balance and only six days to solve a mystery that he didn't have the first clue about, you'd have thought Merlin's first instinct would be to go off and start investigating. That's because you'd have assumed Merlin was a normal sleuth. I knew better.

"Same old opening, I see, Gildas. You're nothing if not predictable," he chided me as he pondered the board, then mimicked my very move, pushing his own king's pawn to king's pawn four.

"We're both pawns of the king, aren't we?" He made the same joke he had made the last time we played. "And we're both moving in the direction he wants. So tell me, young Gildas, what do you suppose our first move should be in our quest to prove the innocence of the very earnest Sir Florent?"

"Well . . ." I thought about it, not having really considered it before. "Talking to Sir Florent, I guess. Wouldn't he be the one to give us the clues to his own innocence?"

Merlin's great heavy brows lowered in disagreement. He sat with his elbow on the table and his chin in his right hand, his index finger laid aside his long nose and the knuckles of his left hand drumming on the table. "I can't see much value in it. If he had any evidence of his own innocence, you'd think he'd have brought it up at his trial, wouldn't you? You say he was carousing in Caerleon with some other squires but left the group. Next thing he knows, he wakes up in the woods, the same woods where this Bess was assaulted, and he's got his shield next to him—the same shield she identified in the throne room as having been carried by the knight that attacked her."

"Right," I agreed. "He couldn't say any more. He didn't remember any more. But maybe if we talk to him, ask him the right questions, we can get him to remember something."

"Or perhaps there are some small things he does remember that seem trivial to him—even if in fact they hold the secret to the entire mystery. Wouldn't that be grand? The problem is, we don't yet know what we're looking for, or what the right questions to ask him would be. Let's think this through. It may be we can come up with the right questions. What are some things that seem strange about this whole case?"

"All right," I agreed, though right now I couldn't think of anything strange. There was one thing that bothered me, but maybe it was too obvious. "The thing I don't understand is, if the rapist wasn't Sir Florent, why did he have Florent's shield?"

"Why indeed?" Merlin asked, as if that was exactly what he'd been thinking. "The simplest explanation is that the rapist was indeed Sir Florent. But we are precluded from making that assumption by the queen, and by the Lady Rosemounde . . ."

"And by our own consciences, which know in all truth that Sir Florent could not have done this deed."

"Even a drunk Sir Florent, who cannot remember his own deeds?"

"Even so," I asserted. "Besides, if he was that drunk, he wouldn't have been able to rear up his horse as Bess said he did, without falling off. He'd have been easy for her to fight off or run away from, if he was that far gone." This had just occurred to me, and I realized I believed even more strongly in Sir

Florent's innocence because of it, much to my own chagrin.

"Granted, then. We cannot conclude Sir Florent is the culprit. The only other alternative, then, is a well-planned scheme to implicate Florent in the rape. The perpetrator would have had to make sure Florent was drunk enough to have difficulty remembering where he was. Then he would have to have stolen Sir Florent's shield with the express purpose of committing a crime where he would be mistaken for Florent, and replace the shield after the crime, and aren't you going to make a move?"

Carried away by Merlin's analysis, I had forgotten about the game. I realized he was pretty intent on getting a game of chess in before we left—that usually meant he'd had no one to play with for a while. I knew Nimue stopped by the cave periodically to converse with the old necromancer and sweep him out of his melancholy if he happened to be afflicted. But by his insistence on the game now, I gathered that the Damsel of the Lake had not been to visit for quite some time. I considered asking him about her, but thought better of it. "King's knight to king's bishop three," I announced, and then I thought about what he had said about the case.

"That would mean almost certainly one of the squires or young knights Florent was with that night is the culprit," I concluded.

"Or was working with the rapist. We can't rule out a conspiracy here, you know."

"You think *that* many people had it in for Sir Florent?"

"I think that many people and more have a grudge against his family. Sir Gawain has been in Camelot long enough to make many enemies, and Sir Gaheris, Sir Agravain, and their brother, young Mordred, do not have pure records either. Your own master, Sir Gareth, has no enemies that I know of, except the Red Knight, but I'm sure there's no connection there. No, I'd say there's a motive here against the clan of Orkney."

"Then it's against me, too, I suppose, since I'm squire to one of them."

"True," Merlin grumbled. "Hadn't thought of that. But look, here's a problem. Florent was caught in the woods. Bess was raped in the woods. The culprit was acting to deliberately implicate Florent. So . . . how did the culprit know Bess was going to *be* in the woods?"

"You mean . . ." I gasped, shocked at the ramifications, "You mean Bess might have been in on the conspiracy? That she staged her own rape?"

Merlin shrugged. "It's a possibility. King's bishop to queen's bishop four."

I thought about it for a few moments and then shook my head. "Bess of Caerleon was assaulted. Her face was bruised. Her clothes were muddied and bloody. She was too distraught to testify. She spent all evening with the queen's ladies-in-waiting and gained nothing but their sympathy. She could not have been in on this, unless she is the world's most accomplished liar, and is willing to do grave injury to herself in order to make her lies seem real. Or, say she was involved; it got way out of hand and she was injured. She would not go on to implicate an innocent man, not if she knew who the real culprit was."

Merlin shrugged again. "I admit, it is an unlikely proposition. But somehow the rapist knew Bess would be there. That means he must have overheard her saying where she was going and when, or he saw her enter the woods about the time he stole Florent's shield as he slept at the edge of the forest."

"Well, that seems possible, doesn't it? Even likely? The rapist, stealing Florent's shield to do some wickedness with it, spots the damsel heading into the forest and thinks, 'Aha, just the thing! I'll rape that maiden and she'll think it's Florent!' "

"Balderdash!" Merlin replied. "You think someone who went

through that elaborate a plan would have left the specific object of the frame-up to chance? No. He knew she'd be there. Knew it before he ever entered those woods. But how? Make your move!"

I looked at the board, and noticed that he'd left his king's pawn unprotected. I could capture it, and my knight would control the middle of the board. I wasn't quite sure what he was doing with that bishop, but it really couldn't do anything that I could imagine, and I could attack it with my knight on the next move. "King's knight to king five," I announced, and took the pawn. He didn't seem at all fazed. I went on to ask him, "So you're thinking maybe Bess said something earlier about heading off for the Lady of the Lake's palace in the morning, and whoever raped her overheard it and was in the woods to head her off?"

"Bess of Caerleon may have been surprised by the knight in the woods, but I will guarantee you she was not in the woods because she was going to the Lady of the Lake about a bill."

"You mean she was lying?"

Merlin scoffed. "Not even a very good lie. How long would it have taken her to reach the Lady's palace? Perhaps another half an hour? She'd have been at the palace long before prime—it would still have been dark. Everyone at the palace would have been sleeping. And there is no possibility the Lady would admit anyone that early. She will not give anyone audience before she's broken her fast and her ladies are at work for the day. It would be terce at least before she would have received the girl."

"I hadn't thought of that." I pondered what he had said. "Then what was she doing there?"

"Nothing for her father, I'll warrant. You said nothing about his being present, either when she came into the throne room with her accusation, or when she named Florent as her attacker the next day. Doesn't his absence seem conspicuous to you, especially when he was the girl's excuse?"

"No, he wasn't there at all. That is quite strange, isn't it?"

"Bess of Caerleon was in the woods that morning for the only reason a young woman would go to the woods by herself before dawn. She was there to meet a man. Doubtless she was not anxious to have that knowledge spread around Camelot, and certainly she was not eager to have her father learn of it—a sturdy carpenter with, no doubt, the solid values of the artisan class."

"So are you saying it's Bess's own fault, what happened to her? She lied about her reason for being there, and she was not particularly pure in her habits?"

"So she deserved to be raped? Don't be ridiculous, boy. It makes no difference as far as the crime goes. But it may well make a difference so far as the suspects go. Think about it—if she was there to meet a man, then where was he? He was late? He never came? He saw what happened but never came forward? That's the fellow we need to find, Gildas. He can tell us a lot more than Sir Florent can. Queen to king's rook five."

I shook my head and looked at the board. When Merlin said it, it all sounded so logical, as if I should have seen it from the first. But I hadn't. And besides, what was he doing with his queen? At this point I really wasn't that interested in the chess game, but was thinking a lot more about the game we were about to play with Mistress Bess, Sir Florent, and everybody else involved.

"So you're saying we should talk to Bess herself first? Get the name of whoever she was meeting and go from there?"

"We certainly need to talk to her. Though I have a feeling she will not be especially anxious to speak with either of us if she has any inkling we are trying to prove the innocence of the man convicted of assaulting her—the man she identified by his shield. But there are other things we need to find out. Obviously, we need to learn the names of every person who was with Florent that night, and we need to talk to them about what happened in the tavern where they were carousing, and what happened afterwards. There's another thing that bothers me, and I think may be a significant clue. What happened to the horse?"

"The horse?"

"The rapist was riding a very striking, white horse, one that Bess says reared up to avoid running her down on the path. I assume the rapist rode off on that same horse when he left young Bess in the woods. There's been no mention of a horse being tied next to Sir Florent when he awoke the next morning."

"The horse must have belonged to the real rapist, then, and not to Florent!"

"Perhaps. In any case, our culprit was riding it, and it wasn't a horse belonging to Florent, of that I'm sure. You are familiar with Florent's horse?"

I thought for a moment. A good warhorse was a serious investment. It could cost even a wealthy knight a quarter of his annual income, and was the one piece of equipment that made the difference between a knight and a simple soldier. Florent had just become a knight, but I now remembered that in anticipation of his knighting, his father recently made a gift to him of a destrier—a dark brown Andalusian beast I had seen him riding on a few occasions. Merlin was right. "Florent's horse was brown, not white."

"Then whose horse was the culprit riding? Suppose we talk to Taber at the castle stables. He can probably tell us who rides a white horse."

I hated to disagree with Merlin. "I don't know of any knight at Camelot with a perfectly white warhorse. And I know the king doesn't own any."

Merlin shrugged a third time. "I'm not saying the culprit

used his own horse anyway. Why give himself away by riding a recognizable animal, in case he was seen by someone from the castle? The girl probably doesn't know much about horses. May not even recognize a warhorse when she sees one. But another knight would have, and the rapist couldn't take the chance of Florent waking up to recognize the horse when he returned the shield."

"Wait a minute!" I slapped my forehead at my own denseness. "Why didn't I remember it before? I guess the girl's rape case drove everything else out of my mind, but listen. On the day she brought her case to the king, there was another case. A free landowner whose horse was stolen. Stabler was his name, Harry Stabler. He claimed another fellow stole his horse out of his barn. The other fellow, a vagabond claiming to be a baker, said he had nothing to do with it, and no one had found any trace of the horse."

"God's eyelids, boy, why didn't you say so before? That's got to be it. Where was this fellow's barn, did he say?"

"First farm northeast of the castle. But we don't even have to go to him to ask about it. Arthur ordered him to give a description of the beast to Robin Kempe of the guard, and Robin was supposed to get his men off looking for it. I say we go to Robin, find out what Stabler told him about the horse, and see whether they've had any luck tracking the animal down. And there's more: Arthur gave the drifter, some fellow from Monmouth, a job in the kitchen. If he knows anything at all about the horse, he's definitely going to be as helpful as he can. The king ordered the cost of the horse taken out of his salary."

"Well, it will take him years to pay off the price of a warhorse. But then, a farmer wouldn't have had a warhorse in his barn either. I'm sure it was a muscular plow horse the maid mistook for a destrier. But this is good. We'll go straight to Camelot and talk to Robin first thing."

"All right," I said, standing up and starting toward the door. I was stopped short by the grand scowl on Merlin's face. He cleared his throat and gestured toward the chessboard with his eyes.

"All right," I sighed, "but as soon as the game is done, we ought to get moving. We've only got six days to prove Florent is innocent. The sooner we get started, the better chance we'll have."

Merlin waved his hand to me, as if to say we had nothing to worry about. "I won't let the little prig hang. Now make your move."

"All right, all right." There sat his queen, vulnerable and out in the open. What was he up to? He could bring her over to attack my pawn, and put my king in check, attacking my knight at the same time. The only move I'd have would be to interpose a piece—move my own queen in front of my king? That would force him to retreat. Or it would force him to take my queen and sacrifice his own. Not a prospect I found appealing. Or I could interpose my bishop. It would defend my king without putting my queen in jeopardy. The only problem was, it would leave my knight open for him to take. I wasn't crazy about that particular outcome either.

But I'd been thinking about that love-day at the king's court and remembering that, before the two men came in to argue about the horse, there was another plaintiff—one that was also useful to us in this case.

"You know, Merlin," I said to him, looking up from the board again. "I just remembered something else. There was another fellow testifying at the king's court that day, right before the two fellows had the argument about the horse. He was an innkeeper from Caerleon, and he was complaining to the king about the way some of the young knights and squires from Camelot behaved in his tavern the night before. He had to be talking about Florent and whoever he was out carousing with, didn't he?"

"It's unlikely there were two big parties of men from the castle celebrating Florent's knighting ceremony, one of which did not include him," the old man said slowly, still glaring at the chessboard with his chin in his hands. I heard sarcasm in his voice, but it was a little too much work to try to figure out why.

In any case, I continued: "He was a really big fellow, name of William Bailey, and he said there were six or seven of them that came to his inn, drank a good bit, and got into a big fight over something. Says they all got angry and left without paying their bill. But this is somebody we really need to talk to, don't you think? He could point out everyone who was there."

"I doubt it," Merlin answered. "Did he know them ahead of time? Did he serve them himself rather than have some wench draw their drinks? I'd be surprised if he could put his finger on more than one or two of the group. But I want to hear more about the fight. He's probably the one to tell us about that. Even if we find out who Florent's companions were, they're not likely to say anything about having a fight, especially if they get wind that we're trying to find out who framed Florent. My guess is that whoever did staged the fight to separate a drunken Florent from the rest of the group, and so give himself a chance to frame Sir Florent the Hapless."

"You're probably right," I conceded. "You know, when Bess pointed out Florent as the rapist, and Florent tried to say where he'd been, none of his companions would say a word. I know full well that Colgrevaunce, Sir Brandiles's squire, must have been with him. He's always doing things with Florent. And Sir Ywain's squire, too, Thomas. He and Colgrevaunce do everything together. But they looked around at the trial when Florent asked for help, as if they hadn't a clue where he was that night."

"And Florent himself never named them. Part of his code of

chivalry, I suppose—never implicate another noble knight, but always expect them to honor the truth themselves. That worked well for him, didn't it?"

"Well, I say we talk to Colgrevaunce and Thomas. They won't out-and-out lie to me if I confront them directly."

"We'll talk to them. They can tell us who else was present as well. But we'll talk to them separately, and time it so we interview them at the same time—I'll talk to one and you'll have to talk to the other, so they don't have a chance to meet and come up with a story together. One thing puzzles me though, Gildas."

"What is that?"

"Why weren't you at the tavern with Florent? Haven't you two been fairly close companions? Especially since you became Sir Gareth's squire, and Florent's been helping you develop your skills in tilting and swordplay? Why weren't you out celebrating with him on that important evening?"

I felt myself going red in the face and looked down, feigning interest in the chessboard. My answer was barely audible, but loud enough for the old man to hear. "I was jealous. I won't deny it. I didn't think I could be civil the whole night through."

"Well," Merlin mused, dropping his cross-examination. "It seems somebody else had some trouble keeping civil as well, by the sound of your innkeeper's testimony. Who was it, that's the question."

"Shouldn't we just talk to Florent to find out who else was there?"

"Well, we've come full circle, haven't we, Gildas? That would be the right question to ask Sir Florent. If we could find him. As I recall, the queen gave him but one week to scour the countryside and find the answer to the question of what women want most. He won't be easy to track down. No, I think we're going to have to start the investigation assuming our chief defendant won't be available for questioning. Blast your eyes, Gildas, will you make your move or not?"

"Oh yes, sorry." I looked at the board again. All right, if I moved my knight, then he couldn't get me into the predicament where I'd lose it if he took my king's pawn. Not only that, but I could move my knight into position to attack his queen, and so force him to either move it back or take my pawn, but without the consequence there would be if I left my knight where it was. "Okay," I said finally. "Knight to king's bishop three."

"Hmmph." Merlin grunted, as if he hadn't anticipated that move. So why did I have the feeling he had known all along that was precisely the move I would make?

"Sir Florent was set up," he began deliberately, not looking up at me or taking his eyes off the chessboard. "And it was a very well-planned trap. He was made to believe there was some kind of serious conflict brewing at the tavern, so much so that he left and spent the rest of the night alone. But the real attack came on a completely different target—on his honor and his good name. He was completely blindsided."

Merlin stood up and stretched. He reached over to where his dark hood lay on the bed and put it over his head. "We should be going. First stop, to see the good Robin Kempe and find out about that horse."

"But Merlin . . ." I said, glancing at the board.

"Oh yes," he said. He moved his queen forward to take my king's bishop's pawn. "Checkmate," he said, and headed out the door.

Chapter Six:
Wandering Horses and Daughters

It was a fine April day, with the sun growing warm and promising better days to come as we made our way out of the woods, across the freshly plowed fields where the peasants toiled at the spring planting. For probably the first of the dozens of times I had passed it, I noticed a small house near a ramshackle barn and stable, and assumed that must be the homestead on the quarter acre owned by the freeman Master Stabler, he of the missing horse. It seemed improbable to me, frankly, that such an unremarkable hovel could possibly be the home of a pure white stallion magnificent enough to be mistaken by Bess—city girl that she was—for a knight's destrier. The great warhorses were huge, muscular, and expensive. I doubted whether even a heavy plow horse could be so badly misidentified, even by a novice. Merlin glanced over at the site, then back to the path. If he had any thoughts similar to mine, he kept them to himself.

It was well after none when we arrived back at the castle. The drawbridge was down, as it generally was during daylight hours, when the traffic from Caerleon, from the country estates, and from distant lands gave the castle a bustling air, and when the barbican that guarded the main castle entrance was manned by archers of the king's guard. After we crossed the drawbridge, I looked up toward the barbican where I knew the soldiers must be sequestered, though I couldn't see them through the narrow cross-shaped windows that gave them just enough room to shoot an arrow through.

"Robin!" I called to one of the slits. "Are you up there? We need to talk to you!"

After a moment or two of muffled whispers and the sound of shifting a loud voice came back at us from one of the window slits. "Robin ain't here now," it called. "His shift's tonight. He's probably trying to catch some sleep. So he's in the keep. Why don't you go wake him up?" At that there were hearty laughs from more than one voice behind that stone wall.

"Thanks, we will," I answered. "And I'll tell him you told me to."

The laughter ceased pretty quickly at that word, and I heard one more half-hearted jibe as Merlin and I passed through the gate and into the outer courtyard, or lower bailey, of the castle grounds. "Sure, you do that. Tell him it came from the Saxon war party what's taken over the barbican. Tell him that, eh?"

I waved my hand as if to say he could count on me to deliver the message, as Merlin and I quickly crossed the inner bailey, making our way to the castle keep.

The keep was the most highly fortified part of the castle. A great tower intended to serve as the last refuge for defense should the castle be under siege, the keep was built of solid gray limestone blocks and loomed above the castle grounds like a colossus—grim, silent, and monolithic. The walls were some three feet thick at the base, tapering to a mere eighteen inches at the pinnacle, where the tower rose to a height of seventy-five feet. Within the circular tower, some fifty feet in diameter, slept the castle garrison. They were Spartan, barracks-like quarters, but in case of attack the keep was always manned this way, even by men on their off hours.

We entered the door of the keep to find a sleepy guard just inside. "State your business," the fellow said to Merlin as we walked in. Merlin gave me an ironic look, as if to say those of us on the king's business—well, let's be honest, it was more the queen's business, but still—ought to be given some kind of special right to move among the castle's occupants and require them to cooperate with us. I waved his look away.

"We have business with Master Robin Kempe," I told the guard. "It is urgent and we come at the queen's mandate."

"Right. Stay here, then. Back in a moment." The guard disappeared into the keep, leaving Merlin and me to cool our heels in the doorway. Merlin let out a heavy sigh and began drumming his fingers on the doorjamb. I wasn't sure it was a good idea to keep a necromancer waiting.

Finally, a yawning Robin appeared, rubbing his eyes as he made his way out to us. His long blond hair was tangled like a rats' nest, and his face was flushed with just waking, making his light yellow mustache look almost white against his lip. He was dressed in his usual belted green tunic and brown hose, and though he had clearly just been awakened by the guard, sleep hadn't dulled his sharp tongue.

"Well, if it isn't the old charlatan and his lackey, young Gildas of Cornwall. What's this I hear about the queen's business? She still trusting you with her personal affairs, boy? I thought she'd given you the boot and forced you to beg for crumbs from Sir Gareth's table."

I answered him in his own style. "I'm too valuable for her to let go of completely. Particularly when it comes to approaching personages of such great honor as yourself."

"Well, then, step into my private chambers and let's hear what you have to say." Robin stepped out into the open air of the middle bailey.

"You're both very amusing, I'm sure," Merlin conceded as we began a slow walk around the keep. "But some of us have actual work to do, so if you don't mind, I'd like to ask some questions."

"Fire away, old-timer," Robin told him. "Feel free to pick my brain to your heart's content."

"My heart is already content that there is little there to pick from. But I do want to find out about the horse you were commanded to search for, the one stolen from the barn of Master Stabler."

"That?" Robin scratched his head, and his blue eyes gazed at Merlin without understanding. "What interest can the queen possibly have in that godawful horse?"

"We have reason to suspect the person who raped Bess of Caerleon stole that horse before he assaulted her."

Merlin glared down at me with the look he reserved for times he thought I'd said too much, then addressed himself to Robin again. "We do not want that story spread around," he cautioned. "We are still in the early stages of our investigation, and it's better none of the suspects know what we infer or do not infer."

"Well, infer all you want as far as I'm concerned," Robin told him. "We haven't found the horse. I know it was a direct command from the king himself, and I swear I've had men combing the countryside from here to Lady Lake and south to the sea. We've turned up nothing. Of course, nobody told us Florent stole the horse to begin with, or I suppose we could have asked him before he went riding out of here this morning."

A sudden flash of insight struck. "Did you see him ride off yourself?" I asked. "What kind of horse was he riding?"

"Well, he wasn't riding no stolen horse, that's for sure. He was on the great new Andalusian stallion his daddy bought him. The little bugger rode off on him right after the queen gave him that quest, you know, find out what women want most? I've been trying to figure that out myself for some time, you know? Hope he comes back with an answer we can all use, eh Gildas? Maybe you can get yourself a new one now Rosemounde's been promised to the rapist, eh?"

Not that I'd expected a lot of sympathy from Robin, whose

main pleasure in life seemed to be finding new ways to get under my skin, but this last barb was not one I was in a mood to react good-naturedly to.

Merlin stepped in before I could take the interview in a direction he had no desire for it to go. "So we've established that Sir Florent did not have the stolen horse when he left here this morning. We've also established that you haven't found the horse yourself. What can you tell us? How did Master Stabler describe the horse to you? What did he say about it?"

"Well, he claimed the horse was large and muscular. Said it was used both to ride and to pull his plow—he's got no oxen, as I understand it."

"Fine, fine," Merlin said, getting a little impatient again. "But he described the color, did he not?"

"Right, the color. Interesting. Said it was an unusual color, so we probably wouldn't have any trouble knowing it was his horse for sure if we found it."

"Unusual, yes." Merlin kept probing. "Because it was *what color*?"

"A kind of pale dapple gray, the fellow said. With a light gray mane. I'll tell you, we've looked high and low and ain't found anything like it. So what makes you think Florent was the one that took it? Why should he, when he's got that brand-new brown Andalusian warhorse?"

Merlin's brows had lowered over his eyes in glum disappointment. *So much for that theory,* he seemed to be saying. But he answered Robin honestly. "We don't think Florent stole it."

"But I thought you said . . ."

"We said we thought the rapist took the horse. Neither of us believes Sir Florent is guilty of assaulting that girl."

"Well, I've got to admit it seemed pretty unlikely to me, too, but you know, the girl recognized the shield, and the king condemned the poor bugger."

"Neither of which proves he is guilty," Merlin pronounced. "But what do you think? Could a girl like Bess, surprised in the dark, mistake a light gray horse for a pure white destrier?"

Robin shook his head. "Who knows? I don't suppose in that kind of darkness colors are really easy to see. Everything probably looks washed out—white probably looks gray. But gray looking white? Who knows? Maybe."

"Find the horse," Merlin advised Robin. "Find it and then we'll see. Perhaps we can get Bess to take a look at it and see whether she thinks it might be the same one."

"We'll keep looking, old man. I'll send you word if we find the beast. Now if there's nothing else I can do for you two fine gentlemen, I hope you won't think me discourteous to excuse myself, but I've got to get some more sleep. I'll be on guard all night, and I don't think it sets a good example for the men if I snore through my shift." We had circled the keep in our walk and were back at the front door. Before he went back in, Robin turned to us with a last comment. "Good luck to you, though. You know, Sir Florent's no big favorite of mine, but I'm thinking there's somebody in this castle that's got away with a pretty godawful crime, and I'm buggered if I want to see that happen. We'll do what we can to help you." And with that Robin disappeared into the dark of the castle keep.

The streets of Caerleon were narrow and muddy, and most of them radiated outward from the cathedral. Merlin's long dark robes trailed in the dirt as he led me through the town to a side street where stood a row of shops, each with a wooden sign in front tokening the trade followed inside: a mortar and pestle indicating an apothecary, a tankard of beer denoting a brewer, a spinning wheel marking the shop of a clothmaker, and at the end of the street, a hammer and saw designating the shop of a carpenter.

I was dragging after the long day I'd had, but Merlin seemed as active as ever. It was after compline and I knew the shop would not be open, but as most of the shopkeepers lived in the back of their stores, Merlin seemed determined that we would be able to speak with Bess's father tonight.

"I'm not going a step farther," I told him finally. "If we don't get hold of the old fellow here at his shop, I'm going back to Camelot and going to bed."

"Oh, shut your yap. You should be able to keep going for hours yet, a young whippersnapper like you. Where's your stamina? How are you ever going to be a knight if you can't stay awake any longer than the sun?"

"Look, old man. I hardly got any sleep last night, because of . . . well, just because. And I was up at the crack of dawn this morning to witness Bess's announcement of her attacker. And I've been running around ever since, first to find you, then to help you. All to save Sir Florent's skin. And I don't even *like* Florent."

"No, but you like his fiancée well enough." Merlin glared down at me. We'd reached the door of the carpenter's shop, and sure enough, it was locked up tightly for the evening. But Merlin seemed unfazed, and didn't even slacken his conversation. "Look, my young Cornish knothead. Whatever our motives, we must clear Florent's name as promised, and there are only six days to do it in. And a lot of territory to cover. So by your leave, we'll clear up this little problem as soon as we're able." Merlin used his fist to pound as loudly as he could on the door, but there was no response from inside.

"Fine, we'll talk to the carpenter. I hope it's more successful than our conversation with Robin about the horse. But how are we going to get in? Your knocking doesn't seem to be having any noticeable effect. Or am I just being obtuse?"

"You're never anything but, my boy," he answered me. Then,

with a look of deep concentration, he fixed his dark eyes on the door latch and waved his hand over it, uttering in tones of an incantation the word *aperio*. The latch responded to his touch, and the door opened easily.

I knew better than to play into his hand by acting impressed. "All right," I said to him. "So was that actual magic, or do you just have some clever knack for picking locks?"

"Always keep 'em guessing, boy. That's one of the great secrets," Merlin responded, and stepped cautiously into the dark shop.

I shook my head as I followed him across the threshold, and then noticed a head peeking through a door opened a crack in the back of the shop. The carpenter was peering out to see whether his shop was being robbed, and seeing an unlikely pair of thieves.

"Come out, fellow!" Merlin called in a commanding tone to the shadow behind the door. "We're not here to rob you, just to ask you some questions."

"Right!" came a scornful reply. "And my aunt's buttocks are made of green cheese."

Merlin looked at me with his tangled mass of eyebrows twisted quizzically. Then he looked back to the door. "I suppose they are if you say they are. But come out, I need to ask you about your daughter. You can see I'm not armed and am not about to overpower you."

"Yeah, what about that young thug you've got with you there? 'E looks like 'e'd just as soon kill me as look at me. Got that evil glint in his eyes, 'e does."

Another quizzical look from Merlin, and even more tangled eyebrows. "Listen, Master Carpenter, I am Merlin, advisor to the king, and my companion is Gildas of Cornwall, squire to the valiant knight Sir Gareth of Orkney. Neither one of us has any intention of harming you. If you'll simply come out of there, you'll see it's safe. We only want to ask you some questions."

"Oh, right. If you're that bloody Merlin, you'll probably turn me into a horny toad or some such thing. And squire guild-arse there will likely knock me over the head with his sword hilt. I'll stay right where I am, thank you very much."

"God's kneecaps, man!" Merlin exploded. "I swear I'll knock you over the head myself if you don't come out of there right now. This is the king's business we're about. Now get yourself out here." And with that, the old necromancer stepped forward, yanked the door open, and pulled the carpenter out by the front of his smock.

"All right, all right, you've made your point, ye great bloody bearded bully. Let me be now, and I'll answer your questions. Just let go of me."

There was a wooden chair in the shop, and Merlin shoved the carpenter into it. "Sit there," he told him, "and talk to us. We only want to find out some things about your daughter."

"That little tart," he scoffed. "I might 'a known she'd be the cause of a band of ruffians breaking into my shop and terrorizing me. No damn good, that wench, I tell ye. Just like 'er mother."

Merlin was beyond frustration with the carpenter's paranoid imagination, so he skipped over it and went straight for the information he was after. "You are Bess of Caerleon's father?"

"Course I am, that's what I'm telling you, ain't it? Name of John, John the carpenter of Caerleon. Bess is my daughter, though I scarcely like to claim it. Bess was her mother's name, too. That slut left me fifteen years ago with a little girl to raise by myself. Think of it! She run off with a traveling band of players that come into town one day. What do you think of that?"

"Hard to imagine anyone leaving a prize like yourself," I couldn't help remarking. He really wasn't much to look at, I noticed as I stared down at him squirming on the edge of his chair. He was bald on top with long, stringy white hair encircling that dome. His nose was bulbous and his eyes small and shifty. He slouched and wrung his hands as he spoke, and his skinny legs were bare under his dirty white smock. He was holding a scrap of brown bread in one hand that he now gnawed on with what few teeth he had remaining in his head—we must have disturbed him during his evening meal.

"Look, old man," Merlin asked him with a strained kind of calm. "We understand you did some work for the Lady of the Lake recently. Is that true? Just tell us yes or no."

"She's a great queen, the Lady," John answered, a kind of awe in his voice. "Sent one of 'er maids to fetch me to 'er palace. That was something to see, let me tell you. She wanted a library built—shelves to house 'er great books. I made it out of solid oak—a beautiful bookcase. Pleased 'er quite a lot, it did. She gave me a nice price for it."

"She paid you? Paid you immediately?" I asked.

"Course she did. What, you think the Lady is a welcher? Not bloody likely. No, I told 'er I'd be happy to do work for 'er again. But what's that got to do with my daughter? You people aren't making any sense whatsoever."

Merlin followed that lead immediately. "Bess told us—told the king, that is—that she was out in the woods some time after lauds a few mornings ago because she was on an errand for you, to collect payment from the Lady of the Lake for some work you had done for her. You're telling us that isn't true?"

He shook his head and scowled in disgust. "I was paid on the spot when I finished the job. If Bess was out in the woods that time of morning, it weren't for anything *I* sent her after. What's that tart done now?"

"Does she live here with you? Are you aware when she comes and goes?" Merlin asked, beginning to get a picture of what Bess's home life must be like.

"I'm stuck with her until she's married, worse luck," John replied. "But she listens to me about as good as a deaf Irishman listens to his dumb Welsh wife. She comes and goes pretty much as she pleases."

"Not here right now, then, is she?" I asked.

"Right. She's out there in the kitchen right now with the queen of Sheba and Attila the Hun. Maybe they've got room for you too, sonny."

"Well, as her father, don't you exercise some control over her?" Merlin asked, innocently enough.

"Oh sure I do. Spoken like a true childless bachelor. She was done listening to anything I had to say when she turned thirteen. Slut stays out all hours—I never know when she'll pop in or when she'll leave."

"Are you aware," Merlin asked slowly, trying to decide what kind of reaction to expect, "that Bess appeared at the king's love-day court yesterday, claiming she'd been raped by a knight of the Round Table?"

The look on John's face made it abundantly clear that this news came as a complete surprise to him. There may even have been a moment of concern for his daughter flashing across his face before he took a deep breath and grumbled loudly, "Wouldn't you know it? After all I put into raising her, some landed knight comes along and without so much as a 'by your leave' plucks her just when she's ripe enough to finally attract some husband to take 'er off my hands. Now nobody'll want 'er. Blast! It's 'er own fault, ain't it? Like you said, she's wandering about the woods at night, what's she expect? Alms from the squirrels? I'm stuck with 'er for good now, I s'pose, unless I can get the convent to take 'er. Or the brothel. One way or another she can fend for 'erself that way . . ."

It was almost more than I could stomach, and I felt like throttling the old whiner just to shut him up. "Keep your grousing to yourself, will you? Haven't you got any sympathy for your own child? What have you got against her, anyway? She's not her mother, she's your daughter."

"Ah, now it comes to it." He turned to Merlin. "So now your brute of a companion'll throttle me, is that it?"

"I'll throttle you myself if you don't stop the moaning. Just answer his question, will you?"

"She's 'er mother's daughter, that's the truth. Ever since she began working as a hostess at that William Bailey's inn, she's been out all night, almost every night. Who knows what she's doing for the customers in that place, eh? No wonder she was out in the woods before dawn. Nothing wholesome in that, I can tell you."

Merlin and I looked at each other, dumbstruck. We needed no words to realize that we both had the same thought.

"Well, thank you for your help, Master Carpenter. We will leave you in peace now, and apologize for disturbing your evening repast." Merlin gave a courteous nod of his head and turned to stride out the door. I followed close behind.

"Well, isn't that just like all you snotty gentles from the castle. You stop by, but will you stay awhile to keep me company? No! My company isn't good enough for you. Oh, you're far too good for the likes of me. . . ." His voice trailed off as the door closed behind us. Merlin was walking with long strides back up the street and toward the castle, so that I had to jog to keep up with him.

"Now there's a pleasant fellow," I said. "But it was worth our time, wasn't it? So Bess actually worked for the same establishment where Florent and the others were carousing the other night. What do you think of that?"

"William Bailey's inn," Merlin said, sounding strained and looking more tired than I had seen him in some time. "Yes. It confirms some of our conclusions, does it not? If she was a hostess there, then everyone at the party would have . . ."

He trailed off. He kept moving, but not so quickly as before. I completed his thought. "Everyone with Florent may have seen her, may have known where she was going later that evening. It could have been very easy for one of them to overhear her plans and concoct the whole plot against Sir Florent then and there."

"Or even," Merlin continued slowly, "for one of them to make a date to meet her in the woods himself. We should trust no one."

"Now you sound like John the carpenter."

But Merlin was in no laughing mood. He stretched out his right hand and laid it on my shoulder. "Get me to a bed as quickly as you can," he advised. "No more speech. I'm going to be ill . . . it's coming soon." He rubbed his temples with his left hand and I knew what he must mean—one of his great headaches was coming on, and I must get him as quickly as possible to a place where he could sleep. We were still half a mile from the castle, and I led him along that road as fast as I could get him to move. The sun was setting and the long shadows behind us were moving in a macabre, ghostlike dance as we approached the drawbridge and crossed it just before the guards began to pull it up for the evening. The bells in the convent of Saint Mary Magdalene were chiming vespers as we made our way across the bailey to the lesser hall and a cot for Merlin.

As he lay down on one of the benches in the dark, I saw his face—one eye bulged significantly while the other squinted and seemed to turn inward, and in a tired, distant-sounding voice, Merlin uttered words I could not understand:

"Gildas!" he said, grasping me by my tunic and staring at me with that one bulging eye. "The thorns of the rose are darts. The green limb is black."

"Great!" I told him. "Thanks."

I didn't mean to be sarcastic—well, maybe I did, but it's because when Merlin has one of these spells, he becomes useless for at least twenty-four hours. We'd just begun our investigation, and he was incapacitated. Sure, this spell of his caused him to see and pronounce one of his famous prophecies of the future, but as usual, it was steeped in symbol and innuendo, and so was meaningless—and useless—to us in the investigation, unless at some point we figured out the symbols. Looking for evidence and talking to suspects was a lot more beneficial to the investigation, I can assure you. But just in case, I tried to commit the prophecy to memory. Merlin himself wouldn't remember he had said it after he woke up. So . . . thorns are darts, green is black, okay. I guess I had it. But it made no sense to me. And as I lay down myself to the sound of Merlin's snoring, I worried. All we had were six days, and now we were going to lose at least one of them to Merlin's melancholy. We'd better move all the faster once Friday rolled around.

CHAPTER SEVEN:
A STAG PARTY

William of Newcastle was employed in Camelot as Arthur's chief huntsman, a position of vital importance in the court. Hunting was both pastime and passion for the majority of knights, and some of the ladies as well, who saw it as a noble sport. But it was more than sport: It put food on the table and provided furs for the winter months, and in a castle as large as Camelot, with as many retainers as Arthur kept, hunting went on every day. William usually took a group of knights into the woods north of the castle early in the morning, and spent the majority of most days beginning in the late spring tracking hinds or stags. For William it was a serious profession. For the knights, it was an occasional pleasure and occupation, and a chance to exercise their horses and dogs.

Sir Gareth woke me soon after lauds. He had planned an all-day hunt with William and was keen on my coming along. "Merlin is for it anyway today," he told me as I shook myself awake and looked over at the old man, who slept curled up on a pallet next to me and showed no sign of life. "He's having one of his spells, and won't be able to do any investigating today, you can count on it. So up you go! We need to pick up the queen's greyhounds before we leave."

Aeneas and Dido, the queen's pampered dogs, loved to join in the hunt when they had the chance, and Sir Gareth must have promised Guinevere he'd take them today. "All right," I said, pulling on my green tunic and hood for the adventure.

"Who else is coming?"

"Gaheris and Agravain, and their squires. Sir Ywain and Sir Palomides. And their squires, of course, and William's apprentices to handle the dogs."

"Then why don't they pick up Aeneas and Dido?" I wanted to know as I got up and followed Sir Gareth quietly out the door of the lesser hall.

"Oh, my boy, you know the queen. She specifically asked that you be the one to watch her dogs. How pleasant it must be to be so well loved."

That was hours ago. We'd got the dogs and I'd stood still for a lot of tail wagging, jumping up, and licking from Aeneas and Dido, who hadn't seen me for some weeks. We'd picked up our horses, not destriers but smaller and swifter palfreys for chasing the quarry, and met the other members of the party at the barbican. There were thirteen of us altogether, all on horseback except for Tom and Henry, William's two apprentices, who held on to his hounds, and took Aeneas and Dido's leashes from me to hold with William's two bloodhounds or lymers, and two other greyhounds belonging to Sir Agravain.

Each of the knights and squires was dressed simply like me, in a belted and hooded green or brown tunic, each carrying crossbows with wooden darts, of the kind that could be easily fired from a galloping horse. If in fact anything could be easily fired from a galloping horse.

We'd made our way well into the woods, and now sat in a circle, anxious for the day's sport to begin and waiting for Tom and Henry to catch up with the dogs. It was now a bit after prime, and Bertrand de Toledo, Sir Palomides's squire, was passing out cold meat, bread, and bottles of wine for us to break our fast.

"The fare is simple," Sir Palomides admitted modestly. "But I think you'll find that the spices I've seasoned the meat with will make up for the ascetic meal."

I bit into a piece of cold beef and couldn't believe my good fortune. I hadn't had anything that tasty in months.

There were moans of pleasure from all around me as the others bit into their sliced beef as well. "Palomides, you Moorish devil, what kind of magic did you work on this meat?" Sir Ywain raved.

"Curry is the key," Palomides confided. "And a few other spices native to my homeland. But I'm not giving away all my secrets."

While the nobles chatted over their light picnic breakfast, William met his apprentices and the dogs. He took his two bloodhounds by their leashes and began to circle the camp, letting the dogs sniff about for signs of a stag. William was dressed in leather boots and thick leather leggings over his hose for protection against brambles and the like. In the belt that girded his green tunic was a long sword to be used for killing wounded game, and a sharp knife for skinning the animal. A leather thong was also tucked into his belt for later, to slap against his boots and signal the dogs—but more important for that purpose was the ivory horn that hung around his neck. Sir Gareth, acting as lord of the hunt, carried a similar horn himself.

I sat with Sir Ywain's squire Thomas on my right, and Baldwin, Agravain's squire, on my left, silently chewing the tasty beef and the fine white bread, washing it down with a bottle of Bordeaux that we passed among us. I watched William and his lymers, who seemed to have found something. William was crouching down, examining the fumes that the dogs had found, noting the size of them, and the size of the stag's tracks. He stood up then to look at some of the nearby bushes, noting where any of the stag's velvet antler covering may have rubbed off. He seemed satisfied. He picked up something from the ground (I assumed it was animal droppings) and put them in his horn to carry back to the circle.

William approached Sir Gareth on his right side and bent over to speak in his ear. Gareth was across the circle from me so I couldn't hear what was being said, but William was pointing to the contents of his horn and holding his hand up about shoulder high to indicate how large he thought the stag was whose trail the hounds had picked up. Gareth looked pleased and nodded.

"We're ready!" Sir Gareth said as he stuffed one last crust of bread into his mouth and stood up, dusting off his hands. "William has found us a good-sized stag. Let's get mounted!"

As the rest of us quietly mounted our horses to await the signal, William and the apprentice named Tom took all six dogs and began to make their way very quietly toward the place where they knew the stag must be, trying to outflank him and get to his other side to head off any escape route the animal might contemplate.

As I sat my horse, holding the reins with one hand and a loaded crossbow in the other, ready to let fly a dart at the unsuspecting prey, I was struck for a moment by how strange and unnatural the scene seemed: Eight men on horseback lined up in the woods, neither man nor horse making the slightest sound, while six dogs circled one poor stag as quietly as *they* possibly could. Since my mind was preoccupied with the case anyway, I began to wonder how much Bess of Caerleon might have been like that unwary stag—alone in the woods, suspecting no foul play, but about to be surprised and assaulted. And how many others might have been in that wood at the same time, and her unaware of their presence? Certainly Sir Florent had been nearby. And the rapist. Could someone else have been in the vicinity? Why not? The woods provided perfect cover for all kinds of mischief, unsuspected by even those, like the stag, who made their home there.

Suddenly, two loud notes from a horn a quarter mile distant stirred me from my reverie and put everything into rapid motion.

At the sound of the horn, William let slip the dogs, and the speedy greyhounds drove immediately for the stag. The quarry came rushing away from the dogs and toward the hunters and its own doom. Catching sight of the men on horseback, the stag bolted toward our right, and we all spurred our horses to the chase. By now Dido and Aeneas, the swiftest of the hounds, had caught up to the stag and were leaping upon it, hindering its pace. Gareth, out in front of the flurry of riders, leveled his crossbow and shot the animal. Close behind him, Bertrand, Sir Palomides's squire, loosed a shot of his own.

Gareth's dart caught the stag high on the neck, while Bertrand's sharp arrow whizzed through the air and lodged in the stag's right flank. The beast flinched, stumbled, and then the dogs were upon him. Sir Gareth blew a note of triumph on his horn, and we all let out a rousing cheer as William and his apprentices rushed in to pull the dogs off. William then yanked the sword from his belt to finish off the stag quickly and mercifully.

While we passed around another wine bottle to celebrate, William and his two helpers began to skin and dress the animal. They were careful to lay out the liver and heart on a skin for the dogs to devour, as their reward for a job well done.

The scene was repeated three more times during the day, until we had more meat than we could carry back to the castle, and William sent his youngest apprentice Henry back to Camelot for a wagon to help transport the carcasses. Meanwhile we built a campfire and set up a spit on which to broil venison for a great feast after a hard day's hunt. It was nearly compline and time to rest, and to enjoy our own reward. The day of exercise had nearly taken my mind off my troubles, and while the meat sizzled on the spit and we sat around the campfire, we were in the mood for some impromptu entertainment.

"Sir Palomides," Sir Ywain called to the Moor. "Why don't you regale us with one of those love poems of yours? Haven't you set them to music?"

Sir Palomides's dark eyes widened and he smiled at Ywain, pleased to have his talents recognized. "Oh, for this audience I've got the perfect poem, set to a good troubadour melody. But I don't sing them myself. That's one of the reasons I have Bertrand."

Without waiting for an order from his master, the squire Bertrand de Toledo got up and went to his horse, where in a bag under the saddle he had brought a lute to accompany himself in song. There was more cheering, and more passing of the wine bottle, as Bertrand began to play a few chords on his instrument. He was probably a little older than I was, about eighteen years old, and his features were dark—not, admittedly, as black as Sir Palomides, but clearly reflecting the Moorish heritage of his home city. His hair was black and his eyes a deep brown almost as dark. His nose was hooked and his chin strong and protruding. When he spoke, his eyes half-closed, he didn't open his mouth all the way, so that sometimes it seemed only his lips moved.

"Which is it I shall play?" he asked Sir Palomides, with a trace of an accent typical of a Spanish Moor.

"Play the song about the hunt. You know the one," Sir Palomides encouraged him.

"Ah!" was Bertrand's answer, and he gave a close-mouthed smile as he played a few introductory notes on the lute, and then began in a high, sweet tenor:

> *My lady flees me as a deer*
> *Runs from the hunter's dart.*
> *And I pursue my love with just one thought:*

97

That either I will force her to be caught
Or pierce her heart
With my love's rigid spear.

The lady roves within the wood
And I ride close behind
I prick my horse hard in the amorous chase
Till, coming close by her, I see her face.
Will she be kind,
And be for me the highest good?

Like passions wild within my breast
The horse and hounds run free,
And my pursuit now holds my love at bay,
And she becomes my weakened, yielding prey
She gives in to my plea,
And I find I am more than blest.

I load my bow and my shot strikes home,
My arrows pierce her side.
I mount again and prick away at will,
And find that she is dying for me still
And opens her mouth wide
Blowing my horn so to her I come.

There were loud guffaws and some rude remarks as Bertrand finished his song. I shook my head with a wry smile and looked over at Thomas, who was wide-eyed with astonishment at the lyrics, and Baldwin, who was actually rolling on the ground with laughter. Sir Gareth, though smiling indulgently, was shaking his head at the loose talk, and holding up his hands for quiet.

"We need to thank Bertrand, and Sir Palomides, the author of the song, for this entertainment. But it is not seemly that here in the woods we make so bold with the idea of woman's virtue." As he said it I couldn't help remembering the plight of Bess of Caerleon and the hunt in which she served as quarry but a few nights ago in these very woods. I wondered whether Sir Gareth was reacting to the irony of that situation or whether he merely scorned such ribaldry as a mark of discourtesy. But he continued: "In these woods, where it is women who can do the hunting!" At the puzzled looks from the faces around the fire, Sir Gareth nodded and then, taking a swig from a bottle of which he'd already had a little bit too much, he stood up and I realized it was all a lead-in to one of his stories. Smiling, I leaned back in the grass, letting my elbows support me, and got ready for the tale I knew was coming.

"These woods belong to the Lady of the Lake, and never forget it," he told us. "Do not be disrespectful of the power of the Lady. Her presence is everywhere hereabouts, and even the king has learned to respect it."

"The king?" Thomas asked, startled. "But his power is the greatest in Europe. Why should he worry about this Lady? What power does she have?"

"There are many stories I could tell you that would turn your blood cold," Gareth began, as the shadows began to close around us and the venison crackled over the fire. "You've all heard about how the Lady gave Arthur his sword, Excalibur, with which he's won every battle he ever fought since, haven't you?"

Clearly we hadn't, as the squires looked at one another wide-eyed and shrugging with ignorance, while Ywain and Gaheris nodded knowingly.

"Well, that's a story for another time," Gareth continued, as I let out an exasperated sigh. "But let me tell you about Sir Launfal. I suppose you've heard of *him*, at least?" The rest of us shook our heads; even Ywain did not seem to know the story.

"Well, Sir Launfal was a foreign knight . . ."

"Oh, from where?" Sir Palomides asked eagerly. He had been everywhere, and nothing, at least nothing other than cooking, interested him more than exotic places and people.

"A Bohemian knight," Gareth answered. "He was noble born back in Prague, you see, but he was a second son, so he inherited no land. But he had a good horse and arms and so he set off as a wandering knight-errant, looking for some great lord that he could attach himself to. And that's when he came to Arthur. In those days, Arthur was still looking for eager young knights to help him in his wars, and he took on Launfal gladly, for Launfal had a good strong arm and was of noble blood.

"Well pretty soon Launfal got to be a favorite among the knights. He was as friendly a fellow as you'd hope to find, and generous, too. They say that he no sooner had a farthing but he'd spend it on some gift for a friend, or a bottle of wine to go around. Launfal was a knight of the Round Table, but before too long Arthur didn't think that much of him. He thought Launfal was a great spendthrift, because he always seemed to be in need, but that was because he was a lot more generous than he was practical.

"But Arthur thought Launfal wasn't worth giving gifts to, because he'd just go and waste it, and after a while it got so Sir Launfal was down to nothing but the horse and arms he'd come with. His robes were threadbare and his horse wasn't so well fed either, and he didn't have quite so many friends now that he had nothing to be generous with, so he got to thinking maybe he'd be better off to head out and look for some adventures on his own, preferably adventures that would earn him a little more to live on than he was getting at the castle.

"So one day he rides off, into the woods north of Camelot, right where we're sitting now . . ."

By that time the meat was cooked, and William and Tom

were taking it off the spit and carving it into portions to divide among the nobles. As they passed the helpings out, Gareth went on with his story.

"So riding through the woods, he starts hearing this music, and he can't quite figure it out, because it sounds like stringed instruments—lutes and the like. So he follows the sound and he comes to the stream that runs to Lady Lake." I knew that stream well. It was the cold stream I had to cross to get to Merlin's cave.

"Across the water," Gareth continued, "was a great and colorful pavilion, and at the door of the tent are the two most beautiful women he's ever seen: one fair-skinned, golden-haired, and blue-eyed, the other olive-skinned, black-haired, and brown-eyed, both wearing jeweled tiaras and dressed exotically, like Saracen women." He glanced aside at Sir Palomides, who gave a little half-smile.

"They stop playing the song when they see him, and they just stare at him, not saying a word. Well, Launfal is mystified, and he wants to cross the brook to come to the tent, but the horse balks at it. So he dismounts and ties his horse to a tree, and crosses the stream on foot. When he gets to the other side, the ladies come up to him and each one takes an arm and they lead him into the tent.

"Well, there in the middle of the tent is a woman even more beautiful than the other two, reclining on a pile of luxuriant robes and dressed like the others but even more richly, with jeweled necklace, bracelets, and rings and an even more stunning tiara. Her eyes are a bright green and her hair a rich auburn, and her skin is the fairest Launfal has ever seen. And she says to him, 'Come, Launfal, I have been waiting for you. I've been watching you for years, and I know your good heart and your generosity. Of all Arthur's knights, you are the most selfless. You care so little for your own well-being that you give away all you have. The king and others misunderstand but I can see: Your largesse is too fine for the world of men and so they call it impractical. And therefore I am here to offer you my love, for you of all men deserve it.' "

"And that was the Lady of the Lake?" piped up Hectimere, Sir Gaheris's squire, who no one remembered saying a word all day up to that point. He was a blotchy, freckled fifteen-year-old Scotsman with a mop of red-blond hair and quizzical blue eyes, and the very beginning of a thin mustache on his upper lip that he was exceedingly proud of. But he never said much.

"Precisely!" Gareth teased him. "You're right on top of things, young Hectimere!" The squire reddened, then slumped down sullenly and crossed his arms, determined to say nothing more until the tale had ended.

While we all took another bite of venison, Sir Gareth went on with the story. "The two ladies-in-waiting closed the door of the pavilion and left the Lady and Sir Launfal to their privacy, as I will as well. But I don't have to tell you Launfal accepted the Lady's offered love. And you will have no trouble believing he was quite as happy as it is possible for us poor mortals to be. But after several days in the tent with the Lady, waited on hand and foot by the two beautiful maidens, who always kept their silence, Launfal was told he must leave his paradise.

" 'You can't stay here in sloth forever,' the Lady told him. 'You need to make your name in the world. Go back to Arthur's castle, for that is the place where the world's most courteous knights dwell, and there you can win honor. But we will not say goodbye. You have only to go into a lonely corner of the castle or the grounds, where no one can observe us, and call my name, and I will appear there instantly to be with you. And I give you this.' And so saying, she held out to him a rich, fur-lined leather purse filled with gold pieces. 'My Lady!' Launfal cried. 'Such generosity! This is more gold than I could spend in a lifetime!'

"The Lady laughed at that, because she knew him better than he knew himself. 'You'll go through it in a month, my love,' she said to him. 'But that is the beauty of the gift. Whatever you spend from the bag will be replaced the next time you reach into it. It is a bottomless purse that will enable you to be as generous as your nature demands.'

"Well, Launfal went down on his knee and kissed the Lady's hand, and pledged his eternal love for her. But before he left she stopped him. 'One more thing,' she told him. 'When made public, love rarely endures. For my sake, we must always keep our love a secret. The moment you mention me to another living soul, that is the last moment you will have my love.'

"And with that the Lady, her pavilion, and her two magnificent ladies-in-waiting all disappeared, and Launfal was left alone on the shore of the stream, looking across at his horse, who was shaking his head in baffled silence. If it hadn't been for the bag full of gold coins he was still holding, Launfal would have thought it was all a dream." Now Sir Gareth paused to take a breath, and another big bite from the haunch of meat he held in one hand, the nearly empty wine bottle in the other.

"But it wasn't a dream, and over the next few weeks, Launfal was happier than he had ever been. He called for his Lady at least once a day, when he found a private place and a quiet moment, and she always came to him and spent time with him as only lovers can. And the fur-lined bag was never empty, so that Launfal's reputation as the most generous of knights was rekindled and even advanced, as people were amazed by the kind of gifts he showered them with.

"At the same time, Launfal was becoming one of Arthur's most valuable knights. Sir Launfal helped Arthur win the Irish war, and the Gaulish war. He earned respect as a noble knight and a brave one, and Arthur began to look on him with friendly eyes again.

"Now this went on for some two years. Launfal was acclaimed, he was beloved, he was happy. But his reputation started to become a problem for him because the court got to wondering why he never seemed interested in any of the ladies. Keep in mind that this was early in Arthur's reign, before he married the queen. His half-sister, my aunt Morgan le Fay, was here in Camelot acting as the First Lady." Sir Gareth took another swig from his bottle and I could tell he was getting more and more loose-tongued as the story progressed. He went on.

"Well, good old aunt Morgan was a lot like her sister, my dear departed mother, in that she never worried much about morals where love was concerned."

At that Sir Gaheris rose and glowered at Gareth. Remembering how it was Gaheris that had struck off their mother's head when he found her in bed with Sir Lamorak, I wondered that Gareth would flaunt his mother's indiscretions the way he was doing, at least in front of Sir Gaheris. But Gaheris stalked off without a word, standing by himself at the edge of the trees, and Gareth's story continued.

"So one spring day in the inner bailey, while most of the court is out walking or playing on the green, enjoying the sunny weather, Morgan gets Launfal alone and says to him, 'Sir Launfal! I've long admired your courage on the battlefield and your generosity in court. The knights and ladies all look up to you. But I notice you haven't got a lady, and that's a shame. So I'm going to offer you the best thing you can imagine: I offer you myself. Look at me! Don't you find me beautiful? Come to my bed tonight and I'll show you what you've been missing all this time.' " At that I heard Sir Ywain sigh, and remembered with a jolt that Morgan was in fact Ywain's own mother. But everybody knew Morgan's reputation, so Ywain didn't bother to raise any protest. He knew Gareth's story to be true.

"Launfal tried to hold back his words. How could he answer her? To refuse her would make him seem discourteous, but her offer was not exactly a courteous one to begin with. But he didn't want to insult her. She was, after all, the king's sister. He tried a courteous refusal: 'My lady,' he told her, 'I dare not deem myself worthy of even imagining the kind of love you suggest. Surely you are saying these things merely to test my courtesy, and I hope I have passed your test by acknowledging your beauty and my own unworthiness. I beg your leave to return to sport with the other knights and remove my undeserving dross from the shining sun of your presence.' "

Thomas whistled, and Baldwin, Sir Agravain's squire, let out a scornful sneer. "Fawning like a puppy!" he scoffed.

"It didn't last long," Sir Gareth cocked his head at Baldwin, and added, "because it didn't work. Morgan saw right through that courtly mask. 'So you are denying me?' she cried. 'Me? My royal blood and beauty you reject? How dare you insult me in this manner!'

" 'But my lady, I meant no insult,' Launfal answered. 'I simply do not think I am the man for you.' Well, let me tell you, Auntie Morgan was not about to take this kind of treatment. 'What can possibly be your reason for this insult? You must be one of those knights that doesn't like women, is that it? One of those who likes to have his pleasure with little boys, that's you, Launfal, eh? Well, I won't have your kind of degenerate in this castle. I'm going to the king and reveal what kind of person you are, and have you thrown out of Camelot.'

"Well, Launfal had taken just about enough of that woman's vile tongue. He was angry enough to forget everything else but Morgan le Fay's insults, and without thinking he blurted out an answer to her charges. 'My lady, you are quite wrong. I rejected your offer because my own dear Lady is my only love: Even her lowest handmaid is more courteous and more beautiful than you are, and I would never betray her for the likes of you!'

"You won't be surprised to learn that Morgan was furious. She was so livid that she turned pale and couldn't even speak at his insulting speech. Launfal took his leave of her with a curt nod and as he started away, Morgan croaked out just these few words: 'You will pay for this insult.' "

"Served her right, the damned slut," Sir Agravain piped up, visibly moved by the story that he seemed to vaguely know from having been told many years earlier. "I've met my aunt Morgan le Fay a few times, but that was long after she'd moved out of Camelot (by the king's request, as I recall) and set up housekeeping in her own castle. Always acting like she was the queen and not Guinevere, and never a kind word from her, either, so this doesn't surprise me."

"But as you describe her," Gareth went on, "you can see she isn't the kind of woman you would want to cross, or the kind of woman to take a perceived insult without striking back. And she struck back at Sir Launfal with everything she had. She went straight to the king and told him Launfal had tried to rape her. When she denied him and fought him off, Morgan told Arthur, Sir Launfal scoffed at her and insulted her by saying he had his own woman whose lowest handmaid was more beautiful than she was.

"Now, you know the king. You know he would not let the kind of charge she made against the knight go unanswered or unpunished. Besides, he remembered his old dislike of Sir Launfal for his loose spending, and was perfectly willing to believe the word of his sister in the matter. The next day he called Sir Launfal up before the whole court and told him of Morgan's charges, asking him if he had any answer to them.

"In the meantime, Sir Launfal had called on his beloved Lady to come to him and give him solace after the incident with the king's sister. But as you can probably guess, he got no answer. Remember the Lady had given him only one condition, that he not reveal their love to a living soul. He had broken that one condition of their love, and she abandoned him as she had warned. So when Arthur questioned Launfal about the charges against him, he was pretty indifferent. He'd lost his lady, his only reason to live, and was indifferent now to his own welfare. He denied any attempted rape of the Lady Morgan, but reiterated his insult: 'The charge of rape is ridiculous,' he told the king. 'I have no desire for your discourteous and foul sister, because, as I told her when she tried to seduce me, my own mistress's lowest handmaid is far more courteous and more beautiful than that witch.'

"Not the smartest way to address the king, at least not if you want to come out of the trial with your life, but as I said, at that point Launfal didn't really care. The king, being as fair as his temper would allow, gave Sir Launfal one week to bring back a defense, and if he couldn't prove he was innocent of Morgan's charges, he would hang.

"Launfal couldn't have cared less. His purse was empty, and he knew that was a sign his Lady had deserted him. He'd lost her love because he couldn't keep his mouth closed about their secret."

"But surely the Lady knew he'd been provoked . . ." Thomas complained. He was perhaps a little too involved in the story, as if by arguing he could change the outcome of it.

"Provoked or not," Gareth went on, "he was definitely forsaken by his fairy mistress. He languished in his cell in the castle all week. Some of the other knights, who hated Morgan le Fay and loved Launfal for his generosity, visited him and tried to get him to take some interest in his own defense, saying they'd vouch for him, but he was indifferent to life or death without the one thing that gave him any reason to be alive: his beloved Lady.

"The week passed, and the day came that Launfal was to come back before the king to defend himself against Morgan le Fay's charges. But just as the court began to assemble to hear the king's dispensation in the case, a young woman entered the gates of the castle riding a gray palfrey. She was dressed in the finest blue samite and wore a crown of silver upon her head, and her golden hair flowed long and free around her shoulders. Everyone who saw her was agape. They had never seen such beauty in their lives. The lady dismounted and walked into Arthur's throne room, where the court was gathered for Launfal's case, and the king asked her if she wished to speak. All the knights there assembled said to each other, 'Aha, this must be Launfal's Lady! She's as beautiful as he said, and she'll vouch for him now!' But Launfal, standing with his hands tied before him, only looked at them and shook his head, as much as to say they were wrong, this was not his sovereign Lady.

"The golden-haired beauty, whose name was Nimue, only curtsied to the king and said to him, 'My Lady is on her way to see you, my lord King. I come ahead to ensure a courteous welcome for her.'

"Well, Arthur was pretty impressed by this, and gave a courteous reply, saying the Lady would indeed be welcome and he looked forward to extending to her the service of Camelot.

"Just at that moment another rider entered the gates. This one rode a dark brown palfrey. She was dressed in magnificent black samite that matched her raven hair, and her brown eyes sparkled almost as much as the gold crown she wore. She, too, dismounted and made her way into the throne room, and the knights, convinced that this lady was even more strikingly beautiful than the last, now all whispered to each other that this must be she, this must be Launfal's mistress, come to clear his name. But the captive knight only hung his head, because of course this one wasn't his Lady either.

"But the dark-haired beauty, Amaryllis, curtsied to King Arthur also, and the young king nodded back to her as she addressed him: 'My lord King,' she said, 'my Lady is coming, and I am here to see she is received with the greatest of courtesy.' So Arthur looks her up and down and says, 'For your sake as well as for her own, we will endeavor to greet her with all the courtesy due to one of such noble rank.'

"Just as the king was answering the maiden Amaryllis this way, in through the barbican gate of the castle rides the most magnificent woman anyone in this age can possibly imagine. Dressed in pure white samite with a crown of precious jewels, she sat upon a huge snow-white palfrey, her auburn hair flowing like a cloud on the breeze, her eyes like bright emeralds fixed straight before her in a gaze that seemed to regard all around her as beneath her notice. She left her white horse directly beneath the door of the throne room, and mounted the steps like an angel floating through the door and into the court. At the sight of her, women gasped and hid their faces behind fans or nosegays for shame; knights and squires stared dumbfounded and some swooned, unable to sustain the splendor of her visage or the radiance of her presence."

At that Sir Gaheris, who had moved back into the circle, rolled his eyes and shook his head. "Just tell the story," he muttered. "You don't need to embellish it."

Sir Gareth scoffed. "This from somebody who puts his own wife to sleep when he tells her the story of his love." Sir Ywain broke into a huge guffaw at that, and Hectimere, looking timidly at his master, did not know whether to laugh or to answer in anger, but when a smile crossed the face of Sir Gaheris, Hectimere too let out a raucous laugh.

Gaheris gave Gareth a mock bow. "I beg your pardon, little brother, I didn't realize how sensitive you are about your role as minstrel. Pray continue, in whatever vein you choose."

"The knights that were still conscious all looked to Sir Launfal," Gareth continued, as if nothing had intervened. "And they were assured that this was indeed his Lady when his eyes filled with tears at the sight of her, though he had lost all hope that his beloved would ever be his again. Even King Arthur was astounded. He bowed to the Lady and welcomed her courteously, but she launched into a tirade without even acknowledging the king's words:

" 'King Arthur, listen to me and be sure your reputation for justice and statesmanship does not vanish as a result of this case. This knight,' she pointed at Launfal without looking in his direction, 'has been falsely accused by that woman,' and here she pointed at Morgan le Fay, who sat against the wall opposite Sir Launfal and glared fiercely at the Lady. The Lady returned her gaze with a look of disdain and went on. 'Her claim that Sir Launfal attempted to rape her is an utter lie. It was she who tried to seduce him, and when she could not, berated him with insults that goaded him into a discourteous response. But her charge that he told her even his mistress's lowliest lady-in-waiting was more beautiful than she is in fact legitimate. You may judge for yourself whether Sir Launfal's statement was true.'

"With that a buzz went round the court, and every knight and squire there present agreed it was clearly true: Anyone could see both Nimue and Amaryllis exceeded the beauty of Morgan le Fay in the same way the morning star exceeds the brightness of all other stars in the heavens. But Morgan sputtered in rage, and the king looked down, ready, no doubt, to ask the Lady how she came to know what had passed in private between Launfal and Morgan. He never got the chance to do so. The Lady, having given her testimony, spun on her heel and left the throne room as abruptly as she had come in, followed by her two maidens. As everyone stared at her open-mouthed, through the open door of the room, she mounted her white palfrey and prepared to leave. Before she galloped off, however, she gave one glance backward. Her eyes caught those of Sir Launfal, standing near the door, and with an almost imperceptible motion of her head, she invited him to come.

"All the knights were too busy watching the ladies leave to guard Launfal closely, and in an instant he sprang out the door and up unto the great white horse, behind the Lady. The pair of them were last seen galloping back through the barbican gate and off into the land of Faerie." Gaheris looked at him askance at that. Gareth shrugged. "Or at least, through the woods and across the brook to the Lady's palace on Lady Lake. But Launfal has not been seen since. And the king's anger was so great against Morgan le Fay that this was the beginning of the end of her influence at the court.

"And that, my friends, is why you should never speak ill of ladies in these woods. So, young Bertrand of the ribald lyrics, mind your tongue in the future!" Bertrand nodded gravely, so sobered by the tale that he forgot to say it was Sir Palomides, after all, who wrote the song.

By now dinner was over and vespers were ringing, and Henry had returned with the wagon from Camelot. He and Tom and William loaded the venison into the wagon and the rest of us doused the fire and cleaned up the campsite; the Lady, Sir Gareth told us, would not approve if we left the site a mess. Letting Tom take Aeneas and Dido, I mounted my horse and moved next to Sir Gareth and we began the short ride back to the castle.

"My lord Gareth," I asked him as we rode together quietly, the cart bringing up the rear. "This story of Sir Launfal and the Lady of the Lake—how much of it is true?"

Sir Gareth laughed. "Well, young Gildas, you know I was not a part of the court at the time. I heard much of the story from my brother Gawain, and bits and pieces from the real old-timers like Sir Kay and Sir Bedivere. But I admit, there might be a few of what Gaheris calls my 'embellishments.' "

"I can't help thinking about Nimue. This is the same Nimue that Merlin is besotted with?"

"The same." Gareth nodded. "And there was no need for embellishment when I spoke of her beauty, I assure you."

"And Sir Launfal? It's true no one has seen him since the day of his trial?"

"No one from Camelot has seen him. I think he must have washed his hands of what he saw as a corrupt court. But sometimes men have seen a lonely hunter in these woods, and there are rumors that it may be Sir Launfal himself, exercising himself and his great white horse, taking a break from life in the palace of the Lady of the Lake."

I nodded again, and then asked him the question I'd been contemplating all along: "And this story—the false accusation of rape against the innocent knight—I suppose it's no co-incidence that you're telling me this now? Are you meaning to suggest that the case Merlin and I are looking at might be a similar situation, a false accusation against an innocent knight?"

The corner of Gareth's mouth twisted into a slight smile and he shrugged. "Something about this is very fishy, young Gildas of Cornwall. It is not even remotely possible that my nephew did this deed, and that means someone is lying. I don't know who, but that's what you'll have to figure out." And with that he rode ahead as we approached the drawbridge, which Robin on watch in the barbican had left open for our return.

CHAPTER EIGHT:
SECRETS AND LIES

Colgrevaunce was a hapless fellow, eager to please and always with an earnest look, but somehow not quite the one you'd pick to lead a company of knights or deliver an important message or go on a vital quest. Somebody else always looked brighter, stronger, more competent. In that way he was not unlike his master, Sir Brandiles, who though he had been at Camelot for many years—was, in fact, one of the knights Sir Lancelot rescued from the renegade knight Sir Turquin at the time Lancelot first joined Arthur's table—he had never distinguished himself in any particular way. He'd served fairly competently in the ranks during Arthur's Irish and Gaulish wars, but I knew of no tales about him and his prowess or his adventures. Colgrevaunce of Rochester, a Kentishman like his master, had been squire to Sir Brandiles for three years, and though he was now seventeen I had no doubt it would be at least a few more years before he was ready to assume the mantle of knighthood. I had to smile inwardly when I remembered the sight of him charging the quintain in jousting practice and missing it altogether, only to bump it with his shoulder and be unhorsed by the weighted sack on the other end of the stick as it spun around and struck him from behind. That had not been his finest hour.

But my goal for this Friday morning was not to rate Colgrevaunce's chances of displacing Lancelot as the kingdom's greatest knight. It was rather to get him to speak frankly about the night Bess of Caerlon was raped, and, once I got him to admit he was with Sir Florent in the inn, to give me the names of everybody else who was there. There were four days to go before Florent's retrial, and at this point we didn't know anything at all about the case.

Sipping from a glass of watery beer, I leaned against the stone wall near the castle kitchen, where I could already smell some exotic sauce that Roger, the chief cook, was preparing for the midday meal, the main meal of the castle day. I'd caught Colgrevaunce heading for the stables to get Sir Brandiles's horse saddled and ready for him to go hawking later that morning with Sir Kay. Taking a bite out of the bread and cheese I'd begged off Roger for breakfast, I casually asked Colgrevaunce if I could tag along. Without the slightest hint of suspicion, he said, "Suit yourself."

"Off to the woods for hawking today, eh?" I began, falling into an ambling pace with him.

"Right. Sir Brandiles wants to see what his new bird can do. He's got a wager going with Sir Kay that his new gyrfalcon brings down more game than Kay's best bird. Winner gets the whole day's takings."

"Hmmph," I said. "Different kind of hunting altogether than the kind that took place here a few nights ago, eh? The one with Bess of Caerleon as the quarry?" Smooth transition, I thought. But right away Colgrevaunce began looking at me like I had three eyeballs or something. Looking up at him—he was a good four inches taller than I but skinny as a rail, which is partly why he was so clumsy on horseback—I could see in his hazel eyes an earnest look that betrayed his inherent inability to recognize irony.

"I don't see as how it's any kind of a joking matter, Master Gildas. What happened to that young woman is a terrible crime, and ain't nothing to speak lightly about."

"Right. No, you're absolutely right, Colgrevaunce. It's just that I have a hard time not thinking about it. I know Florent's been convicted and all, but I just can't believe he's the culprit."

"Sure, I know," and now Colgrevaunce hung his head so that his long, greasy brown hair hung in swaths before his face. "But she said he's the one what did it. And even though we've been his friends for a long time, we're gonna have to bloody well accept it. I can't say as I have yet, but I'm trying. You're gonna have to try too."

"But if only you'd stayed with him a little longer that night, instead of letting him leave the tavern alone, you'd have seen where he was."

"Yes, if only I'd . . ." Suddenly Colgrevaunce stopped his shuffling step and his head sprang erect. "Hey, wait a minute! I never said I was with him that night. How would you . . ."

"Oh," I waved it off as if it was nothing. "People talk, you know? But like I said, it's too bad you didn't go off with him instead of letting him take off by himself. Without anybody there to vouch for him, old Florent was caught without an alibi."

"Yeah." Colgrevaunce bemoaned the situation, and taking my word that people were already talking about it, he let go any further notions of keeping the events of that party secret. "If only I didn't have that fight with him . . ."

Things were falling into place nicely, and I didn't want to jinx it. But I had to try one more trick: "Sure, but then, why would it have had to be you? I mean, Thomas was there, right? And what's his name . . ."

"You mean Bertrand of Toledo, Sir Palomides's squire? Right, him, and Baldwin as well, Sir Agravain's. So that's two . . . four . . . five counting Florent . . . and then the two knights."

"Of course. Sir, um . . ."

"Sir Sagramore was there, of course. He's one what never misses a party. The other one was kind of a surprise to me, though. Sir Tristram almost never lets his hair down, and yet there he was, pensive as usual but doing his part to help us polish off that keg of ale."

"Tristram?" I was taken aback. "That is a surprise. He's the least likely of knights to go carousing, especially with a bunch of squires . . . no offense, Colgrevaunce."

"None taken, I know what you mean. But he didn't really say much, just sort of sat drinking and looking at us with a kind of quizzical smile the whole time. That is, until we started to get a bit rowdy. He left pretty soon after that."

"The tavern owner said you boys were pretty unruly."

"Too much to drink, Gildas. I don't need to tell you, the next morning my head felt like a horse had kicked it. But too much of that ale pretty much dulled our wits that night, I guess."

"Why? What was it you were about?"

Colgrevaunce shrugged and kept looking straight ahead toward the stables. He was silent for a moment and then he admitted, "We were gambling, Gildas. Betting on rolls of the dice. That's where it all started. That's when Sir Tristram left us—said it was not seemly for knights of the Round Table, or even their squires, to spend their time on that kind of drunken, villainous behavior. Said he'd have nothing to do with us more that night. But Sir Sagramore, now he wasn't quite so particular. We were a little sheepish after what Tristram said to us, and Florent himself told us Tristram was right, that we should put the dice away."

"Good old Florent," I said with a grim smile. "True to character every time, isn't he?"

"But as I say, Sir Sagramore told us as long as we didn't gamble for money, there was nothing unbecoming a knight in the game of chance."

"So if you didn't roll the dice for money, what did you roll them for?"

"Drinks." Colgrevaunce shrugged again. "Loser had to down

a pint of ale as quickly as he could. I lost a few times. Thomas, he lost even more often than me. But Florent, he lost nearly every time."

I rolled my eyes. "Well, Colgrevaunce, it's a complete shock to me that a party like *that* degenerated into a brawl." Colgrevaunce blinked at me. I'd forgotten his irony impairment. "So who was it brought the dice, anyway?"

"Oh that," Colgrevaunce shook his head. "I don't remember. It's just, all of a sudden there they were, in somebody's hands." He hung his head as if thinking. "In Sagramore's, I think. But I don't know that he brought them."

"Well, as far as that goes, it's probably not important," I conceded. "But tell me what the fight was all about, will you?"

Colgrevaunce stopped and turned to me. "The fight?" Again he hung his head. "Well . . . it was . . ." then he glanced to his left and finally looked up at me. "It was that stupid game what did it," he admitted. "You see, once it got going, we weren't content to just make the losers drink. We decided, in honor of good old Florent's knighting ceremony that morning, that anybody what lost the wager would have to down a pint of ale before we all counted to fifty, and anybody what failed *that* would have to undergo the *colée,* right? Just like Florent had from the king that morning."

"Mother of God, Colgrevaunce, are you telling me you whacked Florent on the shoulder with a sword? No wonder it ended in a fight. You're lucky it didn't end in bloodshed. And considering it's Florent we're talking about, you know perfectly well it would have been your blood, too!"

"I'm not saying it was smart." Colgrevaunce rolled his head about and resumed his walk across the bailey toward the stables. "But by then we were about as drunk as we could be and still be conscious. So almost anything sounds like a good idea, right? Anyway, Florent loses the next roll, as usual, and he's too full of

ale to drink another pint, whether we were counting to fifty or
to five hundred. So I tell him kneel down, boy, and receive the
colée. And he kneels just as he's told, and I'm out with my
sword and give him a good whack with it. Well, up he springs
and says I hit him way too hard for something intended for
sport, and he's got me by the front of my tunic, see, and is
shaking me. And he says something like I've always been jealous
of him, or something like that, and I tell him I don't know what
he's talking about.

"Well by then, the others are pulling us apart, and Florent
holds up his hands and says he's had enough, so off he goes.
The rest of us figured he was heading straight back to the castle,
and he was so mad that none of us wanted to go with him."

"Um-hmm." I weighed Colgrevaunce's words. He seemed
open enough, and his story fit pretty closely with the story William Bailey told the king about the row in his tavern that night.
And after all, this was Colgrevaunce; he was too simple to lie to
me, and he had no reason not to trust me, a fellow squire. But
one thing still bothered me—what was left unsaid. That morning, when Merlin burst out of bed recovered from his spell and
ready to take on the entire army of Gaul, he gave me one charge:
"I'm going to question Ywain's squire Thomas. Your job is to
find Colgrevaunce and question him. We know they were both
with Florent the night of the crime, and we know they think we
don't know it. We need to surprise them, get them to tell us
what happened, and then compare stories. They won't have had
time to confer about it, and so we know anything they tell us
that agrees is the truth. But the chief thing we've got to find out
about is the girl. Did they know Bess of Caerleon from the inn?
Did they recognize her when she came to report the rape to the
king?"

And there was nothing in Colgrevaunce's story that touched
on Bess of Caerleon. But how could I get him to tell me?

"Colgrevaunce," I said to him just as we were approaching the doors of the stable. "Tell me. Why didn't you say anything when the tavern wench from Bailey's inn came into court to tell the king she was raped that night?"

He stopped and spun toward me. He hadn't foreseen that question. "How did you know that?" was all he could say.

"I told you, people talk. So you recognized her? Then why keep quiet?"

"Thought it was best for Florent, you know? With her claiming he'd raped her, I didn't want to make it worse by telling everyone he'd spent half the night in her tavern right before she was attacked. That'd look even worse for him, wouldn't it?"

"He was convicted, Colgrevaunce. How could it have looked any worse?"

Just then the stable doors opened and out came Taber, the chief stable hand, leading a light brown palfrey, Sir Brandiles's mount. "Heard you was comin', Colgrevaunce. Here's that palfrey of your master's."

I looked Colgrevaunce in the eyes for what seemed an eternity. Then he blinked and looked away. "Well," I said, patting him on the shoulders in forced camaraderie. "I'll let you go about your duties, old sot. I'm glad we had this talk. Sometimes when we're feeling bad about something, it's a good idea to just talk about it among friends."

"Right," he responded. "I'll see you later," and led the horse away.

"Gambling over drinks and dice. A charming party for a bunch of courteous gentlemen, eh Gildas?" Merlin's eyes were laughing as I related to him my interview with Colgrevaunce. We had taken a walk back to his cave where we could speak privately, and where he wanted to rest and have a game of chess. But that could wait until later. Right now we needed to go over what we'd learned from the two squires who, as far as we knew, were the last to see Sir Florent before he wandered off into the woods on the night of the crime. As Merlin sat upright on his narrow bed, while I sat in one of his wooden chairs, my elbows resting on his table and my chin in my hands, I'd just related to him everything Colgrevaunce had told me.

"He really didn't say much about Bess, though," I told Merlin. "He was pretty surprised we knew about her being the tavern wench at the inn. As if that would have been difficult to find out! But the only reason he gave for not bringing it up at the trial was that he wanted to protect Sir Florent."

"Yes, protect him right into a hangman's noose," Merlin grumbled. "But Colgrevaunce has always been a blockhead. Anyway, I'm not sure his story is true. At any rate, it's not the whole truth."

"How do you mean? Did Thomas say something different?"

"Well, Thomas corroborates most of Colgrevaunce's story. His list of characters is the same: Besides Florent, himself, and Colgrevaunce, he says two other squires, Baldwin of Orkney and Bertrand of Toledo, were there along with two knights of the Round Table."

"Sir Sagramore and Sir Tristram, yes, just as I've said."

"Sir Sagramore and Sir Dinadan, to Thomas's recollection." Merlin chuckled at my look of bewilderment.

"You mean they can't even agree on which knights were there? We're talking to a couple of really reliable witnesses here, Merlin!"

"Well," Merlin replied, smiling indulgently. "Thomas does agree with Colgrevaunce's story about the drunkenness. And when you've been drinking that much, having one of the party slip your mind is not such an unusual occurrence. Anyway, the whole game with the dice and the drinking, that's something

Thomas admitted to as well. He even says Florent was the big loser."

"What about the girl? What did Thomas have to say about Bess of Caerleon?"

"That's where we have a real difference of opinion between Thomas and your friend Colgrevaunce."

"What, you mean Thomas says Bess wasn't there at all?"

"No no, he says she was there all right. And he says she was being especially friendly with young Colgrevaunce himself."

"With Colgrevaunce!"

"Paying him extra attention every time she refilled their drinks. Whispering in his ear, things like that. Even ended up in his lap once toward the end of the evening. Faked slipping and falling onto him, to hear Thomas tell it. And that, young Gildas, was the cause of the fight between Colgrevaunce and Florent, according to Thomas. Nothing to do with the drinking game at all."

"You mean they fought about the peasant girl?"

"Merchant class," Merlin corrected me. "But yes. Florent told Colgrevaunce he was acting in an unseemly way for a gentleman, that he needed to leave the girl alone and that he'd had enough to drink and should go back to the castle."

"Sounds a lot like the Florent I know," I admitted. "So Colgrevaunce tried to fight him then?"

"Even drew his sword on Florent, and, according to Thomas, swore he'd run him through if he didn't stop preaching at him. Told him he was jealous that Colgrevaunce had a wench as lovely as Bess interested in him."

"Hmmph," I snorted. "In Colgrevaunce's version, it was the opposite. Florent accused Colgrevaunce of being jealous of *him*. Who do we believe?"

"God's elbows, Gildas, think about it, will you? Who's got the most to gain by lying? Does Thomas have anything to lose whichever version we accept?"

"I know what you're getting at," I told him. "Colgrevaunce looks guilty of something if we accept Thomas's version, so he looks like he's covering up for himself. But if Thomas is really the attacker, he'd want to cast suspicion on somebody else."

"That he would, Gildas, you're right," the old man conceded. "But Thomas didn't know we were questioning Colgrevaunce at the same time. And if Colgrevaunce's version of what happened is the true one, then Thomas could have told it in such a way as to implicate Colgrevaunce. Either way you've got the fight with Florent and Colgrevaunce with his sword out. Either way Colgrevaunce has a motive to frame Florent for the rape. There was no reason for Thomas to lie. Besides, he had to know I'd be asking the other witnesses. He wouldn't want to get caught in a lie."

"But wouldn't Colgrevaunce know the same thing?"

"If I had questioned him, perhaps. But you? He just thought you were passing the time with him and were curious. You never told him you were investigating, did you?"

"No, I didn't. You're right, Merlin, Colgrevaunce must be lying. But how could he be the one we're looking for? He seems so . . . so inept."

"Well, we can't assume he's guilty. But he knew he'd look guilty if you found out the truth about the argument with Florent. No, he's definitely a suspect, but his lies don't necessarily mean he's the rapist."

"But he's got motive, it seems. He was angry with Florent. Maybe, if what Thomas says is true, he was even jealous of Florent and saw him as a rival for Bess. Besides, if he was admiring Bess in the tavern, and she encouraged him . . ."

"And then cut him off after the fight, perhaps he was also angry with her. Colgrevaunce could very well have a motive for both the rape and for framing Sir Florent."

"And he had the opportunity, didn't he? I mean, after they left the tavern, did anybody see him go back to the castle?"

"I don't know, Gildas. What did he say?"

"Well . . . I didn't ask him that."

"Gildas! You had the chance to ask him but never found out what happened at the end of the night?"

"Well, I didn't think he was a suspect at the time! I'm still not so sure. It never occurred to me I'd need to find out about his walk home. So what did Thomas say about it?"

Merlin was quiet for a moment. Then he changed the subject. "What I'm most curious about is the difference of opinion about the knights who were there. Why would Thomas forget about Sir Tristram? And why wouldn't Colgrevaunce mention Sir Dinadan?"

"The knights? But you just told me that wasn't important. What about—"

"Well, I've been thinking about it, and I've decided I was wrong. All right, don't act so shocked. Sometimes even I make a mistake. If Colgrevaunce really was covering something up, then it may be Sir Dinadan was somehow mixed up with this quarrel in a way Colgrevaunce would rather not have anyone know. It might be a very good idea to talk to Dinadan ourselves and get his version of events."

"And what about Sir Tristram?"

Merlin shrugged. "He's a knight of impeccable character, as far as anyone knows. One of the three greatest knights of the Round Table. It's hard to imagine anything about him that could possibly rouse our suspicions."

"Except that Thomas left him out of his story," I reminded him.

"Yes, and while it's more likely Colgrevaunce was hiding something, we can't rule out Thomas's deliberately altering the truth. Besides, it would be good to get the perspective of someone like Tristram. We definitely need to talk to him as well."

At that Merlin rose from his bed, stretched, and looked out the door of his cave toward the lake shore and, further off in the mist, the mansion of the Lady of the Lake. "You know," he said in a low voice, only half intended for me. "That book of Aristotle's I've been reading—the one concerned with the idea of tragedy . . ."

"Yes," I answered. "What about it?"

"Aristotle says the tragic hero is a man more noble or in some way superior to the majority of men. He brings about his own downfall through some significant error of judgment. I can't help thinking such a description applies only too well to Sir Florent. A young man of royal family, more skilled at chivalry than any of his peers, who finally achieves his dream of knighthood, yet through the mistake of drunkenness, he causes his own downfall. But we feel his punishment exceeds his own deserts. If we agree that Florent did not rape the girl, then his punishment far exceeds his fault that night. Indeed, he seems a tragic figure."

"Only if the queen does not save him," I ventured.

"No, even then. For he will be branded a criminal all his life. His fall will still be complete. Never again will he be the promising young knight he was. No, it's only the two of us who stand between him and the fall that will ruin his life."

"Merlin . . ." I changed the subject. "You said you made a mistake when you dismissed the two versions of the knights who were present."

"Yes, I did. Hard to believe I'm not infallible, is it not?"

"Well, what about your not finding out from Thomas whether he went home with Colgrevaunce after the quarrel? Wasn't that a mistake too?"

Merlin glared down at me from beneath the jungle of his

eyebrows and then, with a good-natured growl, answered, "Don't burn me with the facts, boy. White or black?" And he walked over to sit at the chessboard.

CHAPTER NINE:
LA BELLE ISOLDE

Sir Tristram and Sir Dinadan were unlikely companions, but they were often together, and seemed particularly likely to enjoy one another's company in tournaments and similar knightly pastimes. It may have been that they complemented each other: Sir Tristram's rosy view of chivalry was kept from degenerating into naiveté by Sir Dinadan's sarcasm, while Dinadan's ironic worldview was prevented from overwhelming him by Tristram's uncompromising ideals.

With only three days left before Sir Florent's retrial, Merlin and I sought out Sir Tristram as soon as we were able, once we found out that Tristram was at the rowdy celebration of Sir Florent's knighthood. When we found Tristram, he was with Sir Dinadan in the Great Hall, where with the help of Tristram's squire Kurneval, they were gathering up clothing and arms in preparation for a long journey.

"Bound for Brittany," Sir Tristram told us, his green eyes looking at us eagerly and his open, clean-shaven face showing all the excitement of a boy about to enter his favorite game. "Duke Hoel has announced a tournament there to take place in a fortnight, and we intend to uphold the honor of the Round Table against all comers."

"And while there, no doubt, you'll be staying with your wife, Isolde of the White Hands?" Merlin asked politely.

"The love of his life," Sir Dinadan deadpanned with heavy irony. "She's never out of his thoughts, is good old what's-her-

126

name." Dinadan's dark brown eyes twinkled, and the half-smile that twisted his mouth looked more like a sneer than anything else. Dinadan had a black mustache and goatee, with close-trimmed black hair that contrasted sharply with Sir Tristram's shoulder-length, naturally curly auburn locks.

"We will certainly stay at our castle there with the Lady Isolde of the White Hands," Tristram answered, ignoring Dinadan's barbs for the moment. "I look forward to seeing her again, and besides, my duty requires it."

"Wow!" Dinadan scoffed. "There's a declaration to warm the cockles of her heart. Stop, Tristram, you'll turn her pretty little head!"

"Don't show disrespect to my wife," Tristram warned the other knight mildly, "or you and I will end up with a score to settle."

"No," Dinadan agreed, "I would never disrespect your wife. There's enough of that going around without any need of it from me."

Tristram looked darkly at Dinadan, but Merlin thrust himself in at this, since he had not come to listen to banter but to gather relevant information. "Well, I wish you good luck, my lords, but before you go I need to have you clear up some questions about last Monday evening," he began. Tristram looked at Dinadan with a puzzled expression as Merlin continued, "I've learned the two of you were present at the celebration held for Sir Florent at the tavern in Caerleon."

"That is true," Tristram conceded. "How does this concern you, Old Man?"

"On the queen's orders," Merlin decided to pull rank a bit, "young Gildas of Cornwall and I have been investigating the events of that evening."

"Trying to find an out for young Florent, are we?" Dinadan asked. "Can't have the king's own blood running through the veins of a rapist, now can we? What would the other kings say when they all get together at meetings and such?"

Taking his cue from Tristram, Merlin seemed to have surmised that the best way to deal with Sir Dinadan's taunts was to ignore them, and he went on as if nothing had happened. "As I understand it, aside from several squires, the two of you were present, and also Sir Sagramore le Desirous, is that correct?"

Tristram nodded, but he hadn't taken his eyes off me since Merlin introduced me. It wasn't as if he had never seen me before, but something about my presence here today was affecting him somehow.

The mention of Sir Sagramore gave Dinadan a new target for his irony. "Ah, the aptly named Sagramore the Foolish," he began. "Another paragon of courtesy, to be sure. And what do you suppose he was doing a few weeks ago, coming out of the Lady Elaine's bedchamber just after prime, his face reddened, I suppose, by that rising sun? And she his own betrothed? How does the old song go . . . 'To pluck a flower in season, I trow it is no treason'?"

"Oh, give your venom a rest, can't you Dinadan?" Sir Tristram said. "Sir Sagramore was not to blame in the incident you're referring to. He told me all about it. He says he was walking through the castle late that night, after everyone had gone to bed. A strong gust of wind blew into the corridor and extinguished the torch he was carrying. Having no way to relight it, he had to grope his way through the corridor to find his own door. Coming on a door he thought led into the lesser hall, he opened it and entered the room, lay down on the first couch he found, and went off to sleep. When morning came, he realized he'd entered the room of the queen's ladies-in-waiting, and had spent the night next to the Lady Elaine. Both of them were embarrassed, and he tried to leave before anyone caught sight of him. Apparently, someone saw him leaving the chamber and spread those lies about him."

"Right." Sir Dinadan nodded. "Your version is far more likely to be the truth. How silly of me."

"Sir Sagramore's indiscretions, real or imagined, are not my concern," Merlin said, trying to steer the conversation back to his own investigation. "All I need is to know why you three knights happened to be at the revel in the first place, and also what your view is of the events that took place there."

"Oh, that." Dinadan scoffed again. "I'll let Tristram give you his version of the story. It really was all his concern from the beginning. Me, I'm heading over to the stables to see if our horses are ready. We have some hard riding to do before we get to Brittany. Though I don't expect Isolde of the White Hands anticipates any hard riding, does she, my lord Tristram."

Now truly angry, Sir Tristram flung a challenge at Dinadan's back as he fled the room. "Get your foul tongue out of here before you provoke me to use my steel on you!" With that he reached for his sword.

The sound of Dinadan's mocking laughter was all that answered Sir Tristram's outburst. His ire punctured by Dinadan's scorn, Tristram lowered his sword and simply looked depressed. The squire Kurneval, who had said nothing to this point, stared after Sir Dinadan with a cold fire in his eyes, and muttered under his breath, "Boor."

"I mean no offense, my lord," I couldn't help saying, "but why do you spend so much time with Sir Dinadan? He's no pleasant person to be around. I rather marvel you haven't run him through yet."

Merlin looked at me with a bit of impatience. No doubt he thought it was none of my business, or he thought I was taking the conversation away from the investigation, or both, but Sir Tristram sighed and answered me in a far-off voice, as if he was speaking not to me but to an invisible audience of everyone to whom he felt the need to explain himself.

"Dinadan is my penance," he said through a kind of mist that seemed to cloud his eyes. "He is the constant reminder of how far short of the chivalric ideal I have fallen. He reminds me how much my own sin prevents me from judging the sins of others."

"And not being judgmental . . . that's a bad thing?" I asked.

"Not in itself," Tristram admitted. "But we should not be allowed to comfort ourselves that a good effect justifies a bad cause. For Dinadan, he never allows me that luxury. And yet he is a good companion in other ways: brave, loyal, and honest to a fault."

"Yes, I believe we have seen that fault," Merlin interjected. "But my lord, that is not to our purpose, and while I have no desire to appear rude, I must press my own agenda, particularly since you are planning to leave very soon. You can help us a great deal if you would give us your version of the events that took place the evening of Florent's ceremony. You were there, in the tavern, and saw how things got started. Can you tell us what you saw? What you believe caused the quarrel between Sir Florent and Colgrevaunce?"

Tristram shrugged and shook his head. "I didn't witness the quarrel. I'm afraid I left quite early. The young squires were all drinking too much, and Dinadan and Sagramore both were egging them on. They had brought a pair of dice and were gambling for drinks. I thought their behavior was unbecoming to knights or squires of the Round Table and told them so. Florent at least, I thought, would support me. But he was too far gone with drink, and so I left them all and came back to the castle alone. I didn't see any of them again until the next morning."

"Then you didn't witness the quarrel, or the departure of Sir Florent?" Merlin pressed.

"Neither, I'm afraid. I left far too soon for that. Sir Dinadan, though, as I understand it, was present until the end of the evening, and so would have seen the quarrel as well as who left and when."

"All right," Merlin answered, a bit grumpily. Obviously as far as he was concerned, the wrong knight had left the inn. "He'll be coming back here?"

"Yes, he'll be back to get his gear, and the squires will bring the horses." With that Kurneval nodded and left the room, apparently hearing the hint of a command in Sir Tristram's voice.

"Then perhaps you can answer another question while we're waiting for him," Merlin went on. "If you'll pardon the impertinence, my lord, what were you doing at that gathering? I mean, Sagramore is always ready for a pint, and Sir Dinadan has been known to throw a wet blanket on many a party. But you yourself have never been one to go carousing with young squires, or to frequent public houses in Caerleon or anyplace else. What is Florent to you that you would break with your usual custom to attend a party in his honor?"

Sir Tristram gave Merlin a sidelong glance and turned up his mouth in a grim smile. He looked back at me again in the same manner that made me so uncomfortable, and then he answered.

"When you introduced your young apprentice to me as a native of Cornwall, Old Man, it put me immediately on my guard. I have been trying to determine whether he is a danger to me or not. And I'm still not certain. There are those associated with the court of my uncle King Mark who would gladly see me dead, and no questions asked. It is no secret that King Mark would mourn precious little for my passing."

Taken aback by this admission that seemed to come out of nowhere, I paused a few seconds before babbling, "I . . . I have no connections in the court of Cornwall. My father is merely an armor-maker who wanted something better for his son. King

Mark doesn't know me from Adam."

"But there is one in the court of Cornwall, or so the rumor goes, that would mourn greatly if the heart of Tristram would beat no more: La Belle Isolde." Merlin, tired of talking around the subject, had chosen to attack it head-on. That Tristram brought it up himself in response to the question of why he was in the bar that night meant it was about to become a part of this investigation. "Tell us, Sir Tristram. What does your affair with Queen Isolde of Cornwall have to do with your presence that night in the tavern?"

Tristram sighed, though I thought there was a look of relief in his eyes. The strain of keeping quiet about what was essentially an open secret showed in his often pained expression. But as he spoke now, he appeared more relaxed, less on his guard, than I had seen him before. He sat on a bench along the wall and began to speak, the words pouring forth like a torrent released by a burst dam.

"I was at the tavern that night to meet Sir Sagramore. It was only by chance that we joined with the party of squires who had set up the revel with Sir Florent. Sagramore just returned from Cornwall. He was there as my eyes and ears, and he was bringing me a message from La belle Isolde, a message to the effect that King Mark had sent an assassin to Arthur's court with the express orders to murder me."

"Murder you!" I gasped.

"Yes . . ." Sir Tristram looked at me guardedly. "King Mark, though he is my uncle, is no Arthur. His ways are devious and conniving. He insinuates behind your back and encourages treachery. He smiles while an unsheathed dagger waits under his cloak. That is King Mark's way."

"But why should he want you, his own nephew and the greatest of Cornish knights, dead?"

Merlin sighed at this and raised his eyes to Heaven, exasperated, I suppose, at my ignorance of what seemed common knowledge in Camelot, as well as the fact that I was getting Tristram off the track of Merlin's investigation.

But it wasn't that I was ignorant. As the queen's former chief confidante, I was privy to every juicy bit of gossip that ever made its rounds in Camelot. Everyone knew Tristram was in love with the fair Isolde, his uncle's queen. No, my surprise was the extent of Mark's outrage, and the manner of his revenge. Some kings would ignore the affair for the sake of the greater good of their kingdom. Most kings would insist on revenge, and meet their rival in open combat in the lists. King Mark, however, seemed to enjoy devious maneuvers and covert mischief. That's what he thought of as politics.

"First, I am not Cornish by birth, but the son of King Melyodas of Lyonesse. My mother was sister to King Mark, but died giving me birth, and so I was named Tristram, the sorrowful-born. When I was eighteen, I sought out my uncle's court in Cornwall, and strove to become his champion. For him I killed Sir Marhault, brother of the Irish queen, in single combat and thereby ensured that Ireland would pay the tribute they owed Mark. But my wounds would not heal; there was a spell on the Marhault's sword such that any wounds it gave could be healed exclusively by medicines known only to his sister the queen and to her daughter, apprentice to her arts."

"And so you traveled to Ireland?" I asked. "But how could you obtain the healing salve if the queen knew you were her brother's killer?"

"Well, that was the problem, wasn't it? The only thing I could do was hide my identity and pretend I'd got the wounds in some other way. I disguised myself as a wandering jongleur, playing music and singing poetry that praised the beauty of the Irish queen and her fair daughter, La Belle Isolde. My songs won over the fair Isolde, and she first healed the wounds of my body and then, in her kindness, healed the wound of my heart by giving me her love."

"Very sweet," Merlin commented. "But . . ."

"But how did she end up marrying your Uncle Mark? How could you let her slip away?" I don't have to tell you I was thinking then, as always, about the fair Rosemounde, and I needed to know how even a knight of Tristram's prowess and fortune could not win the hand of the woman he was in love with.

Tristram scowled and shook his head. "I returned to Cornwall with one purpose—to ask my uncle to negotiate for the hand of La Belle Isolde. I thought what an ideal match it would be. The Irish princess marries the heir apparent to the throne of Cornwall—cementing our new relationship as allies rather than as bitter adversaries. I praised the princess in glowing terms until my uncle gave in. He liked the idea of allying himself with the Irish, and he liked my descriptions of the princess Isolde—so much so that he decided she should be his own bride. And to make matters worse he sent me back to Ireland to negotiate for her hand."

"No!" I couldn't help feeling for Sir Tristram. What was it like? I didn't have to wonder. Here I was, trying to prove the innocence of Sir Florent, the man about to be married to my own beloved Rosemounde. How much the same must have been Tristram's anguish when he returned to the Irish court in order to negotiate a marriage contract between his uncle and the woman he loved. "What did you do?"

Tristram sighed. "What duty required. I set off the next morning across the Irish Sea again, to beg my lady's hand for another man. This time I went as myself, and received no fair welcome in that court, I assure you. But King Angwish was as conniving a politician as Mark himself, and knew the importance of political allies as well as the next man. He was more than willing to let bygones be bygones (even if his wife wasn't), and marry his daughter off to ensure an alliance. But first, I had to face a challenge from the other suitor for Isolde's hand . . ."

"The Saracen Knight, Sir Palomides," I chimed in.

With a look of some surprise that I seemed to know so much about his personal affairs when, after all, I was the one that asked for the story, Tristram nodded. "Yes, and a more valiant knight I have never faced. We met in the lists the day after I asked for the lady's hand. His armor was gold plated, and his horse was the swiftest Arabian stallion I had ever seen. He put no armor on his horse, relying more on speed than power to win his battle. When I galloped toward him to knock him from his saddle, he skittered out of the way and harassed me with his sword from all sides before I could move out of reach. He'd have beaten me and shamed me, if I hadn't done the only thing I could to win the fight: I ran his horse's unprotected flank through with my spear. Palomides tumbled from his mount, and I was able to ride him down and force him to yield. Thus I won Isolde from him, and so he has never forgiven me for her loss. Nor would I have done so had he beaten me.

"But I had won her hand. Certainly the queen never gave me a fair look, and Isolde, her mother's daughter, lamented her affection for me once she discovered my true identity. She was more than happy to marry Mark in that case, if for no other reason than that it caused me pain—me, the murderer of her uncle. But underneath, I saw her love still smoldered, and I held my own in check only through the severest effort."

"Then the story of the love potion and all that, that I've heard rumors about—that's just a story somebody made up?"

Sir Tristram cocked his head at me and narrowed his eyes in thought. "The love potion did its magic—that is a true story. Though it was hardly necessary. The way it happened was this: The fair Isolde's lady-in-waiting, Brangwen, had brought a love potion for Isolde to drink for her wedding night. The queen had mixed it for her, believing that as long as Isolde must marry King Mark, she may as well love him. But Brangwen made a mistake, and on our crossing from Ireland to Cornwall, served Isolde and me each a glass of the potion, thinking it was wine. That potion was our downfall. It was a witchcraft neither of us could fight against, and we consummated our love there and then in the cabin of the boat en route to Isolde's wedding with my uncle."

"God's earlobes, man, what did you do when you got to Cornwall?" Merlin, taken up by the story, had forgotten to press his investigation and now was as interested in Tristram's tale as I was.

"The wedding took place without a dissenting voice. It was a beautiful and formal ceremony in the cathedral there at Exeter. I was in attendance to do homage to my new sovereign lady—though in truth she had been my own sovereign lady for many months already. But the new Queen Isolde was in desperate straits in anticipation of the wedding night. How could she face the embraces of that odious old man when her heart belonged only to his usurping nephew? I don't have to tell you about my own thoughts. Guilt and shame, jealousy and distrust, love and joy all mixed together and made it impossible for me to think through what steps I should take. I was even contemplating bursting into the royal castle that evening and rescuing the lady Isolde from her conjugal debt at the point of a sword, adding regicide to adultery in the catalog of my crimes. But that did not prove necessary.

"It was Brangwen who came up with the solution we could all live with. She loved her mistress, and could not bear that she should be shamed. The lady volunteered to take Isolde's place in the bridal bed, once the lights were put out. Mark had no way of knowing what Isolde would be like, and having just met her at the wedding could be easily fooled in the dark into thinking that the Lady Brangwen (being, as she was, of approximately the same size and coloring) was in fact La Belle Isolde herself. And the Lady Brangwen was a virgin to boot, something King Mark had been assured was the case with my Lady Isolde."

"And King Mark was fooled by this?" Merlin asked.

"Desperate times called for desperate measures. The king had commanded that Isolde come to his bed that evening, so Brangwen brought Isolde by candlelight into his chamber. When the candles were put out, it was Brangwen and not Isolde that climbed into bed, while Isolde waited, with veiled face, outside the chamber door. Brangwen left the king's bed before dawn, and she and Isolde went back to the queen's chamber, protected by the night."

"So that worked for the first night; I can see how it could," I interrupted. "But how long could you keep up such a ruse? It had to be dangerous."

"It was. But we were mad with passion and recklessness. The king, an old man when he married her, demanded Isolde's presence perhaps once a week, and each time Brangwen was able to deceive him and escape undetected in the dark. On the days that her presence was not required in the king's chamber, I was able to sleep with the lady Isolde in her own room, guarded by the faithful Brangwen. But you both know how difficult it is to keep any kind of secret within the walls of a castle. Rumors soon started and talebearers were at Mark's ear, telling him he was being deceived, telling him the queen was unfaithful, that his nephew was cuckolding him. So listen to what he did one night a few months after his marriage.

"He had two armed knights stationed quietly in his chamber one evening and called for Queen Isolde. She came as usual, with Brangwen, and as usual it was the lady-in-waiting that slipped into bed with the king. Isolde had just started for the door when the knights moved into action. One held a sword at Brangwen's throat and the other barred the door so that Isolde could not exit. At the sound, a third knight threw open the door and entered with a torch to throw light on the scene."

"Were the ladies safe?" I asked, my eyes large with vicarious fear.

Tristram sighed. "My Lady Isolde has always been quick-witted and quick-tongued. She saw the situation at once, and immediately invented a plausible story to stem the old man's wrath. 'My lord,' she told him, 'I did not want to reveal this to you so soon, but I can no longer hide it. You must know that an illness I contracted as a child has left me barren. None of my mother's great healing charms has been able to restore my fertility. My father was not aware of this when he agreed to your marriage terms, and I foolishly allowed my excitement at being the wife of so great a king to cloud my judgment. I believed I could still give you children if you sired them with my faithful lady-in-waiting, Brangwen. Knowing your great virtue, I knew you would never consent to sleep with a woman who was not your lawful wife before God, so I felt the need to deceive you; thus when Brangwen gave birth to your son and heir, I could have her delivered in secret and convince you and all the world that I was your child's natural mother. Forgive me my foolish-ness. I know now that I never should have tried to deceive a king so great and wise as yourself.'

"Well, King Mark was just vain enough to fall for that explanation. He told the knights they could leave, and even agreed to keep sleeping with Brangwen and trying to have a child by her. Of course, the joke was on him in more ways than one, since in fact Brangwen is the one that doctors have said is barren. But that really wasn't the point. When Isolde told me about this the next day, we both agreed it had been a very nar-row escape and we must take steps to ensure our safety. It was agreed that I should flee the court, and take Brangwen with me, since she would be a prime target for the king's wrath once the whole truth came out. Once free, I could search for an opportunity to come back and steal Isolde away."

"But you never have done so," Merlin said. He said it in a matter-of-fact way, not accusing, not commending. He let Tristram interpret things his own way.

"It's not for fear of King Mark, or his armed guards. But being away from La Belle Isolde, I'm able to think more clearly about things, and am not so swept away by our passion. I realized that at this point, there is only suspicion on Mark's side. There has been no proof of the lady's adultery or my treachery. I am trusting that you two can keep my confidence, since I know Merlin of old to be honest and no gossip. As for you, Gildas of Cornwall, I still don't know whether to trust you. But if you do have connections in King Mark's court, you already know these things. If not, I trust that Merlin's judgment will keep your tongue in line.

"It comes to this, then: Were I to spirit the queen away from my uncle, it would be tantamount to an admission of guilt, and would shame us both forever in the eyes of the world. So I have not returned. I came to Arthur's court and placed Brangwen in the care of the sisters of the Convent of Saint Mary Magdalene, and became a knight of the Round Table. In my adventures, I traveled to Brittany, as is well known, and helped my friend Sir Kaherdin fight a war, for which he gave me a fief and the hand of his sister, Isolde of the White Hands, in marriage. I couldn't refuse the lady, but I have never consummated the marriage. Sir Dinadan knows this and has consistently abused me for it. The irony of my wife's name is a constant reminder of my hopeless love whenever I am with her. And so I spend most of my days at Camelot or riding in search of adventure. And now you know all."

"And so Sir Sagramore . . ."

"Has been my consistent spy in the house of King Mark. You see, in my early adventures, I defeated Sagramore in a joust when I met him in the forest, and as a condition of his defeat I required of him that he should visit the court of my uncle and offer his services to the king and queen. Well, Mark was flattered (he loves that kind of thing) and Isolde knew it was her chance to send me a message. Since then, Sir Sagramore has been my liaison with the Cornish court, and regularly brings me messages from there."

"Yes, Sagramore is a spy, we use him as we will," Sir Dinadan's voice suddenly interrupted. He had returned from the stables and was clearly anxious to be gone. "But I'm sure you've got all the information you could from Sir Blabbermouth here, so we'll be off for Brittany then. Come on, Tristram, the horses are ready."

"Two questions before you go, Sir Dinadan." Merlin stood before the door to block the knights' escape. "It should not delay you long, and I need the answers for my investigation."

"Well, let's have them, Old Man, I'm restless and ready to leave. If we don't get on the road soon, we're going to miss high tide and be delayed a day before we can sail for Brittany."

"It won't take long. First, what was it that caused the quarrel between Florent and the squire Colgrevaunce?"

"Oh, is that all," Dinadan scoffed. "It wasn't anything. They were both too drunk to be thinking clearly. But it had to do with that woman. She was a real flirt, you know what I mean? She was coming on to both of them. You know, trying to get them to notice her, giving them the eye, and all. Florent was like a fish on the hook, but Colgrevaunce was sure the lady wanted him more. So he calls Florent some kind of dirty name, and they're at each other. The lady disappeared then—she didn't want any part of that kind of fracas. Florent left right away once she'd gone, and the party started breaking up."

"So you're saying everyone else left right after Florent did."

"Within a quarter of an hour, I'd say. I believe I was the last to depart."

"The others had already left? Did they go together?"

"Not really, no. Colgrevaunce went off alone, as I recall. The two squires, Thomas and Baldwin, left separately, and then Sagramore went off with that Moorish squire Bertrand. I trust that by that time there was so much bad feeling between them, none of them wanted to be with any of the others the rest of the night."

I could see Merlin's face fall at that. Not much help there, that was for sure. He looked down at the floor thoughtfully, and with that Tristram and Dinadan made their way toward the door of the hall. Dinadan called back, "See you when we return, Old Man. We'll be off now . . ."

"What about Sir Sagramore?" I interrupted. "Do you know where he is now? We should talk to him . . ."

Perhaps mildly annoyed by the impertinent questions of a mere squire, Sir Dinadan merely shrugged. "I haven't seen him since Bess of Caerleon's accusations in the king's hall. Perhaps he's gone back to Cornwall."

Before they got to the door of the hall, though, Merlin's head shot up. "Sir Tristram!" he called. "Tell me one more thing: Who did Sagramore name as the assassin sent by King Mark?"

Sir Tristram looked back over his shoulder and called back, "He had no name. All he said was that it had to be someone intimately connected with the court. Perhaps even one of the group of squires in Sir Florent's circle." He looked me in the eye. "Gildas of Cornwall, for all we know." And with that he left the room.

CHAPTER TEN:
THE INNKEEPER'S STORY

There were only two days left after today before Sir Florent stood for his retrial before the queen, and that being the case we really could not waste any time on things unconcerned with the investigation, if we could possibly help it. And so even though the bells of the Convent of Saint Mary Magdalene had struck none some time hence, Merlin insisted we spend the rest of the day on a walk into Caerleon again, to talk with William Bailey, proprietor of the inn at which the famous revel had taken place on the evening of the rape.

"Everything seems to focus on what happened at the tavern that night," Merlin opined as we approached the gate to pass under the barbican. "It may be that this William can shed some light on the situation. From what we've found so far, it seems he may have been the only one present at that ruckus who had no particular agenda of his own."

"Which means he had no particular reason to pay any attention at all to the group," I suggested.

"Well, he had some interest, since he needed to keep track of what they were drinking in order to give them their bill."

"Which, you remember, he didn't do, since they all seem to have left before he billed them. Remember, he had to come complaining to Arthur to be paid."

"Well, if you've got any better suggestions, now's the time to—"

"Well, if it isn't the old charlatan himself, and his moron apprentice Gildas the Godawful!" came a familiar taunt from the window of the barbican.

"Robin Kempe, so they still pay you to sleep on duty up there?" I answered in kind as I gazed up toward the black window slit in the tower above the gate. "King Arthur must be having a lot of difficulty finding actual guards these days. Or are you just one of his charity cases?"

"Oh, the king asked me whether I wanted to command the barbican or train the current crop of squires to be actual knights, but I decided I wanted a job where there was at least some chance of success, so that's why I'm up here."

Knowing Robin, he probably knew exactly how low that blow had hit home, but before I could answer this time Robin continued on a track that really piqued our interest. "Say, you know that horse you were so keen on finding out about—the gray that was stolen from Stabler's barn the night of the rape?"

"Yes, what of it?" Merlin answered impatiently. "And give us a straight answer, none of your little jibes, you young blockhead!"

"Seems it's turned up after all. Master Stabler came in and told me about it not more than an hour ago. Seems the big fellow came back this morning, just wandered in all by himself like as if to say, 'Well, I'm back. So what's the news?' If anybody else had told me, I'd have thought they were having me on. But it's true."

"And is there any evidence at all as to where the horse has been these three days?"

In my mind's eye I could see Robin shrugging his shoulders up there behind that little black slit of a window.

"I'm buggered if I know," came the reply. "All I know is, Master Stabler said he was covered with brambles and dry leaves, like he'd been in the forest. But that's no big surprise. If he'd been out in the open, we would've seen him before now, wouldn't we?"

"Right," Merlin answered, and began to hurry off across the bridge. "Let us know if you hear any more." And the old man was off.

I stared back at the tower one more time and called, "We shouldn't be too late. But keep the gate open for us, will you?"

"Oh right," Robin called after my retreating figure, bent on getting the last word. "Like I live to serve the likes of you! Bugger off, will you?"

I caught up with Merlin as he strode purposefully along the path that veered toward the city. Without looking down at me, he muttered, "I do want to get back before dark. It makes me suspicious, this returning horse. Where's it been? Who's had it? Is it the same horse that the rapist rode?"

"If Bess thought gray looked white in the moonlight. But you don't think it just wandered home on its own? Why would somebody turn it loose now if they'd had it for those three days? And where did they keep it? And why?"

"All questions without answers at the moment," Merlin admitted. "What's worse, we don't even know if this horse had anything to do with the rape. It could just be a wild goose chase."

"What's bothering me more right now," I said, "is the whole situation with Sir Tristram. King Mark hired someone to act as an assassin, and that someone is likely to have been one of the squires at that party. What's the connection? Is there any link between the assassin and the rapist?"

"More good questions," Merlin remarked. Usually he liked to think things through out loud, and as we hiked briskly toward Caerleon, I felt a tirade coming on.

"God's knuckles!" Here it came. "This case keeps getting thornier and thornier. We've got Colgrevaunce lying to us about his fight with Sir Florent. We've got Thomas lying to us about Sir Tristram and Colgrevaunce lying about Sir Dinadan. We've got somebody stealing a horse and then letting it go. We've got one of the squires, or somebody else in the court, covering up about being sent as an assassin to Sir Tristram. We've got somebody framing Sir Florent for a rape and we've got Bess lying about being in the woods for a lover's tryst, with we-don't-know-whom. And do we have any suspects?"

"Um . . . everybody at the party, it seems to me?"

"They all had opportunity, it seems. They all saw Florent leave alone. And anyone there could have made arrangements to meet Bess later in the woods."

"Anyone but Tristram, I'd say."

Merlin raised his shaggy brows and sighed. "If he has yet to consummate his marriage because of his faithfulness to La Belle Isolde, it seems unlikely he'd throw that faith so lightly away on Bess of Caerleon. But Dinadan and Sagramore may have had no such compunction . . .'"

"Particularly if Dinadan's version of the story of Sagramore and the Lady Elaine is true, as opposed to Sir Tristram's."

"Nor can we rule out Thomas as a suspect, for he did lie about the party. We have not questioned Baldwin of Orkney or Bertrand of Toledo. What do we know of them?"

"Bertrand is a singer and a Moor. As far as I can tell, a faithful squire to Sir Palomides, who is a faithful knight of the Round Table. Of course, I've known him to sing some ribald songs. I wonder how much that might translate into discourteous behavior?"

"Anything's possible, and worth checking up on. And what about Baldwin?"

"Quiet. Even surly sometimes. Not unlike his own master, Sir Agravain."

"Oh yes, Agravain." Merlin looked thoughtful, scowling under the weight of his heavy brows. "Agravain has always borne watching. Perhaps his squire does as well. We do need to think about questioning those two at least. And ultimately perhaps Sagramore too. But it'll have to wait."

We were just coming into Caerleon. Ahead of us rose the Gothic towers of the cathedral's westwork, marking the center of the city. Here at the first cross street into town, however, was a colorful sign of a smiling red fox—the sign of William Bailey's hostelry. "Here we are, lad," Merlin said. "Let's see what we can find out, shall we?"

"Welcome, my lords!" a booming voice greeted us as we stepped in the door. Bailey himself stood before us, his huge frame dressed very much as he had been a few days ago at the king's love-day hearings. His leather belt held a sack-like brown chemise in place, and his hair was close-cropped on his round, brown knot of a head. His nose was red and bulbous, and he had a few days' growth of beard on his chin. But he was clean and orderly, much like the room itself, and his eyes twinkled kindly as he met us. "Sit yourselves right down at a table here, and I'll have my wife set you up with drinks. In from Camelot, are you? It's my Lord Merlin, is it not?"

"Master William, it's kind of you to remember me. Yes, we've just been in town on some castle business," Merlin began, on his best manners. We sat down on one of the small wooden benches close to the door. It being still well before vespers, we were William Bailey's first customers of the late afternoon, though a few long tables were already set up, awaiting the crowd that was anticipated every night in the most popular hostelry in Caerleon. Merlin, ever mindful of catching those he questioned off guard, had clearly decided to give William the impression we were just visiting town and had stopped in for a drink by chance. "Why don't you have her pour me a nice claret, then? Perhaps the same for my young friend here, or perhaps you'd rather have a pint of ale, Gildas?"

"Ale would be fine, thanks," I answered, looking quizzically at him.

"A glass of claret and a pint of ale. So, Master William, the word around the castle is that you had some excitement in here the other night. A fight that some of the squires got into, or some such thing? What was that all about?"

"Ach, it wasn't so much that people need to be talking about it," William answered good-naturedly, waving his hands. "Just a few drunken squires. The one, I guess, was Sir Florent—the one got caught for raping Bess, my serving girl. Terrible thing, that. Now we're short-handed; she's not been back to work and I can't blame her. Why come back to the place where you served drinks to the man that assaulted you just a bit later? For heaven's sake, if I'd known what would happen, I'd have thrown 'em out long before that fight they had."

"No doubt, no doubt," Merlin said, his eyes darting about as if searching for another question that might open things up.

"We heard the fight was all about the woman," I broke in, trying to help Merlin out. His eyebrows lowered at me in a warning not to say too much.

"Did you now?" William answered me with genuine interest. "Now that I hadn't heard. All I know is, the two of 'em started grabbing for one another and even going for their swords, and then the older fellow, the one with the black beard, he steps in and stops it. And that was the last of it. Excepting they all left pretty much after that."

I was about to jump in again and ask whether he noticed who left when, or whether they all left together, but Merlin's threatening brows convinced me to hold my tongue. That would have sounded too much like an investigation, and not enough like a casual question.

"Well, I'll send Moll over with those drinks, then," William said, and then backed up into the kitchen.

"That went well," Merlin grumbled, the corner of his mouth twisted down with irony.

"Do you think he's covering something up? You'd think he'd have a better idea of exactly what's happening in his own tavern, especially if it gets rowdy enough for a fight to break out."

Merlin shook his head. "No, I just think he's a particularly simple fellow. I don't think we'd get any more out of him even if we put him on the rack."

I had to admit Master William did not seem to know any more than he was telling. My gaze wandered around the tavern. It was dark and not especially roomy. I counted some fifteen benches set up along the boards that served as tables, in rows that ended at the kitchen door. A fire was just heating up in the fireplace along the north wall, and the south wall was hung with a large tapestry depicting a hunting scene. The only window was next to the door to the street on the west wall, and it was shuttered. Light came in from a few windows on the second floor, where there seemed to be several sleeping rooms for travelers who lodged here.

The kitchen door opened and Molly Bailey came through. She carried a small tray and strode to where we were sitting. She stopped short and looked down at us with flashing black eyes and a frightful scowl, and then launched into a tirade. "You think you have fools in hand, do you? You may fool my husband—a simpler soul never breathed as what he is—but you're not fooling me!"

Molly was dressed much as her husband, with a long, brown linen chemise that rode high on her neck and came down well below her knees. It was belted in the middle with a leather thong. Her hair was covered by a gray woolen veil pulled around her face and under her chin, and hanging down to the middle of her ample chest. Moll was not by any means undergrown.

She slammed the flagon and tankard down at our table so

that some of Merlin's wine spilled out. She tsked and wiped up the spill with her sleeve, and then looked over at what must have been my bewildered face. "Close your jaw, boy, you'll catch flies," was all she snapped at me, but on Merlin she turned her considerable ire. "What do you mean coming in here and lying to us? All of a sudden you have this uncontrollable desire to taste our wine, do you, after how many years at Camelot? Just happen to be in the neighborhood, do we, and need to pass the time by askin' about the night of the rape all casual like? Out with it, you charlatan. Who sent you? What do you want with us? You think somebody here knows about that attack? Come on, out with it, I said!"

Taken aback by the frontal assault, Merlin was briefly speech-less—a rare occurrence for him. He stammered at first under the glare of Moll's unflinching eyes as she put her hands on the table and leaned forward, glowering at him.

Merlin recovered quickly, though. "Madame, we are sent to investigate this crime by the queen herself, who has taken a personal interest in the case. I have found it puts people at their ease if I speak with them casually rather than making them feel they are being interrogated."

"Oh sure," Moll scoffed. "A lot easier to trick them if they don't know why you're asking the questions, ain't it? Well, let's hear your questions, then. Just what is it your precious queen wants to know from us?"

"Well first," Merlin replied, falling easily into his role as inquisitor, "tell me about the knights. Had you seen them before? How did they behave generally during the revel?"

"How in blazes do you think they behaved, you old fool? They were young men drinking and carrying on. They were loud and boisterous and they kept drinking. But we have that kind in here all the time—that's our business. Even when they came to blows, it wasn't especially unusual. Some might not think so of squires and knights, but I know as well as anybody they're all just men underneath, so it's no surprise they'd act like it."

"Came to blows?" Merlin probed, his eyebrows raised.

"The tall red-haired fellow that seemed to be the center of attention. He and the other one—he was tall too, but skinny, and long brown hair, that looked like it could stand a washing."

"Colgrevaunce," I muttered.

Molly shrugged. "That might'a been his name. I didn't catch it. But that one, him I've seen in here before."

Merlin's eyes widened with interest. "You had seen Colgrevaunce before?"

"He'd come in here almost every night for a whole week before that party," Molly replied. "Course, he ain't been in here since. But he was always wantin' Bess to wait on him. He'd taken a fancy to her and no mistake, I could see it in his eyes. I kept telling her to take him upstairs for a tumble; she could make some extra money and I'd only charge her for the use of the room. Close that mouth again, boy, you look like a fool."

I was rather shocked at the implications of Molly's revelation, though Merlin seemed to take it in stride. I did indeed close my mouth as I heard him ask her, "Is Master Bailey running a brothel here, then?"

Molly laughed and scoffed at the idea. "My husband is a simple man, as I've already told you. He thinks the men come here purely for his good wine and ale. I tell him only what he really needs to know."

"And Bess, did she regularly take part in that aspect of the business?"

Molly scowled again and shook her head. "Our Bess was a hard worker and a good barmaid. She'd been with us about two years, but even though I could see the way people looked at her, she never did do more than flirt a bit, with the customers of rank. Our last barmaid before her was a game little slut and had a nice business on the side, and she drew a lot of customers in. But I could never talk Bess into taking part in that kind of transaction. She was a bit of a priss and a romantic besides—thought her knight in shining armor would come some day and carry her away. Well, that's not exactly what happened, is it?"

"But you said Colgrevaunce—the tall skinny squire—was in for several nights admiring her. Did she think he was going to be her knight?"

"Oh, that may have been her thoughts," Molly answered. "But I could see that weren't the way of it. That Colgrevaunce fellow had one thing on his mind, and it wasn't hearts and flowers. I figured at least she could make some ready money off of it. But she wasn't interested."

"The fight, though—we heard it was a fight over her," I interrupted.

"You heard right, then. I could see it comin' all night. Bess was waiting on them but needed my help a lot of the time, so I could see what was going on. The red-haired knight, he made a point of complimenting Bess every time she came to the table. Told her she was beautiful and graceful and I don't know what all. Well, I could tell there was nothing behind it, it was just a way some of those knights had of complimenting a person, but Bess, she didn't know better and I could see he was turning her head. She kept blushing red as a flame every time he talked to her."

"And Colgrevaunce didn't like this?"

"This Colgrevaunce—he was a lot bolder that night than he'd been the other times he came in. Those times he was by himself and so he just sat quiet-like, watching Bess, always watching every move she made. But that night he was boldened by having all his friends around him, I guess, and too by all he was drinking, and it was a pretty lot, I'll tell you that. But he kept calling Bess things like 'My pretty wench' and 'lusty dame,' and playing with her hair when she brought him his drinks, and he even grabbed her backside once when she bent over the table."

"And Bess?" Merlin asked.

"Well, she wasn't complaining. I think she felt flattered to have the two of them flirting with her like that. But Colgrevaunce was doing more than flirting. He whispered something in her ear later in the evening that made her look pretty shocked and turned her redder than anything the red-haired one said. She scurried away from the table after that, and it wasn't much later that the fight started."

"So," Merlin said. "You think the fight had to do with something Colgrevaunce said to Bess? Something Sir Florent—the red-haired knight—objected to?"

The woman shrugged. "Might have been. I wasn't close enough to hear what he said in her ear. She was off in the kitchen, all red-faced. So she wasn't near when it started. I did hear the red-headed fellow shout 'villain' and 'churl,' and something about 'discourteous behavior,' all that kind of thing. The other one, the skinny one, was drunker even than the redhead, and was shouting louder."

"And what was he saying, if you heard it?"

"Talked about how the redhead was jealous, that he, I mean the skinny fellow himself, didn't have a rich and famous father and didn't have his pick of all the women in the court, and how what he did with this one—I mean, what the skinny one did with Bess—was none of his business, and he'd show him just how much it wasn't any of his business."

"And he took the first swing, did he?"

"The skinny fellow made a fist and swung it at the redhead, but that one was stronger, and wasn't as drunk. He ducked and gave the skinny one a hard blow right in the midsection.

Knocked the wind out of him, it looked to me. Then Skinny goes for his sword, and the redhead starts to go for his sword as well. But then the knight with the black beard jumps up and grabs the redhead by the arms, and the other knight, the jolly one with the red face . . ."

"Sagramore?" I looked at Merlin. He nodded.

"He gets in between them and says it's gone far enough. At that word the redhead shakes off Blackbeard's grip and stalks out the door."

"Madame," Merlin asked as politely as he was able. "This is very important. Do you recall whether Sir Florent, the red-haired knight, took his shield with him when he left?"

Molly Bailey studied Merlin through a deep scowl. "What's that to the purpose?"

"Please, my good woman," Merlin continued. "We know the rapist had Sir Florent's shield. If Florent left the shield here in the tavern, then any one of those remaining knights or squires could have taken it and committed the crime, disguised as Sir Florent."

Molly let out a derisive puff of air. "That red-haired gentleman didn't rape nobody," she opined. "He was the best behaved of the whole bunch, and didn't like any of the others behaving like we wasn't ladies waiting on 'em. You want to watch that skinny one, is what I say. That's the one looked out of control from what I saw."

"Your point is well taken," Merlin answered with patience. "But did Sir Florent leave with his shield?"

Molly screwed up her face in an effort to remember. "Seems to me only a few of them had shields. They'd come from the castle and weren't all armed, except for their swords. But the couple that did have shields laid them against that back wall. And when I remember him leaving—seems to me he did pick up a shield on his way out."

Merlin looked meaningfully at me and then back at the woman. "Did you happen to notice which of the other men left soon after? And who was the last to leave? And also, if you know, were any of them riding horses?"

Molly looked down at him and her face suddenly became a blank. "Didn't notice," she said. "The rest all left about the same time, not long after. Far as I could tell, they were pretty much all on foot. There might have been one horse out there, I don't remember for sure. But it's not that long a walk back to the castle. That's all I can tell you."

Merlin, seeing he had got all he could from her, finished the interview. "Thank you, madame. You have been a great help, and the queen thanks you as well."

"The queen can go whistle for all of me," Molly answered with a snort. "I just want you two out of here before we get any of our real customers for the night. Nothing hurts business like spies from the court. So finish your drinks and adieu to you. And don't let the door hit you too hard in the arse on the way out."

She snatched up the two coins Merlin had laid on the table and stalked back to the kitchen, still in a huff. Merlin looked thoughtful as he finished his wine, and I didn't speak for fear of interrupting his thoughts. In a few moments, he was ready to leave and we arose. Neither master nor mistress of the inn bade us goodbye, and we found our own way out, back on the street where it was approaching nightfall. I thought I had heard vespers ring while we sat inside, and suggested we ought to get back within the castle walls as quickly as possible.

Unfortunately, Merlin had other ideas.

"Florent had his shield with him. He fell asleep in the woods, and someone, almost certainly one of the knights or squires at that party, followed him closely enough to see where he lay, steal his shield, and rape Bess."

"While riding a big white warhorse," I added. "Which none of them had with them."

"Maybe," Merlin answered, drawing the word out. "Still, there's something our lady Molly was not telling us. Something she knew about who left the tavern when. I'm not sure what it would have been, but it could be important." We had reached the end of the road where we were to turn off toward the castle when Merlin stopped dead in his tracks.

"Young Gildas," he said to me, raising his hefty eyebrows in a look that seemed almost apologetic. "We can't go home yet. I think it's time we talked to Bess."

CHAPTER ELEVEN:
BESS OF CAERLEON

"Leave 'er alone, ye great bearded bully!" her father shouted, brandishing a broom handle he had grabbed from the shop. "Go back where you come from, and take your thug of a lackey with you!"

The interrogation of Bess of Caerleon wasn't going very well.

When we arrived at her house, she recognized us from the window and dashed into the back rooms of the carpenter's shop before we were through the doorway. Merlin called to her that we only wished to ask her some questions about her attacker, but she shouted back through the closed door, "I know why you're here, and I want nothing to do with you! Get out!" After which her father came in from the outside, saw us apparently cornering his daughter in his own living quarters, and began threatening us with cleaning implements. It wasn't exactly a warm welcome.

"No one's going to hurt her, sir, we only want to find the person that assaulted her, and see to it he's punished," I tried to explain, reasonably and calmly, while dodging the broom handle that swooshed over my head as the agitated carpenter danced about, all the while screeching like a hoot owl.

"Out, I tells ye! She's not goin' to speak with the likes of you, ye murderin' thievin' lyin' vandals!" In the meantime, Bess kept shrieking from behind the door as if we had come to murder her in her father's house.

Merlin stood motionless in the center of the carpenter's shop, glowering darkly. He seemed for a moment to fold within himself, as if gathering his strength for a great effort. Suddenly, his arm shot forward and he cried, "Incendia!" At which a bolt of fire exploded right in front of the carpenter. He froze, struck dumb by the blast. From behind the closed door, Bess peeked slowly out to see what the awful noise had been.

Having got their attention, Merlin proceeded calmly. "John of Caerleon, listen to me now before I blast you into a cinder. Our mission here will do no harm to your daughter, nor to you. We wish to interrogate her peacefully, but if it must be through force then it shall be. Make no mistake, we *will* interrogate her. Now send her out to me before I turn you into a stoat."

John glanced over his shoulder to see Bess peering from behind the door, and answered Merlin in a defeated voice, "There she is, tell the slut yourself. Never comes to see me until she's got into trouble, now it seems my 'ouse is the only place she can stand to be."

"I know you," Bess said defiantly as she stepped around the door. She stood, arms folded across her simple gray smock, in the center of the shop. Merlin gazed into her eyes and she stared right back at him. "You're in league with that bitch of a queen, the one that let my rapist off with his life. Why should I speak with you? You're just trying to say what happened to me didn't really happen. You're trying to whitewash the whole thing because I'm a simple artisan's daughter and that bastard who raped me is the son of a prince. I'm not about to tell you anything! I don't care what you blow up!"

"That's right, you tell 'im, Bess old girl. Don't let 'im bully you, him with his gray whiskers and his great pointy nose. Nothing but the queen's lapdog, isn't he! What? And what about you, boy? 'Ow's it feel to be the lapdog of a lapdog?"

"Will you shut up!" Merlin turned on him again. "So help me, I'll have Gildas here gag you if you speak again!"

At that John squinted at me and then retired to the back wall of the shop, grumbling incoherently as I glared at him in what I thought might be a menacing manner.

"My dear young lady," Merlin began, in what was, for him, an incredible show of courtesy. "I have no intention of minimizing the pain you have been through, or denying that a serious crime has been committed against your person. Please believe me when I tell you that all I want to do—all the queen wants us to do—is to find out the truth about what happened to you that night."

"So you are calling me a liar!" Bess flared up again. "You think I haven't told the truth?"

"That is not what I said, Bess." Merlin spoke in conciliatory tones. "Your story of the rape is true, I have no doubt. I do believe there are more things you could tell us that might give us insight into why this crime was committed, and who is guilty."

"Florent was convicted! It was his shield. Why would you defend such a person? Have you no decency? Have you no shame?" Tears began to flow down Bess's cheeks. She stiffened, fought them back, and drew herself up to her full height. I half expected her to come down upon us with unchecked fury, but the acid calm and pure hatred in her voice as she spat her next sharp words sent more of a chill down my spine than rage ever would have.

"You are here to make the charade complete." She bit off the words like a snarling wolf. "To make me say I was mistaken when your precious Florent brutalized and violated me." Her voice rose to a shriek at the end, and once again I feared a murderous explosion. With effort she contained herself.

"Madame, you have mistaken us." Merlin bowed in deference to the artisan's daughter, though she remained unimpressed. "We want nothing more than to find and punish your attacker."

"He *is* found." She spoke with quiet malice. "Punish him."

I started to speak, but Merlin stopped me with a glance, and continued his cautious approach. "We are as afraid as you are that your attacker may go free. And *that must not happen,* do you understand? The rapist must not be allowed to slip undetected through the fingers of Arthur's justice."

"The queen is trying to make that happen even now!"

"Not so, madame!" Now Merlin rose to his full height and spoke with all the authority that age and position gave him. "The queen demands justice for women more vociferously than the king. But she also demands truth, and we have reason to believe another man raped you. Do you want that man to escape?"

"I saw what I saw! The shield condemns him!" Bess was uncowed by Merlin's display, and spoke now with the authority of the wronged and the demands of the innocent. Merlin, seeing he was getting nowhere, changed course once again and plunged directly into a cross-examination.

"We know you were in the woods that night to meet the squire Colgrevaunce. Did he ever appear, as he had promised?"

Now that was something Bess of Caerleon had not expected. She paled and stood open-mouthed, the smallest of tears forming again in the corners of her eyes. My stomach sank into my shoes in sympathy for what she must feel. But when she spoke again her confidence was undiminished.

"That lying, cowardly poltroon—if he had been there, that villain never would have raped me . . ."

"Possibly," Merlin agreed. "Or perhaps we would have Colgrevaunce's murder to solve as well. Or, perhaps—and have you considered this?—your attacker was Colgrevaunce himself."

Bess stared at Merlin with outright scorn. "You have a reputation for wisdom, old man, but age must have turned you into a dotard. Why, in the name of all that's holy, would a man take by brute force what I had invited him into the forest to freely give him?"

Her answer was like a punch to my midsection. I had never considered that aspect. Colgrevaunce could not be guilty.

Merlin's eyes flashed under his ponderous brows, and the corner of his mouth gave the slightest twitch upward. I could see he was impressed, and was growing fond of this independent little wench. So was I, for that matter. But Merlin, with another slight bow of his head, demurred. "It would depend on the man, madame, but certainly Colegrevaunce would not do so."

"Right." I had been quiet as long as I was able, but this was too much. "But what of Florent? What motive could *he* have had?"

Now I felt the weight of those steely eyes boring into me. "Jealousy," Bess answered simply. "I asked Colgrevaunce, not him, to meet me in the woods. They quarreled. He left angry."

So Colgrevaunce's version of the affair may not have been so unbelievable after all. At least, Bess saw things the same way. For my part, I still had doubts. "Forgive me, my lady." I realized after I said it that I was giving her quite a promotion in class. "But why would you, or any other woman, choose Colgrevaunce over Sir Florent?"

Merlin scowled at me with undisguised impatience, but Bess, in all her anger and frustration, actually laughed. "Sir Florent treated me like a lady, it is true. But he had no real interest. He saw me only as a lowborn girl, an object in a world that he maneuvered using his courtesy as a map. I was to him simply a thing to be moved around correctly in the game he calls his life. He wins if he scores all the points for courtesy and marries the most eligible noble girl."

Now it was my turn to blanch. Bess saw my reaction and lifted a questioning eyebrow, though she said nothing. My heart sank to think that perhaps Bess had sized up Florent correctly—

and that my Lady Rosemounde would only be one more object in his world, one more pawn in his game, that led to success and honor and, in his case, a kingdom.

"But for Colgrevaunce, I was much more. I had no illusions the silly fellow was in love with me, but I was more to him than a piece in a game. His desire for me was palpable. I was a prize. I was the reward at the end of his quest. And I could broker that desire into something more. Him, I could manipulate. Him, I could work into a benefactor who would raise me out of this sty . . ."

At that a loud and inarticulate cry of objection emerged from the far corner where John had retreated.

Bess ignored it. ". . . And make me a lady. I was that close. But now where am I? No one will want me now—not even the brainless churls of my own class."

I bristled a bit. As the son of an armor-maker, I was certainly of the same artisan class as Bess. Though like her, my ambition—or at least my father's ambition for me—had given me a different set of social connections.

"As to that," Merlin answered, with, for him, uncommon courtesy, "no reasonable man will find your virtue or character diminished in any way by what has happened to you."

"Oh, right," came the carping from the corner. "And I've got a solid-gold big toe, too!"

All three of us glanced at the carpenter with puzzled expressions. "My father has a point," Bess said. "It is not character or virtue men look for in wives, but rather alliances and unspoilt goods. I never had the first quality and have lost the second."

Merlin seemed momentarily at a loss for words, but I could see he was switching tactics again. This time he tried sincerity.

"My good woman," he began, "be all that as it may, I cannot give back to you what is lost. But I can promise you justice. I give you my sacred word that justice will be served in this case.

But I cannot bring justice about if you do not help us."

Somewhere behind those fierce eyes I could see a wall had come down in Bess's soul. Her answers were still tentative, but she did allow herself at least a rudimentary trust as she answered Merlin. "What is it you want from me, old man? I have told everything I know."

"I want to know more about what happened before the attack—what went on here at the sign of the Red Fox Inn. Can you help us there?"

Bess sighed. "I will answer what I can," she conceded. "But I've already told you what matters. Colgrevaunce and Florent both paid special attention to me. I made plans to meet Colgrevaunce in the clearing in the woods after their party ended. It was that, as I understand it, which caused the quarrel between Colgrevaunce and the knight."

"Florent heard you making the agreement?"

"Florent was on the other side of the table. Only those on either side of Colgrevaunce would have heard us. But the story spread round the table very quickly, as far as I could tell."

"Now this all happened after Sir Tristram left? Sir Tristram was the tall—"

"I know who Sir Tristram is," Bess interrupted. Then she blushed and looked down. "Sir Tristram is a regular visitor to Master Bailey's inn. But his visits have nothing to do with this business."

"Indeed?" Merlin raised his weighty brows. "How can you be so sure?"

"Sir Tristram is a great knight and a great gentleman. And he kept out of any arguments or unseemly behavior among the party assembled that night. As you said yourself, he left long before the quarrel broke out."

"Nevertheless, madame, in investigations of this nature, it is my experience that the slightest details, even if they have no apparent relevance to the investigation, may turn out to hold the most valuable clues."

I snorted a bit at that (very quietly, I assure you) since to my knowledge Merlin had only been involved in what he called "investigations of this nature" on one other occasion. He was probably just trying to justify his own nosiness.

Bess was turning redder by the second. I was about to say something, to try to alleviate her embarrassment and perhaps deflect Merlin's question, which seemed to me to be off the subject. I was willing to take her word that Tristram's visits had nothing to do with the crime we were investigating and were probably just between him and Bess. Then she suddenly burst out, "He told me of his impossible love for the Queen Isolde. It was a beautiful tale and I sympathized with him. And then he asked me to agree to receive letters that he would write the queen, in order to pass them on to a messenger who would travel between Caerleon and Cornwall. I was also to receive letters from the Lady Isolde and pass them to Sir Tristram."

Merlin nodded without comment. He was doing some quick calculating, as far as I could tell. "And how long, Bess, had this been going on? Some months?"

"A year and a half," Bess answered.

"And that means—Sir Sagramore would be the messenger you're talking about?" I now realized there certainly was a connection between this and the party. At least in terms of participants.

"Yes. Sir Sagramore has brought several messages to me since I began working at the Baileys' inn. Sir Tristram stops by once a week, when he feels he can come in unobserved, and asks whether there has been a message. Sometimes he brings a letter for me to give Sir Sagramore. But that is all I know about them."

"And both those knights were at the raucous party the night you were attacked. I have a strong feeling there was more going on at that table than a quarrel over you, Mistress Bess. I wonder whether there is some connection . . ."

"No, old man, there is nothing to think about there. Sir Sagramore and Sir Tristram are gentlemen. They would never seek to harm me. Besides, I didn't speak to either of them that night. Once they came in and met in the tavern, they talked between themselves. I had no cause to act as a go-between. You need to concentrate on Florent, old man. He's the one whose shield I saw. It was not Tristram, or Sagramore, or Colgrevaunce that raped me. I would have known it."

"Known it?" I couldn't help interrupting. "But you said you never saw the attacker's face . . ."

"I saw him ride the horse. I saw him dismount and come toward me. I know Colgrevaunce and Sir Tristram and Sir Sagramore well enough. I could recognize their walk, their demeanor, even with veiled faces. I'm sure I would have recognized one of them!"

"Let us go back a bit," Merlin said, stroking his beard while he pondered this latest news. "Let us recreate the table that night. Sir Colgrevaunce was on one side, and Sir Florent on the other, correct?"

"Yes." Bess let out an exasperated sigh. "I've told you before."

"But tell us now where everyone else was seated. Sir Tristram and Sir Sagramore?"

"Sir Tristram was off to the side, a bit away from the table."

"By himself?"

"No, that other older fellow with the dark beard was with him."

"Sir Dinadan, was it not?"

"I don't know his name. He had a sarcastic tongue, though— never ceased beleaguering Tristram, or me, or anyone else that came to his attention. Sagramore was at the table, sitting to the right of that dog Florent. But I don't know what good all of this does."

Merlin shrugged. "Maybe none at all. But I want to know who did what that night, as closely as possible. Now aside from those we've already mentioned, there would have been the other three squires: Bertrand of Toledo, Sir Palomides's squire; Thomas, Sir Ywain's squire; and Baldwin, squire of Sir Agravain."

"Three others, yes," Bess said slowly, thinking back. "But I did not know their names. There was one very dark one, a Moor I believe . . ."

"That would have been Bertrand," I encouraged her.

"He sat to the left of Florent. The other two sat on either side of Colgrevaunce. One had black hair and eyes and a trim black beard . . ."

"That's Baldwin. The other, sandy-headed fellow, that's Thomas."

"All right," she concluded. "So you know where everyone was. Now what, old man?"

"I wonder," Merlin said, still pondering and stroking his beard, "if you can tell us what no one else has been able to. Exactly when did each of them leave the tavern?"

Bess scoffed. "This is what you are wasting my time with? How is this going to get me justice?"

"Good Mistress Bess," Merlin cajoled, quietly and patiently, "I give you my word you will have justice. But please, humor me in this. Can you tell me the order in which the men left the party that night? We have already been told Tristram left first, and Florent was next to leave after the quarrel."

Bess, with another impatient sigh, rolled her eyes as she thought back and then began enumerating on her fingers. "Well, the one you called Thomas left soon after Florent did. And the other squire, Baldwin, soon after that. Colgrevaunce would have left with them, but he hung back a few moments to make sure I still planned to meet him in the woods. He had plenty of time to get there. I thought he would go to the clearing and wait for me right then."

"And the other three?" Merlin asked.

Bess looked down. "Sir Sagramore went off after those two squires left. The black-bearded knight, Sir Dinadan, did not leave right away. He came and spoke a word in my ear: He had some private business to conduct with the mistress of the house, Madame Bailey, and I directed him to one of the upstairs rooms in the inn."

I was taken aback at that, but Merlin was unmoved. "And did Sir Dinadan conduct that kind of business with your mistress often?" he asked calmly.

Another shrug. "It was something he liked to do when he was here in Caerleon. He seems to be rather a randy knight."

"So it seems, indeed," I said, and looked quizzically at Merlin.

Merlin had one more question. "And when did Bertrand leave?"

"Oh, the Moor. Well, he waited at the table after the other squires went away—seemed to be waiting for Sir Sagramore a moment—and then when he saw the knight was about to leave, he followed after him, and left without a word."

"Ah," was all Merlin said. "Well, I thank you for your pains, good Mistress Bess. I assure you, though what you've told us may mean little to you, I think it helps us a great deal. And I beg you, remain optimistic. I have given my word I will bring your attacker to justice. That has been enough for kings in the past."

"Yes," Bess snarled, clearly unconvinced. "Kings who had never been raped. You bring me justice, and I'll say you're a better man than I took you for. But I want him hanged, mind you. For what he did to me, he deserves no less."

Merlin bowed again and started out of the shop without speaking again. I turned and followed. But I had one more question that I voiced as we reached the door. "My lady," I asked, giving her that promotion again. "I just want to clear up one small detail. You're absolutely sure the horse he was riding was white? Could it have been, say, a light gray that just looked white in the moonlight?"

"White as snow, boy," she answered. "That much I saw clearly. Whiter than morning milk."

"Yeah, now you've got yer answers, ye great hairy bullies, now leave my shop and the devil take ye! And don't be comin' back here without you've got the scoundrel in tow that raped my innocent Bess!" John the carpenter, his courage returning now that we were out the door, shouted at us as we left.

As we walked off down the dark lanes of Caerleon, I looked back to see Bess silhouetted in the shop window, watching us with—what? Hope? It seemed her only hope for justice was in us. Who else cared about finding the real attacker? Most thought Florent must be guilty. The king thought the affair was over, and saw Guinevere's interference as an annoyance. Only Merlin and I—and the queen—wanted justice based on Truth.

Neither of us spoke as we made our way along the dark street leading out of town. The distant bell of the convent of Saint Mary Magdalene had long since rung vespers and we quickened our pace to cover the half mile back to the castle where, no doubt, the drawbridge would have to be lowered to let us in at this hour. Quiet as he was, I wanted to find out whether Merlin's impressions of Bess and her story were the same as mine. I was about to ask him when what sounded like a giant insect whizzed close by my right ear. Or—but no, it couldn't be.

"What on earth—" I began.

Merlin, quicker on the uptake and readier for action, shoved me to the side of the road and into the ditch. "God's teeth, Gildas, get down!"

"What is it?" I whispered, crouching in the ditch with Merlin lying belly down at my side and peering cautiously up over the road.

"It came from that direction," he whispered, pointing.

"What did? What was that I heard?"

Merlin didn't answer, but held out his left arm. Stuck in the fabric of his robe above the elbow, its tip red with blood where it pierced his flesh, was a crossbow bolt.

I gasped, then ducked my head as another bolt went whizzing past.

"Good lord," I whispered to Merlin. "We're out here with no defense—I haven't even got my sword with me. What are we going to do?"

"Not exactly what I signed on for, you Cornish dunce," Merlin hissed at me. "Look what you've gotten me into now!"

"Is there only one of them?"

"Only one person seems to be shooting. He's cautious, though. He must think we're armed." Merlin looked around. Behind us were a few trees—not much protection, but better than lying here in the open field. "Make a break for those trees! Now!"

I got up and sprinted, but I didn't want to leave the old man behind. He was moving as fast as I'd ever seen him, but the marksman had seen our shadows move, and I heard a cry from well behind us as another dart whizzed overhead. We reached a large tree and a second dart made a loud "thwock!" in the trunk just as we ducked behind it. Looking out from that shelter, I saw the shadow of our pursuer approaching the road from the other side, his crossbow held high. He stood in the road and leveled it toward us.

He seemed a young man, and strong of build to judge from the shadow I could make out. I could probably outrun him if I made a dash for the castle alone, but Merlin would be easy prey. "Merlin! Can't you use your magic? Why don't you throw one of those 'incendia' curses at him and make a good explosion?"

With an exasperated sigh, the old man burst my small bubble of hope. "What, you think I just say it and it happens? Those bursts are a trick I do with Greek fire. I carry enough with me when I leave my cave for one fireburst. I used it already at the carpenter's shop."

"This is not a good time to tell me it's not really magic, old man," I grumbled. "Duck!" We squeezed together behind the tree just as another dart thudded into the trunk. The shadowy figure in the road now made to run toward us. Suddenly, out of nowhere it seemed, we heard the sound of horse's hooves.

The ghostly archer in the road looked to his left with alarm, and saw, just as we did, a great destrier bearing down on him at full gallop from the direction of the castle. He turned and ran off before the horse reached him. Merlin and I dashed out from behind our tree and rushed back to the road to meet our rescuer.

As the horse reached us it reared up on its hind legs and my blood ran cold. It was a pure white warhorse—white as snow, whiter than milk—and on it rode a hooded figure whose face was hidden from us. Merlin gasped as well, but then, as the horse settled down, the rider pushed back the hood to reveal a shock of golden hair, sparkling in the moonlight. A pair of azure eyes gazed down at us with a sparkle of amusement.

Merlin gasped again, this time in surprise and wonder.

"Nimue!" he cried.

Chapter Twelve:
The Lady of the Lake

"Tsk, tsk, such a foolish old man," the damsel purred in gentle tones as she reached her hand out to her devoted servant. "To be wandering about after dark with only a brat of a squire to accompany you." With that she gave me a quick wink. "Don't you know there are dangerous folk about? Do I have to watch you all the time?"

She helped hoist Merlin up onto the great white horse to sit in the saddle behind her. Now that the danger was past, I saw his arm was bleeding heavily—that second arrow must have done more than graze him. He even seemed a trifle faint as he answered Nimue, "Anything to attract your attention, my lady."

She seemed to size me up for a moment, and then she conceded, "You, boy, you look skinny enough. Snowfax here is bred to carry a knight in full armor, I think he can manage the three of us without strain. Hop up, then!"

She reached down and pulled me up as well, to sit in front of her on the great destrier. "And now let's be off," she cried when I'd settled myself in.

"Excuse me, madame," I said, as courteously as I could while riding before her in a saddle built for one. "But where are we off to, exactly?"

"Through the woods to my Lady's palace," Nimue answered. "Your master is severely wounded. He will need our potions to recover in time to continue his hunt for Mistress Bess's attacker."

"Should have stayed in my cave," the old necromancer said faintly from behind the lady, as the horse ran smoothly and effortlessly toward the woods north of Camelot. "Nothing there to bring me danger. All Gildas's fault, the blockhead."

Nimue smiled at my chagrin and then whispered, loudly enough to make sure Merlin heard her, "Don't mind him. It's just his way. He loves playing the part of the cranky old man. It's one of his few pleasures in life."

"Oh, I know that by now," I told her. The glimpses I was getting of Nimue as we rode swiftly through the trees were astounding. I'd heard Merlin praise her beauty (it was for her love that he had chosen to lock himself away in his cave, after all), but seeing it for myself was an experience I'd not trade for a thousand gold pieces. She wore a dress of fine white samite, covered with a gray cloak and hood. Her skin was like carved alabaster in the moonlight, as if she were the statue of a goddess that no flesh and blood woman could ever hope to compete with. Her lips like coral were pursed in worry, belying her free and easy manner, as she showed a real concern for Merlin's welfare—Merlin, her devoted servant, whom she had rejected as a lover but for whom she held an affectionate regard, and regularly visited in his self-imposed isolation. It was clear to me now why Merlin remained her devoted thrall.

"But . . . how do you know about those things? Is the Lady of the Lake so interested in the affairs of Arthur's court that she keeps track even of humble sleuths like Merlin and me?"

Nimue gave a light laugh. "Don't flatter yourself overmuch, Gildas of Cornwall. The Lady has taken a special interest in this case because her name was dragged into it. John the carpenter did some work at the palace, and his daughter used the Lady as her reason for being in the woods the night she was attacked. This my Lady knows. And while Bess of Caerleon lied about her reason, the Lady still takes it personally that one she employed and protected should be abused so abominably."

"Perhaps," I answered as the trees sped by us. "And perhaps it is her Lady Nimue who takes a special interest, since your horse was somehow involved in the crime."

The Lady Nimue hesitated only a moment and then gave another merry laugh. "Well, Gildas," she exclaimed. "You really can recognize a clue when it comes up and carries you on its back!"

"Don't tease the boy," Merlin said weakly from behind. "It's too important. How is it your Snowfax came to be carrying the man that raped Bess of Caerleon? This investigation has yielded more questions than answers, and now it's turning deadly. Tell us, Nimue, who was riding your horse that night?"

The nymph refused to be chastened, but did acknowledge the truth of what Merlin was saying. "You're right about this turning deadly. You're getting paler by the minute, old man. Rest, now, and I'll have us at the Lady's palace in a furlong's way or two. As for my horse, I must admit I have no idea who was riding him that night."

"Somebody stole your horse? From the Lady of the Lake's palace? That would take some courage—or foolishness," I conjectured.

"No, Gildas of Cornwall, it wasn't like that. Let me explain it briefly now; after we get to the Lady's palace we may be able to go over it at more length. But here is the truth: On the night of the crime, I was keeping in view the newly knighted Sir Florent—much as I was keeping you and Merlin in my view tonight."

"Keeping in view?"

"It is what we servants of the Lady call it when we spend nights in our woods, watching with all our senses those for whom we have some special affinity and some cause to protect."

"Wait—you're saying you had some special reason to watch

Florent? Some special affinity with *him*?"

The nymph nodded. Merlin said nothing, and I wondered if he was still conscious. If not, I was glad for him. But it was just a little bit more than I wanted to hear about the lovely and wonderful Sir Florent, who was going to marry my own beloved, and who apparently also charmed the hearts of even the devoted followers of the Lady of the Lake. It was a little more than disgusting, in my view. But I didn't say any of that to her. After all, I wanted to stay on the horse.

"Too bad none of the Lady's servants had any reason to keep Bess of Caerleon in view that night," was what I finally said instead. Then I realized, "But if you were watching Florent, you must know what he did! You must know where he was. You can be his alibi and prove he is innocent of the rape!"

"Of his innocence I have no doubt. But alas no, I cannot be his alibi. I know of his whereabouts only as far as you do: I followed him from Bailey's inn to the edge of the forest, where he leaned his shield against a tree and lay down in the grass to sleep. My intention was to give him the horse as a gift on the day of his entry into knighthood: a magnificent white destrier, as fine a horse as there is in all of Europe."

"You left the horse with him?"

"While he slept. I tethered Snowfax to the tree on which he had laid his shield, knowing he would see it and accept it when he picked his shield up. But that also meant I had to get back to the Lady's palace on foot, so I began walking there immediately, and I couldn't continue to keep Florent in my view."

"So you don't know Florent didn't wake up, pick up his shield, jump on the horse, and ride off immediately to rape Bess of Caerleon."

"Of course I know he didn't. I just can't prove it." As she said this, the forest opened onto a large lake that reflected a thousand moons off its rippling waves, and a magnificent stone façade, shining silver in the moonlight, that led into the great palace of the Lady of the Lake.

The palace was built as a great manor house. It was protected on one side by the Lady's Lake itself, and on the other three by a moat and outer wall of stone some eight feet high. A drawbridge leading to a gatehouse spanned the moat, and though I saw no one in the guard house as we trotted up on Nimue's horse, the bridge closed immediately after we crossed it into the bailey. Inside, we dismounted, and a woman servant dressed in simple peasant garb took Snowfax and led him toward the stables, which I could see to the right of the house. In the bailey were scattered several simple, timber-framed wattle and daub structures: a granary, a dairy, a cattle shed, and a blacksmith shop.

The manor house itself, an elaborate brown limestone structure of two stories, took up the entire rear portion of the enclosure. Nimue led us through the porch and into the great hall, and each room had its own oak ceiling. On my right, at right angles to the hall, I could see a solar, doubtless the Lady's private chambers, and to the left, similarly, was a parlor. To the rear, beyond the hall lay the kitchen and doubtless there was a buttery there as well. Another small room off the great hall, that in other houses no doubt would have been a chapel, was here used as a library. This was the great collection from which Merlin had been allowed to borrow the Aristotle manuscript currently in his possession.

Once in the great hall, Merlin leaned on my shoulder and nearly collapsed. "Nimue," he said weakly, "I need help very soon." And with that, the old man collapsed to the floor.

Alarmed, I looked at his side, where the arrow had wounded him, and saw it had bled freely all the while we rode the horse. "Merlin!" I cried, and when he could not answer, I looked up at Nimue, at a loss. She saw the panic in my eyes and gave back a confident assurance.

"Do not despair, Gildas of Cornwall. This injury will not be the end of Merlin. The arrow has not struck any vital part, and my Lady can heal all wounds." She nodded toward the Lady's solar. There, framed by the doorway and lit by a hundred candles at her back, dressed in white samite even richer than Nimue's and bordered and filigreed with golden thread, her hair flowing loose upon her shoulders and more golden than her gown's embroidery, stood the Lady of the Lake herself.

I remembered well Sir Gareth's tale of Sir Launfal and the Lady that he had told in the woods while we were hunting, and could think only that he had not given her beauty its just due. No one and nothing I had seen before in my sixteen years prepared me for the sight of those flashing blue eyes and that alabaster skin. Truth to say, even the beauty of Guinevere, and of my own Lady Rosemounde, paled in comparison.

I could think of nothing to do other than fall to my knees and bow to her. "My Lady, your powers are legendary throughout the earth. Please, help my friend and your servant Merlin the Mage, advisor of kings. He—"

"Your courtesy does you credit, young Gildas of Cornwall, and your own reputation precedes you," came the Lady's soft, musical voice. I felt transformed to another sphere, where all was harmony and where the beauties of Nature have their home beyond the ravages of Fortune, where the Lady and all she stood for reigned under God's loving gaze in an unfallen Paradise.

Or at least, that's what I felt, looking at her in that dress, in that light. But it lasted only for a moment. The Lady stepped from her doorway and came toward the fallen Merlin. A half-dozen serving women followed her, and as she reached the old necromancer's prostrate body, she crouched down to give him a cursory examination. Then she stood and quietly commanded,

"Lay him on the couch in the library."

The six women lifted Merlin and carried him into that small front room, whose walls were lined with bright tapestries depicting a unicorn hunt. On the fourth wall was a large case of shelves, in which stood more manuscripts than I had ever seen before in one place.

The women laid their burden on a cushioned bench and then stood back as the Lady stooped over him and looked more closely at his wound. "Hmm," she intoned, as much to me as to anyone. "Your friend is a lucky old man, Gildas of Cornwall. Another two inches over and the arrow would have pierced his kidney or his bowel. As it is, I think he will heal and be none the worse for wear. But first we must stop the bleeding."

The Lady beckoned to one of her women, who handed her a white pouch. She reached into it and brought out a number of clean cloths and a small ceramic vial. She set to work immediately cleaning the wound with the cloths, and then rubbed an ointment from the vial into the wound. "This will ease the pain and speed the healing," she promised me with confidence. Then she took a much longer strip of clean, white cloth and wrapped it around Merlin's torso. Watching her work, I was reminded of the story of Sir Tristram, and how only the Lady Isolde or her mother could cure his wound. Were they healers like the Lady of the Lake? It seemed the Lady, expert in all the remedies found in Nature, and learned in the opinions of the great authorities of the past (I saw Galen and Avicenna on her bookshelves), might have some other magic as well, secret and privy among her devoted followers in this fairyland palace of hers, that made her arts superior even to those storied others adept in the healing arts.

In only a few moments she was finished. She nodded to Nimue and to me as she left the room, followed by her entourage of serving women. "Watch with him tonight, Gildas," she told me. "Call out if there is any change, though I do not expect that to happen. In the morning, I will send Nimue to you. You have much to discuss. The old man should be conscious by then and able to converse, though he'll probably be somewhat weak."

"My Lady, I give you all my thanks."

"I do not particularly need them all," the Lady told me as she swept toward her room. "Find me the violator of that poor young woman, and do it soon. That is the thanks I require."

And with that she disappeared, back into her solar, and the six serving women disappeared with her. Nimue, bearing a candle out of the great hall, nodded a good evening to me as she too left, taking a staircase off the great hall toward the second floor, where there must be several smaller solars for devotees of the Lady who, like Nimue, stayed with her to serve her and be educated in the arts and sciences of the Lady's domain.

I sat in the dark next to Merlin's bed, listening to the old necromancer's even breathing that told me he was sleeping peacefully after the Lady's ministrations. Confident as I now was that Merlin was all but out of danger, I still fretted inwardly about the fate of Sir Florent, now but two days away from his second trial before the court. We knew little more for certain than we had when we began this inquiry, yet what little we had discovered only made me more certain that Bess of Caerleon was assaulted by someone else, someone without the ethical base that Florent's courtesy gave him, or someone easily persuaded to abandon chivalry for personal gain, or for jealousy, or for revenge. The motive was unclear, but the culprit almost certainly had been among the group at the Red Fox Inn on the evening of the attack.

As I sat pondering motives, the candelabrum at the head of

Merlin's bed cast flickering specters in the gloom. Suddenly, among the shadows on the far wall, the apparition of a human face appeared. I started back, having heard nothing to warn me of anyone's approach, and feared at first that the face I saw was not of this world. I snatched up the candelabrum and held it out toward the face, and made out more distinctly the shape of a man, clothed in a long, dark dressing gown, standing with arms crossed against the wall and gazing intently at Merlin's prostrate form.

"There's no need for alarm," the figure interjected in low, whispered tones just as I opened my mouth to cry out. "No harm can come to you in the Lady's palace. I had heard the mage was our guest, and for old times' sake came down to get a look at him. He's even older than I remember."

"You . . . know him?" I stammered. "Who, or what, are you? You live in the palace? You serve the Lady?"

The thin smile on the pallid face was ethereal, and the man's eyes seemed to look past me and into some other time. "I serve the Lady as best I can, and with all my heart, and will do so until I die. Or until the end of time. Whichever comes first." His soft laugh indicated he was making a private joke. When all he saw on my face was bewilderment, the pale shadow sighed and with a resigned look began an explanation more direct and to the point.

"Twenty-two years I have lived with the Lady here in the palace of Avalon," he began. "In all that time, neither I nor she nor any of her ladies-in-waiting have aged by more than a minute. I believe this palace is somehow outside time—that with the virtue of the earthly Paradise, the Lady keeps us safe here from the ravages of time. For myself, I still take a great interest in the matters of the world, especially those of Arthur's court. To be completely cut off from the world of other human beings provides us no opportunity for generous deeds. I flatter myself that the Lady and her disciples feel more inclined to pay attention to worldly affairs because of my own small influence."

"I still don't quite understand," I murmured, partly to stave off the sleep to which his low, quiet tones were enticing me. "What are you doing here now? What is your interest in Merlin?"

"Like my mistress, I have a particular interest in this case of yours, the assault on the girl from Caerleon," he went on, ignoring my questions. He looked directly and earnestly into my eyes as he continued. "For you see, I know exactly what it is to be falsely accused in court, and to be condemned without hope of deliverance. Florent must be delivered, for his own sake, for the girl's sake, and for the sake of justice."

"Are you saying you know something of this affair? Can you give me proof of Florent's innocence?"

The visitor's face clouded. "No. That I cannot do. But listen to me. Perhaps what I say may be of some help. Nimue thought it might, in any case. Know first that I often go riding in the woods at night. The woods belong to my Lady, you know, and I think of it as patrolling for her. Few have ever seen me, as I wear dark hunting clothes and ride my black palfrey Sharka, but I like to keep the forest free of outlaws and thieves, and therefore safe for . . ."

"For people like Bess?" I said, with some acid in my voice. It was beginning to annoy me that so many people were in the forest that night, and nobody had been in the right place to either help Bess or clear Florent. But the soft-spoken shadow was not easily fazed.

"That night there were too many intruders to keep track of them all. What I can tell you is this: Besides myself, there were three other riders: One was Nimue on Snowfax. The other was the tall, lean squire, riding a borrowed gray stallion. The third was the knight that I often see riding in these woods, out toward the west and then back again, from wherever he goes."

"Knight? Which—Sir Sagramore? He apparently took messages between here and Cornwall regularly. Is he the one you saw? Red-faced chap? Jovial?"

"Neither his face nor his mood was visible to me, but I did recognize him by his arms. His shield bears the symbol of the royal house of Cornwall, the green tree on a field of white. It would suggest that he is the knight you speak of, bound to or from Cornwall."

"Yes," I said, frowning. "That must be him. But the other rider—that must be Colgrevaunce. So it was he that stole the gray horse? He certainly left that part out of his story." I was talking mostly to myself now. I realized that, in the short time we had left before Florent's reprieve expired, we must question Colgrevaunce again, and confront him with his earlier falsehoods.

Looking up, I realized the mysterious stranger had vanished, again without a sound, into the shadows of the palace. I wondered momentarily whether I had indeed seen a kind of phantom of the night, or whether perhaps I had been dreaming. But then I also realized with a start that the gentle, regular sound of Merlin's breathing had ceased. I looked down at his face and was astonished to find his eyes wide open and staring at me.

"Did you see him too?" the old enchanter asked quietly as he exhaled.

"Who?" I whispered.

"Sir Launfal."

Ah. Now it all made sense. And I was encouraged not only by the knowledge that I had not dreamed the conversation, but also by the bits of evidence Launfal had supplied. "Merlin!" I cried. "We have to question Colgrevaunce again! There's a good deal he's not been telling."

"Indeed," said the old man as he began drifting off again into sleep. "But I wonder, too . . ." he mumbled just as he passed into oblivion, ". . . where is Sagramore?"

Chapter Thirteen:
Colgrevaunce's Second Thoughts

By myself and only today and tomorrow left to clear Florent's name.

Merlin had been too weak to rise this morning, and I decided to let him sleep. In the interest of speeding the investigation along, Nimue had risen early and offered to bring me back to Camelot riding behind her on her great white destrier Snowfax. We galloped through the awakening woods and then through the main street of Caerleon just as it began to bustle in the early morning light, the wind cooling the sensations I felt as I held myself close to the breathtaking figure of Nimue before me in the saddle, the horse gliding beneath us with the grace of a sprinting stag. We covered the three miles from palace to castle in the time it would have taken me to rise, dress, and come down to breakfast from my quarters in the castle itself, and in a matter of minutes Nimue halted Snowfax as he reared up before the moat at the castle's main gate. It was still so early that the drawbridge had not yet been lowered for the day.

I jumped from Snowfax's back and thanked Nimue, who arrested me with a sharp look: "Find this culprit, Gildas. Time grows short, and justice must be served. Florent must be saved." With this last word, I thought I saw her blush as she trotted off, back toward Lady Lake. I turned and looked across the moat, up into the barbican, and shouted toward the slit in the wall from which I knew the archer on guard was watching me.

"Lower the drawbridge! I am Gildas of Cornwall, squire to

Sir Gareth, and I am come on the queen's business."

"Looks like the business of the Lady of the Lake to me," came the immediate answer from the alert guard in the tower above the gate. "I know you, young Gildas. Hold on, then, while I have the bridge lowered."

After what seemed an eternity, the bridge began to creak downward, lowered by chains attached to the windlass that two of the guards turned within the gatehouse. The moment it touched ground on my side of the moat, I trotted across, waving my thanks to the guards without looking back. I needed to make my way, first, to my own quarters in the lesser hall, outside the solar that served as bedchamber for Sir Gareth and his brother Gaheris. I needed to see Gareth, and to see how willing he was to help in our efforts to clear his nephew's name. Without Merlin, there was only so much I could do alone. I could confront Colgrevaunce myself—even, perhaps, pressure him a bit—but I had no authority to undertake the questioning of a full-fledged knight of Sir Sagramore's stature. Nor did I have the first idea how to find him, but I realized Merlin was right: I had not seen or heard from him since the morning of Florent's sentencing, when all the knights stood with their shields on display before the girl from Caerleon. As I recalled it, Sagramore had held out his own coat of arms that day (a swan argent on a field purpure) and not the arms of the royal house of Cornwall, the green tree on the field of white, that the mysterious Launfal claimed to have seen him bearing in the forest the night before. I had no idea what that all meant, but I knew Sagramore was a witness to the argument in the Red Fox that seemed to hold the key to this business, and there was a good chance he could shed light on the affair that others may have missed.

Sir Gareth was just stirring, standing in the door of his solar and rubbing his eyes, when he saw me rush to my place. "Well, young Gildas, don't tell me I may actually have the service of my own squire for a change! Nothing you need to be doing for the queen? Nothing the old wizard needs from you today?"

"Um . . . I'm afraid I'm still working on the investigation . . ."

"Ah, I thought it must be too good to be true." But Gareth looked at me seriously now. "Have you made any progress? Do you know any more about Florent's involvement in this . . . this nightmare?"

"Not very much," I admitted. "We know a lot about what went on that night, but where Florent was at the time of the attack we still aren't sure, and we're even less sure about who might really have been responsible for the crime. But that's why I'm here: I . . . we need your help."

Sir Gareth straightened and looked more sober. "Tell me," he said, with a quiet resolve.

"Merlin lies in the palace of the Lady of the Lake," I told him. "He was wounded by an arrow last night . . ."

"Shot? Where was this? When?"

"We had been seeking answers in the town of Caerleon, and were making our way back to the castle in the darkness. The shots came on us suddenly in the open field. We crouched down for cover but were in grave danger until Merlin's damsel of the lake, Nimue, galloped over to us and apparently set the bowman to flight."

Gareth looked pained. "This investigation is turning deadly. Take more care, Gildas. But what of the old man? How serious are his wounds?"

"Not life-threatening, thank goodness. But he needs rest and time to recover. The problem is, of course, that we simply don't *have* any time."

"But who shot at you? Did you see anything? Was there one bowman or many?"

"I think if there were more than one, we would be having a

different conversation. I mean, Merlin would probably be dead and . . . and I guess I would, too." I just realized this as I said it. Until now my concern for Merlin and my devotion to the investigation (and, through that, to the queen and to Rosemounde) had blinded me to what was surely my own very narrow escape with my life.

Gareth was looking at me strangely, and he said to me softly, "Sit down, Gildas," his hand gently guiding me to the stone floor, where I sat with my back against the wall. It was then I realized I was shaking uncontrollably.

"Take a deep breath, my young squire," Sir Gareth advised calmly, "and take your time answering. What is it the old necromancer needs me to do?"

I took a deep breath and blew it out but when I answered my teeth were still chattering. "S-s-sir Sag . . . ramore . . ." was all I could get out at first.

"Gildas of Cornwall," Sir Gareth began as he eased himself down to sit next to me. "The day I faced the Red Knight of the Red Lands in mortal combat, I was inspired by love of the beautiful Lyonesse whose angelic visage looked down on me from an upper window of the Red Knight's castle. Under her gaze, I urged myself to the peak of my own courage and strength, and overcame the might of one who had bested forty knights before me. But what I never told my Lyonesse, or anyone else for that matter, was that, moments after I forced the Red Knight to yield and subsequently spared his life, I stood alone within the castle wall and fought off swooning in a cold sweat. In the heat of the battle I had no time to think about what I was risking or what might happen to me. Once it was over, the enormity of it all overcame my imperturbable guise. This will pass, but your body must respond to what your mind denies. In the meantime, tell me what must be done."

"We must speak with Sir Sagramore," I said between gasps.

"He was at the Red Fox Inn the night of the assault, with Florent and three other squires, as well as Sir Tristram and Sir Dinadan, and he was also seen riding through the woods afterwards. But we haven't seen him since. We don't know where he is, and we need to talk to him. That, I think, is what you could do for us. Only a knight can compel another knight to submit to questioning."

"Persuade rather than compel, I think, young Gildas. And I have to find him first." Gareth rose and stretched, and walked into his solar to put on his boots and sword. "And I had better start looking now."

I was getting my breath back and waved weakly to Sir Gareth as he strode off, calling back over his shoulder, "I'll meet you back here before vespers. If I do not have Sir Sagramore in tow, I will know the reason why not." I nodded, and continued to look straight ahead as my hands finally grew steadier.

I stared without seeing, thinking back to the previous night and wondering who could possibly want Merlin (and presumably me as well) dead. Someone did not want the truth of Bess of Caerleon's rape to come out. And that could only mean one thing, I finally realized—that my instincts had been absolutely correct about Sir Florent. He could not possibly have been Bess's attacker. Only the real attacker could be concerned enough about the outcome of the investigation to try to silence those of us involved in it. The image of Rosemounde, her laughing eyes, her smirking mouth, danced before my eyes as I thought about where this quest had truly begun, and my chief motive for engaging in it, and then I began to grow angry. If the violence surrounding these recent events was expanding to engulf Merlin and his somewhat inexpert assistant, how much further could it go, even to the point of engulfing those members of the court with a special interest in the case's outcome—that is, most emphatically, the Lady Rosemounde. That thought burned in my heart even as my glazed eyes suddenly focused on a figure walking in the dim early morning light, along the wall on the opposite side of the lesser hall.

"Stay right where you are, you bastard!" I shouted with sudden ire, and saw the tall, skinny figure turn toward me with his mouth agape. "You lied to me, Colgrevaunce!"

The hapless squire slouched and looked at me with hurt, astonished eyes. "Gildas, what's the matter with you? What are you shouting about?" By now I was upon him, and it was all I could do to keep from pummeling his long, stupid face. I shoved him into a corner of the hall where we might have a modicum of privacy in the shadows, and hissed at him.

"You lied! You were going to meet Bess yourself in the woods. You were fighting with Florent over *her* at the inn! You lied about Dinadan being there as well. What else have you been lying about?"

The corners of his wide mouth turned down as he shook his head, murmuring, "No, but I didn't . . ."

"Yes you did!" I shoved him. By now I was angry and getting angrier the more I thought about it. "Florent never raped that girl! You had the motive to frame him for it! You were jealous and you acted on it! You never spoke up when you could have saved him! And now I've got somebody shooting at me in the dark, trying to kill me and Merlin! Out with it! Who really raped her? Was it you? Was it you who shot at us last night?"

To my surprise and chagrin, Colgrevaunce collapsed in the corner. Tears welled in his eyes and he wrung his hands in helpless anxiety. In my excitement I had forgotten just who it was I was talking to. Colgrevaunce had no cunning. He was too simple to plot or to conspire. His lies were only to protect himself, I realized as I cooled down a bit. Besides, Bess had told us it certainly wasn't Colgrevaunce who assaulted her.

I breathed deeply and waited for my hands to stop shaking again. "Colgrevaunce," I said more quietly and calmly, "listen. I'm helping Merlin investigate the attack on Bess of Caerleon. We're doing it at the request of . . . of the queen. Now look: I know you've been lying about some things from that night. You've got to tell me the truth because this can't go on. Besides Florent himself, there are others in danger. This attacker is now singling out other people—Merlin, for one, who was shot last night. That can only be because he doesn't want us to find out the truth about the rape. Which can only mean we're right about Florent. So calm down and start with one lie at a time. Why didn't you tell me about Sir Dinadan?"

Colgrevaunce looked up at me with red-rimmed eyes that seemed to say, *That was a stupid question, and what difference does it make?* But he gave me a sober answer. "I was ashamed about Dinadan," he said in a quiet monotone. "I didn't want to think about him. Besides, you were just passing the time with me that day; I didn't know you were in any kind of official investigation."

"Would you have told the truth, then, if you knew?"

He hung his head. "No," he admitted. "Dinadan spoke to me privately after Florent left the inn. He told me I was being a fool to fight over a serving wench. He told me she was a virgin and there'd be trouble if I met her later in the woods, as he found out I'd planned to do. He was going to stay, he said, to have a romp in bed with the mistress of the inn, and told me it was safer and less complicated to ease my urgings in that way. He was leering at me the whole time like he understood why I was interested in the girl and all."

By now Colgrevaunce's color had changed from absolute white through pink to red to nearly purple with emotion. He shook his head and spat out, "What did he know, that gross lecher? Bess may not be a lady, like your Rosemounde"—now it was my turn to blush—"but she was a good deal more than a whore one pays for a quick tumble. That's why Florent made me so mad with his 'courtesies' to Bess. He could have any lady, with his money and his knighthood and his face I'd like to smash in . . ." I could see where the anger of the night at the inn had come from. "But me? If I could have had a woman like Bess I'd have been happy. I wouldn't have cared about her class. What? My father may own some land in Kent, but he's got nothing except a single horse, and he uses it to plow his fields alongside his own peasants."

"Look," I interrupted him, "we're getting away from the point. You never met Bess that night. Why not?"

"I know!" he cried out in unexpected anguish. "If I had kept our tryst, she would have been safe! I'm to blame! I'm to blame!" And at that he broke down again. I sighed. It was going to be a long conversation. And I couldn't help agreeing with him. Damn it, he *was* to blame.

I gave him a light slap on the side of the head and tried to get him back to the conversation. "That's not helping anyone!" I hissed. "Tell me what happened. Why didn't you keep your tryst with Bess? Where were you?"

Now it was Colgrevaunce's turn to sigh. "It was what Sir Dinadan had said. I kept thinking about it. When I left the inn I wandered aimlessly in the woods, thinking about what I really wanted from her. Maybe he was right. Maybe I should just visit a harlot of the town and forget about Bess. What might her father do if word of our tryst got around? Would he insist I should marry her? How could that possibly work for me, a lowly squire with no obvious prospects of knighthood or advancement. I'd have had to take her back to my father's estate and plow the fields with him. If he didn't disinherit me, which would be entirely possible. I'm sure he never thought I'd come home with a common wench for a bride when he sent me off to Arthur's court."

"So what are you telling me?" I asked when he paused. "That you just wandered around in the woods and then came back to Camelot? That you never looked for Bess at all?"

"No, no," he said quickly. "That's not it. I wandered for some time, but when I finally came to my senses I realized that whatever happened, I had to at least go and find her, because it couldn't be safe for her to wait in the woods by herself. I didn't completely desert her!" It was all offered in a tone that said, *Look, I may be pretty low, but at least I'm not that low.*

"So what happened?"

"I'd just decided to turn around and look for Bess, when I heard hoofbeats. There was a horse coming through the woods. It was dark and I couldn't see, or even tell by the echo of the hoofbeats which direction the horse was coming from, when suddenly a dark figure on horseback burst out of the trees behind me and knocked me over. I hit my head on a tree, or on the ground, I'm not sure which. I was dazed, maybe even unconscious for a while. I have no idea how long I lay there stunned. By the time I came back to my senses, I didn't know how much time had passed. But I feared it might be too late to meet Bess. I was in a panic. Not far ahead of me, in a clearing in the trees, was a small barn. I know it was not the most knightly thing to do, but at that point I saw no alternative: I opened the barn door and found a sturdy gray plow horse. It was only a matter of moments for me to lead him out and jump on to ride him bareback . . ."

"Wait . . . so you're saying *you* stole the gray horse? Why didn't you admit to *that,* at least, when it came up at the court?"

Colgrevaunce threw his hands into the air. "I just wasn't thinking! Old Stabler came to complain about the horse after Bess had come into the court with her charges. When I saw her, all bruised and bloody as she was, and heard what had happened to her, I couldn't think of anything else. My head was ringing with anger and shame. I knew I should have been there! I knew I should have stopped it. And I hadn't. And she didn't say anything about me to the king. I never heard another thing, I was so confounded by it all."

"But what happened, then, with the horse?"

"I rode as fast as I could to the western edge of the forest near the stream what flows into Lady Lake, where I was supposed to meet Bess. But when I got there I didn't see any sign of her. I got off the horse to look around, and on the ground I found this." From the sleeve of his tunic Colgrevaunce pulled a green wimple of the sort a common girl might keep her hair bundled in. I remembered Bess coming into court that morning, her hair bedraggled, with no covering. This was certainly hers, and she had worn it that night.

Colgrevaunce stared at the wimple and spoke through tears. "When I saw this trampled on the forest floor, I knew something had happened to her. Why would she leave her head uncovered and have dropped this in the woods? I feared the worst. But by then I didn't know what to do. I could see the first touches of dawn in the east, and stumbled back toward Camelot. By then the horse had run away. I got to the castle just as Sir Brandiles was waking up, and I had duties to perform for him. All the while I was trying to work out what to do about Bess. I would have broached it with Sir Brandiles, but I didn't know exactly how to do it without . . . without . . ."

"Without admitting all the things you'd already done that night—drinking, gambling, wenching, horse stealing. It would have been hard to tell the story without looking like a despiser of courtesy itself . . . or at the very least a complete idiot and a craven, which is, let's admit it, a pretty apt description of you based on the events of the evening."

Colgrevaunce nodded. He was too beaten down to even attempt to defend himself. "Don't think I haven't said the same thing to myself, morning and night for the past five days. Nothing I can do now can undo the events in the forest. I would give anything for the chance to relive that night and change every decision I made. If I could find the cowardly brute that did this to Bess, I would challenge him right now to the utterance. Even if he killed me, I would regain my honor, which is now as ground into the dirt as Bess's wimple."

"First we have to find the culprit, Colgrevaunce, and your lies went a long way toward stopping us from doing that over the past few days. But on the bright side," I tried to lighten the intensity of the situation with a little humor, "the horse found its way back to its master! And as for this villainous thug, maybe we can build on what you've told me now."

"Find him!" Colgrevaunce grabbed at the front of my tunic, his eyes imploring. "You find him and then you leave him to me . . ."

"I can't promise that, Colgrevaunce. We need to report it in open court before the queen when Florent comes back to face his sentencing the day after tomorrow. It will be up to the king, finally, to decide his fate."

"Not if I get to the villain first," Colgrevaunce insisted. "Let me help with the investigation. If I stay close to it I'll know before you report to the queen . . ."

I cringed internally at that. Colgrevaunce was not exactly the one you wanted going around asking questions. He could be easily duped and, of course, did not have the best record of decision-making, especially in a crisis situation. He *had* pretty much just demonstrated that.

"I'm not really sure there's anything in particular you could do right now. I need to be able to talk to Merlin about these things. But how about this: You keep your ears open for anything that might be useful, whether it's a rumor about Bess, or her attacker, or Florent, or anybody else who happened to be at the Red Fox Inn the night of the assault. Report back anything curious. We've got to keep gathering information. Right now we really aren't sure what might turn out to be important or not. But first answer me one more question: Do you have any idea who the rider was that rode you down? It must have been deliberate, no? Otherwise he would have stopped to help you."

"I didn't see anything," Colgrevaunce lamented. "It just happened too fast, and it was too dark. Dark rider, dark horse . . . nothing to tell. He wasn't displaying his shield, so there was no coat of arms to identify. But I'm pretty sure I'd have known if it was Florent. Whoever it was, if he deliberately ran me down, then . . . then he must have sought me out on purpose after I left the inn. So it must have been the rapist, isn't that so? Trying to make sure I was out of the way before he committed his assault?" Now Colgrevaunce was excited.

"Yes!" I said, but then, "No. I'd forgotten. The attacker rode a snow-white horse, remember? If the man that ran you down was riding a dark horse, then that can only mean . . ."

"That there were two of them. And they planned it together." Even Colgrevaunce had worked that out. Things had just gotten more complicated. And we were running out of time.

CHAPTER FOURTEEN:
A REPORT TO THE QUEEN

I left Colgrevaunce in the lesser hall and made my way across the lower bailey, the courtyard that ran to the great hall and its adjacent chambers. My plan was to visit the queen in her suite, there to report to her (and, I hoped, to my Lady Rosemounde as well) what progress was being made in the quest to exonerate the newly knighted Sir Florent. But as I passed close to the one-story kitchen below the great hall, the aroma of the midday meal (it smelled like the last of the venison our party had provided a few days earlier) filled my nose. My stomach, remembering I had not eaten at all today and had been too busy to think of eating last night, drew me to the open door of the kitchen where I called for Roger, the chief cook.

The heat from the kitchen was stifling, and I could barely make out dark figures moving within in the great hubbub that naturally accompanied the preparation of a meal for the hundreds of knights, squires, and laborers that made this castle run smoothly. I caught a whiff of the bread baking in the brick oven to the right of the doorway, and boys turning legs of venison on spits in the fireplaces along the wall further down. After a few moments Roger himself emerged from the door and greeted me with a rough friendliness.

" 'Ere, now, if it in't young Gildas, squire to me old scullery boy Beaumains!" Since Sir Gareth had worked incognito in the kitchens of Camelot when he first arrived at the king's court, determined to make a name for himself through his own merits and not through his relationship with the sovereign, he was a great favorite still among the kitchen workers, and so I, by extension as his squire, enjoyed the goodwill of Roger and his staff. Which meant I could generally get a meal whenever I stopped by. Like now.

"Ah, Roger, I'm awfully busy today, on my master's business, and the queen's . . ." It never hurt to name-drop a bit in Camelot. "Could you give me a quick bite that I can eat on the run?"

Roger glanced toward the oven at his left. "Bread's fresh baked," he said. "Just out of the oven, made by that John Potter the king put to work here. I think you'll find 'is bread much to your likin'! I can give you a quick plowman's breakfast o' bread and cheese. We're makin' a bunch o' those up anyway right now for the 'unting party that's goin' out this mornin'."

"That sounds perfect." I thanked him as he handed me a small loaf and a thick slice of goat cheese. As I turned back to head for the queen's chamber and took a big bite of the warm bread, I saw the hunting group. The forester William of Newcastle was in the lead, of course, and Sir Agravain, his dark eyes glowering at me, rode close behind him. I saw Sir Palomides once more, who gave me a smiling nod in greeting, and Sir Mador de la Porte. Their squires followed behind, and when I saw Baldwin and Bertrand riding together, bringing up the rear with their crossbows slung across their backs, I suddenly remembered we had never interviewed the two of them about the evening of Bess's assault. What they could add to what we had already gleaned from the testimony of the other men present I didn't know, but for the sake of thoroughness I approached them as they sat on their horses in a queue of hunters waiting at the kitchen door for their breakfasts.

"Baldwin! Bertrand! I need to ask you about the party at the Red Fox Inn."

"Why?" Bertrand demanded, looking annoyed.

"I'm working with Merlin to investigate the rape of Bess of Caerleon. It's on the orders of the queen."

"I'm going hunting for venison, on the order of my lord Agravain, so piss off." That was Baldwin, with a demeanor as surly as that of his master. The word "courtesy" was unknown to either of them, I had found. Bertrand was a little more forthcoming.

"I don't think either of us has time right now," he said, gesturing toward the hunting group.

"Well, just in the couple of minutes you've got right now, let me get your thoughts. We know Florent and Colgrevaunce quarreled that night over the girl, Bess. And that Colgrevaunce intended to meet her in the woods afterward."

"Colgrevaunce wouldn't have known what to do if he had met her," Baldwin growled.

Bertrand added, "Besides, she said herself Florent did it. Doesn't sound like anything we could say can change that fact."

"Perhaps not. But tell me: Do you remember anything strange about how the night ended?"

"Strange like what?" Bertrand asked, his eyes on the kitchen door, where food was now being distributed to the rest of the party.

I felt rushed, and couldn't think of the right questions to ask, but managed to blurt out, "Who left with whom? Did anyone seem unusually disturbed?"

"Everybody was disturbed," Bertrand answered matter-of-factly. "Sir Tristram left first, he was disturbed about the gambling. Florent took off after the fight, and Colgrevaunce soon after. They were both upset about the fight and about the wench. Maybe they both meant to find her in the woods. Everybody else went off separately, as far as I remember."

He looked to Baldwin for confirmation. Sir Agravain's squire was just picking up his bread and cheese and had begun to trot off with the rest of the group. He called back, "I left alone. Didn't see who left afterwards. Don't give a rat's arse either."

At that Bertrand picked up his own plowman's breakfast and gave his horse a kick. I called after them, "Well, if you think of anything that seems important, let me know, will you?"

"Right," I heard Baldwin call. "You'll be my first confidante." And then the entire party passed through the bailey toward the open gate beneath the barbican.

The queen's chambers were off the great hall and the throne room. The outer chamber had until recently been my own quarters. It was currently staffed by Master Holly, an aged clerk who served as supervisor of the queen's household, and part-time warden of her door, ensuring that no unwelcome visitors surprised her unawares. He sat at a wooden desk, going over the queen's account books with a quill pen. I could hear that in the queen's inner chamber, the ladies-in-waiting were being entertained by someone reading a romance.

"I need to see the queen," I told Master Holly. When he looked up, his squinting eyes did not give the impression that he was happy to see me. Indeed, he seemed quite put out, as if looking at the queen's expenditures on blue cloth over the past several months made the most scintillating reading in the world.

The old man placed his fingers on his lips, as if to disturb the reading would be a boorish act, and whispered, "I'll see whether the queen will grant you audience, Gildas of Cornwall," at which he tiptoed gingerly through the curtains that separated the outer chamber from the inner chamber while I waited, bemused, without. Knowing the queen as I did, I could imagine her having a good deal of amusement at the old man's expense, and didn't seek to cause him any more grief than he already no doubt had to put up with.

When he emerged again, Master Holly nodded assent and whispered, "The queen says you may enter, but keep quiet until the Lady Vivien finishes her reading." With that he sat down again at the desk and was lost in his figures, while I stepped quietly through the curtains.

In the middle of the room, perhaps twenty feet square, five chairs were arranged in a circle, where sat the queen, flanked by the Lady Vivian on her left and the Lady Rosemounde on her right. Across from her, and with their backs to me as I entered, sat the Lady Anne and the Lady Elaine. The women's eyes were all cast downward on their embroidery while Lady Vivien regaled them with a lay in French, read from a large manuscript placed on a low stand before her. The queen glanced up at me quizzically, her eyebrows knit in a kind of scowl, her face asking what was the news. When I glanced at Lady Rosemounde, her face seemed more desperate, her eyes more pleading. To both of them I made a somewhat noncommittal shrug, and waited in courtesy for the Lady Vivien to finish.

Lady Vivien was reading an old story I had heard before, but the plot resonated more with me this time than it had in the past. It was the tale of the legendary singer Sir Orfeo, the king of Thrace, and his Queen Heurodis, who dreams one night that the king of Faerie is threatening to abduct her. Sir Orfeo posts a thousand guards around his wife, but the guards are unable to protect her and she disappears. In his grief, Sir Orfeo leaves his kingdom in the hands of his steward and, taking his harp, walks off into the woods where he lives as a wild man for ten years.

One day, he sees a group of several dozen ladies hawking in the woods, and among them he believes he sees his wife, Heurodis. Naturally, he tries to follow them. They disappear into the side of a mountain, and he slips in after them, only to find a green Faerie kingdom there behind the mountain wall. He makes his way to the castle lying at the center of this kingdom, and begs entrance as a minstrel, since he has brought his harp.

Once in the court, Sir Orfeo sees many folk who were believed dead, including his own wife, who lies sleeping in the corner of the Faerie King's throne room. Well, Orfeo sees his chance to rescue Heurodis, and he entertains the Faerie King with the sweetest song he has ever sung. The king is so moved upon hearing it that he promises to give Orfeo anything he wants in payment. Orfeo, of course, asks to be able to bring Heurodis back into the outside world once more as his queen, and the Faerie King grants his boon.

I thought that was the end of the story, but the Lady Vivien's tale went on, in a kind of epilogue. When Orfeo and Heurodis returned to Thrace, they weren't sure whether they would be welcomed back or whether the steward might try to hold onto the throne for himself. On the street, Orfeo actually runs into his steward, who fails to recognize his former master. But the steward welcomes Orfeo anyway, saying that for the sake of his master, who was a singer himself, he is always kind to minstrels. When Orfeo sings before him at the royal palace, the faithful steward recognizes the harp as Sir Orfeo's, and asks his visitor where he obtained it. Orfeo tells him that he took the harp from the hands of one who had been torn apart by lions, and at that the steward falls down in a swoon. At that point, Orfeo recognizes the steward's faithfulness, and reveals his true identity, rewarding the steward's loyalty by naming him his heir.

The story was familiar to me, but listening to Lady Vivien's reading just then was like hearing it again for the first time. My mind, churning as it was with the intricacies and thorny problems of the Florent investigation, could not help but be struck by the connections between Sir Orfeo's tale and the story of Bess's assault. In both tale and reality, the woods were a dangerous place filled with supernatural forces, though the Faerie world of the tale seemed far more sinister than the influence of the Lady of the Lake. In both cases, though, mortal beings might be forever enchanted by the supernatural power of the wild wood. Beyond that, I was struck by the fact that even a thousand armed knights could not protect Heurodis from the violence brought against her. Could anything have protected Bess? Or was violence against women a part of the nature of things, and only brought out most clearly by the forest itself, where Nature was revealed at its basest and most brutal?

But the Lady Vivian's version of the romance added another element I found illuminating as well. The steward, who does not seem to have been of the royal family, nor even, perhaps, of a noble house, is rewarded in the end for his virtue. I knew Florent and Lady Rosemounde, both of high noble houses, might be thought a natural match, but could not I, the son of a simple armorer, hope for some reward for my own faithfulness, my devotion to my lady? My selfless defense of Florent, my own rival? How that might happen I could not foresee. But it reminded me of Bess's desire to marry a knight and rise from the grinding reality of her own home; and, indeed, of Colgrevaunce's own expressed wish to take Bess as his own despite his family's objections to her class.

Unfortunately, though the lay of Sir Orfeo made me think, it didn't help me answer any of the questions surrounding the case, and the queen interrupted my reverie by clearing her throat and standing up. "Ladies," she announced, "I shall retire for a time into my private chamber with the Lady Rosemounde and our devoted servant Gildas, who is come, no doubt, to bring me news from my Lord Merlin. The rest of you may go about your own business until dinner time. Gildas, with me." She turned and stepped toward the heavy wooden door that led to her own bedchamber, and Rosemounde, rising with her, glanced back at me with a mouth turned down in dread of what I might have to say. The other ladies rose, picked up their embroidery, and filed out, Lady Anne looking down at the floor, Lady Vivien looking oblivious as she sped to catch up with Anne and chat with her under her breath, Lady Elaine with a sidelong look at me and a tsking sound as she walked by, as if I might be about to do something improper to the queen and Rosemounde. With a slight nod to the exiting ladies, I stepped across the threshold into the queen's private chamber, where she and Rosemounde already sat side-by-side on the queen's bed, with the curtains pulled back so as not to interfere with their comfortable situation. Clearly the queen intended that I should stand, which I did, facing the two ladies.

The room was quite small, really, for a royal bedchamber. Perhaps fifteen feet square, with the bedstead in the middle of one wall and a small fireplace opposite. Next to the bedstead was a small table on which stood a candelabrum and a small manuscript book of hours, no doubt for when the queen was having one of her pious moments. Three of the walls were covered in tapestries from floor to ceiling, the one to the right of the bed depicting the story of Saint Agnes, the martyred patron saint of virgins and rape victims, whose own virginity was preserved in a brothel when any man trying to force himself on her was struck blind. I couldn't help considering that it was too bad Bess had no such protection. On the other wall hung a tapestry depicting the life of Saint Ursula, a Christian princess from here in Logres, whose refusal to marry a pagan husband ended in her martyrdom and the martyrdom of the ten thousand virgins who accompanied her on her pilgrimage to Rome. On the back wall, however, behind the bed, hung a tapestry I knew was more to the queen's own liking: In a larger-than-life image was depicted Judith the Jewess of Bethulia, holding up the gruesome head of the Assyrian commander Holofernes, with her bloody sword in her other hand, a look of holy triumph on her face in the knowledge that her act saved her city and her people from destruction.

Above the fireplace hung a shield and a sword in its scab-bard—partly, I assumed, for decorative purposes, but partly as well for the queen's protection. I smiled inwardly at the thought of my Lady Guinevere, like Judith on the opposite wall, wield-ing a sword in her own defense. Then I remembered my former suspicion, which had arisen during my years as the queen's page, that behind one of these tapestries was a secret door, through which the good Sir Lancelot could enter and leave undetected on evenings when the queen granted him her favors. Thus I was sobered to the reality that, in fact, the sword and shield were not for the queen herself, but rather for Sir Lance-lot, kept here against the possibility that, despite the careful discretion of their trysts, he might someday be found with the queen in her private bedroom. Were that to occur, both their lives would be forfeit as traitors to the crown, if Arthur could bear to pronounce such a sentence on his wife or his greatest ally.

"Now then, young Gildas," the queen began, straightening out her skirts and then looking up at me with the eyes of author-ity. "What have you to report?"

"Your Grace," I inclined my head in her direction, and then added, "and my lady," as I nodded toward Rosemounde's earnestly questioning gaze. "Merlin is even now lying in the house of the Lady of the Lake, recovering from a wound received last night while we were pursuing our investigation—"

"No!" the queen exclaimed, appalled. "Will he live? Who did this?"

I put out my hands to calm her, and glancing at Rose-mounde's horrified face, I changed my tone. "He will be fine, he is being tended to by the Lady herself; and no, we did not see who did this thing. Whoever fired upon us was frightened off by one of the Lady's servants. But the important thing is that somebody did not want us to continue our investigation."

"Unless it was a random thief out to rob wanderers in the dark," Guinevere suggested, settling back again onto the royal bed.

"This close to the walls of Camelot? What thief would be so bold?"

"If someone was bold enough to rape a maiden in the woods within three miles of the castle, why not a thief?" Rosemounde interjected. "But what have you found in this investigation?"

"We have found many questions but few answers, my lady."

The queen gave me one of her icier looks. "That news does not fill me with great confidence, Gildas of Cornwall."

"No, Majesty, but it seems to be frightening someone in the castle. Frightening him enough that he tried to end our investigation last night by the most certain means possible—our deaths. That can mean only one thing: Sir Florent cannot be guilty of this crime. The true culprit is afraid we are getting close to exposing him, and is willing to commit murder to prevent that from happening. Rest assured, Florent is innocent."

"We have been sure of that, from the beginning," Guinevere reminded me. "But unless I can bring before the king another name, the name of the true villain responsible for this deed, along with evidence to convince him and Bess of Caerleon herself, then I cannot see how I can save Florent. Give me that name!"

"I can't give you a name right now," I admitted, averting my eyes. "But we must be getting close to the truth. We know Florent spent the evening of Bess's assault celebrating his new status as knight, surrounded by fellow squires and three knights of the Round Table at the Red Fox Inn in Caerleon, where Bess is employed. Colgrevaunce was there, Sir Brandiles's squire, as well, and Sir Ywain's squire Thomas, Sir Agravain's squire Baldwin, and Sir Palomides's squire, Bertrand. The knights Sir

Sagramore, Sir Dinadan, and Sir Tristram were there also. They had met for another purpose but became a part of the celebration. We know, too, that Bess agreed to meet Colgrevaunce in the woods later that night."

"So her story about going to the house of the Lady of the Lake to collect her father's wages was not the truth," the queen said, stating the obvious.

"Yes, and her own father has refuted that claim . . . a fabrication intended, I suppose, to ward off any suspicion of her own lustfulness."

"And why not?" My own Lady Rosemounde bristled. Turning red, she continued, "If Bess of Caerleon cherished thoughts of love for Colgrevaunce, then what bearing could that possibly have on her forced submission to the lust of a brutal stranger? But Bess herself must have known how you men would interpret her meeting with Colgrevaunce! Naturally she would not volunteer that information, knowing how you men would pervert that truth and use it against her. Just because you men will couple with anyone if the lustful urge goads you does not mean that women will do the same . . ." and at that she broke off, tears trailing from her eyes down her now-crimson cheeks.

The queen gazed at her with some wonder, then glanced back at me, eyebrows raised high. The corner of her mouth turned up slightly as she said, "Yes, Gildas? You were saying?"

Confused and feeling blindsided, with no clue how to interpret or react to Rosemounde's outburst, I stammered, "No, my lady, I did not . . . that is, she . . . I meant no . . . what I am trying to say is that Bess has already exonerated Colgrevaunce, saying she would have recognized him had he been the attacker. But she . . . that is, we thought someone else in the room must have overheard her making the arrangement with Colgrevaunce, and thereafter both prevented Colgrevaunce from making his tryst, and attacked the girl. That is all I meant . . ."

I remained bewildered by Rosemounde's outburst, but the queen forged ahead, following my thoughts and anticipating the conclusion. "Therefore you are suggesting someone at that table—someone other than Sir Florent or this squire Colgrevaunce—is the true perpetrator of this outrage?"

"Precisely, Your Majesty. But we can narrow it down further. Sir Tristram left the inn before the quarrel began, and so would not have known of the arranged rendezvous in the woods. We know from independent sources that Sir Dinadan remained at the inn for some time after the others left. Bess herself says she knew Sir Sagramore well enough to have recognized him if he was the attacker. Essentially, that means . . ." and I had not put it this way even to myself until this moment. "That the attacker must have been one of the other squires: Thomas, Baldwin, or Bertrand."

"Indeed," said the queen thoughtfully. "Unless, of course, Bess is mistaken, or someone is lying. Find the truth, Gildas of Cornwall. Find this villain fast." She glanced behind her momentarily at the tapestry of Judith and Holofernes, and added, "And bring me his head on a platter."

At that the queen rose, and I gathered our interview was over. I inclined my head to her, and she started toward the door to rejoin her ladies-in-waiting. She glanced back when she reached the doorway to observe the Lady Rosemounde, who had arisen far more deliberately and kept her own head bowed low, concealing her face. Rosemounde raised her moist eyes to me as she walked by, and spoke in a voice that struggled to muffle her sobbing, "Gildas, you have only one more day! You are my only hope."

Now it was my turn to redden again, and I could not speak. I merely nodded and looked away. She did not need to remind me of the deadline that approached all too rapidly. In my own mind it was before me constantly, and every moment that passed reminded me I had one less moment to find Bess's attacker and save Sir Florent. If love was indeed humbly selfless, how true must my love be, that goaded me to risk my life to save my beloved's fiancé from harm, in order that she could marry him instead of me. For several moments I stood in admiring smugness over my own humility.

As the queen opened her door to step through, however, the three of us were greeted by a turmoil of female voices all raised in alarm and confusion.

"How dare you! Laying hands on the queen's handmaiden!"

"The king shall hear of this! This is an outrage!"

"Let go of me, you great brute!"

"Yes! Unhand her!"

"I mean no harm or insult to the Lady Elaine," I heard a male voice say, and then realized it was my master, Sir Gareth. I darted out the door to the queen's inner chamber just after Guinevere and the Lady Rosemounde stepped into the fray, and blinked at the sight of Sir Gareth, standing his ground and holding the Lady Elaine by the arm, while Master Holly hopped about ineffectually, his hands in the air, and Lady Anne threatened Sir Gareth with her embroidery needles and Lady Vivien made as if to club him with the large manuscript from which she had earlier been reading.

Then I heard an authoritative voice behind me say, calmly but firmly, "Let go of my Lady Elaine, Sir Gareth, and explain yourself this instant." I looked over my right shoulder to see that the queen had ducked back into her private chamber in order to snatch the sword from over the fireplace, and was now holding it with the point toward Sir Gareth, steadily and with purpose.

"Your Majesty," Sir Gareth answered, releasing Lady Elaine's arm and kneeling abjectly before the queen's anger. "Forgive me. I meant no harm to the Lady Elaine. My eagerness to help in the investigation of these charges against my nephew made me pursue my object perhaps more vigorously than was courteous. But I must speak with the lady, will she or nill she."

"I shall be the judge of that," Guinevere insisted, and did not yet lower her sword. "Lady Elaine, please be seated. Let us hear what Sir Gareth can say to explain himself."

"Your Grace," I said, heading off Sir Gareth's explanation. "It was I who asked my lord Gareth for his assistance earlier today. With Merlin incapacitated and our time running perilously short, I felt the need, in carrying out Your Majesty's own command, to enlist the aid of another investigator to help in this inquiry. Because of his keen interest in the case, Sir Gareth was eager to lend his aid, and because of his intimate knowledge of the court, he was the ideal ally in this matter. I first asked him to find Sir Sagramore and get him to submit to questioning. He is the one principal in this case who was present at the inn the night of Bess's attack, but whom we have not been able to question. His testimony may be crucial in solving this crime."

"The difficulty is, Sir Sagramore has apparently disappeared." Sir Gareth took over my explanation seamlessly, bowing his head toward the queen. "No one in the castle has seen him since the morning Bess of Caerleon made her accusation of my nephew, when all knights appeared in the throne room with their shields. All I have been able to determine, Your Highness, is that Sir Sagramore was seen by two or three witnesses speaking with the Lady Elaine, somewhere outside Your Grace's rooms here. The lady is, therefore, the last person known to have seen Sir Sagramore, and since his testimony may be crucial in this case, I approached the lady to ask her what transpired between them on that date, and whether she knew his whereabouts at this moment. But when I accosted her and asked where I might find Sir Sagramore, she turned away without answering and made to escape. That is when I took hold of her arm—"

"And that is where you failed in courtesy," the queen finished for him. But she did relax her grip on the sword and let it fall to her side, all the time looking at the Lady Elaine, who had blushed and was squirming slightly in her chair. The other ladies looked at one another, not knowing what to think, and everyone was silent for a moment. Then another voice exploded from the outer chamber, apparently cowing the dutiful Master Holly: "God's nostrils, man, I don't care if she's entertaining the ambassador from Mount Olympus, I tell you I will speak with the queen!"

I breathed a sigh of relief. It was Merlin.

Chapter Fifteen:
The Lady Elaine's Tale

"Gildas, you dunce of a Cornishman, of course she exploded at you when you tried to blame the victim for the crime against her."

"But that's not what I was doing!" I insisted, trying to at least justify myself to Merlin, since I was not likely to have such a chance with Rosemounde herself. "I was only trying to point out that anyone could have heard Bess agree to meet Colgrevaunce in the woods that night. That's all I was saying."

We were arranging pallets for ourselves in the queen's outer chamber, my old sleeping quarters. She had requested that we both sleep there tonight, desiring to keep us close to be the more easily informed if we made any breakthroughs in the few hours that remained to us.

"And what were your precise words? Do you remember them?"

"Well . . . I think I said we knew Bess had agreed to meet Colgrevaunce that night in the woods."

Merlin raised one eyebrow at me, quizzically. "You're absolutely certain you said nothing else that might have been interpreted as critical of the maid?"

"Maid?" I raised my own eyebrows as Merlin lowered his and glared at me.

"In the eyes of the law and of God," Merlin asserted. "And this attitude is precisely what has put you in the Lady Rosemounde's doghouse tonight. Come now young Gildas, what else did you say to raise her ire?"

"Well," I remembered now a bit sheepishly, "I believe I did follow that up with something to the effect that Bess made up the story of collecting money for her father's work in order to allay any suspicion of her own lustful intent . . ."

"Dunce of a Cornishman!" Merlin said again, rapping his knuckle on my forehead. "And this somehow is confusing to you?"

"All right, then," I admitted. "I see your point. But the way she acted after that—she was angry and seemed to blame me for the faults of men in general, saying men would judge women by the men's own lusts. But she was crying as she said it. I don't understand where that came from at all."

Merlin sighed and looked away. "This may be more difficult, it's true. But it's not impossible. I'm afraid you'll never understand women, my dear Gildas."

"Oh, like you're an expert?" I goaded him. "Have Nimue eating out of your hand, do you?"

I wanted to take the words back as soon as I said them, but after an initial start Merlin plunged ahead. "Just because I understand Nimue's feelings and motivations does not mean I can control them. Or would want to. Particularly since my understanding tells me that the last thing she would want is for me or anyone else to control her. But your problem here with Rosemounde lies in your inability to put yourself in her place. Think of it: Your newly acquired fiancé is suddenly accused of raping another woman. There is, of course, denial: He could not possibly have done this. But there is also shame because you are attached to him, and humiliation because if he *has* done this, he has done this not only to her and to himself but to you as well. And even if he *hasn't*, he's at least put himself into a position to be accused, and that in itself is unforgiveable. And therefore there is anger at the man that did this deed (whoever that may be), at the man who perhaps has not done this deed but stands accused of it (Sir Florent), and at men in general whose own lustful natures have made this deed possible, and whose lustful natures cause them also to misread the nature of the victim (Sir Kay, for instance). All are tarred with the same brush. And you? Gildas of Cornwall is the one that has lusted after her the longest, and so Gildas of Cornwall is an easy target of that anger."

I knitted my brows together and admitted, "I'm not sure I follow all of that."

"Well, never mind then." Merlin shrugged. "Just take comfort in the fact that she does not actually hate *you* specifically. She merely hates the entire male gender. And remember, too, she did tell you that you were her only hope. That should count for something."

"Only if we can solve this case. And we have one more day to do it. Merlin, can we make anything out of Lady Elaine's story?"

"Now we come to it." Merlin eased back onto his pallet. His arm was in a sling, and his body seemed rather more frail than usual. Certainly he seemed more tired than was typical, except when one of his occasional spells was upon him. But the Lady of the Lake had done a miraculous deed in healing him so swiftly, and, knowing how essential it was to the cause of justice that the old necromancer be returned to his investigation in Camelot, had caused him to be brought to the castle by horse cart as soon as he was stable and out of danger, early that afternoon. He had arrived in time to assist in the questioning of Lady Elaine. With his good hand, Merlin was holding a piece of parchment seized from her, on which were scribbled verses from a lover whose name she had refused to give us, and which we had not pressed her for since it seemed irrelevant to the case. What she *had* told us about Sir Sagramore, however, only raised more questions and answered none. The solution seemed to recede from us, deeper and deeper into the mist.

"Sir Sagramore is a noble knight," Merlin began. "He is nephew to the Emperor of Constantinople. His father is a duke, though Sagramore himself is a second son and therefore stands to inherit none of his father's lands in the East. Still, his father saw the potential of wedding his younger son to an heiress who might bring Sagramore his own lands."

"Yes, yes, and the Lady Elaine's father is lord of a sizeable estate in Ireland, and is cousin to the Irish king. Sagramore's father met Elaine's during the Crusade, and the two betrothed their children when both were quite young. All this we knew already," I said. "What we did not know were the lengths to which they have since gone to avoid actually getting married."

"Yes," Merlin mused. "The lady is nearly twenty years old, and so has been of marriageable age for some six years. I found it amusing that for two years she was able to convince her father and Sagramore's that she was considering taking the veil. When it became clear to the abbess of Saint Mary Magdalene that the Lady Elaine had no vocation, she convinced the queen to take her in as a lady-in-waiting. Such a commitment, of course, meant she needed to serve in the queen's household for at least a year or two to make it worth the queen's while and to enable Elaine to learn courtly manners. Her father in Ireland was mollified by that for a short time, at least."

"And Sagramore's father was off in Constantinople. He could learn what was happening only through letters that might take a year to reach him. I'm sure Sagramore's letters were generally quite vague as to dates and plans. How frustrating it all must have been for the Emperor's sister and brother-in-law." I actually laughed a bit at the situation. It had never occurred to me how many ruses might be available for a young couple, betrothed against their wills, to postpone the actual wedding, so long as they were out of the immediate reach of their own families.

"Sir Sagramore contributed his own delaying tactic to the situation," Merlin reflected. "Like a certain Cornish dimwit I know, he dragged his feet in his knightly training, and managed to put his knighting off until he was past twenty-one. That meant, let's see, he is three years older than the Lady Elaine, so when she finished her two years in the queen's service, he embarked on his own knightly adventures, vowing to earn a reputation for chivalry to make himself worthy of Elaine's hand. And cleverest of all, he attached himself to one of the greatest knights of the Round Table, Sir Tristram, who through his own adventurous quests and because of his interests in Cornwall and in Brittany, was seldom at court. And when he *was* at court, Sagramore acted as Tristram's messenger, constantly traveling back and forth to the court of King Mark. And thus, through one trick or another, our two lovebirds have managed to put off any actual nuptial bonds for some six years. There is something admirable about their perseverance."

"But where is he now?" I sputtered with some annoyance. "And what could he tell us? He didn't tell her anything at all, at least nothing she was willing to pass on to us."

"I don't think she was concealing anything of their conversation," Merlin responded. "Why should she?"

"Who knows?" I answered, exasperated. "Everybody's motives in this seem impenetrable."

I thought back to Lady Elaine's testimony. It was Sir Gareth who had asked her about the rumor of Sir Sagramore leaving her bed early one morning some few weeks past. If there was an accusation implied in his question, Elaine had confronted it head-on. "Yes, he spent the night with me. But with no lecherous intent. Nothing was further from our hearts. We are not attracted to one another in that way, and besides, we were both so intent on rebelling against our families' idea of a forced marriage that we would have done anything to avoid that. Lady Anne and Lady Vivien were present in the same quarters at the time and can swear nothing untoward occurred." The two other ladies had been asked to leave the room during the questioning, so that only the queen and Rosemounde remained with Gareth, Merlin, and me. But Elaine's sincerity seemed real, and it seemed pointless to call the other two ladies back to verify her assertions.

In my mind's eye I saw Lady Elaine sit back and put her hands defiantly on her hips. "The truth is simply that we have become good friends over the years, and allies in a single cause: the avoidance of marriage. I was quite comfortable having him there in my quarters, and we talked nearly till dawn about our shared plight. Both fathers were becoming more insistent that the marriage take place, and papers had been drawn up concerning the dowry of land that would come with me upon completion of the nuptials, in addition to the monetary gift with which Sagramore's father was essentially buying me from my family. It sickened us and made our resolve the greater. Of course, we talked about other things as well; it was a long night. One of our topics was Sir Tristram."

She had laughed at that point—a grim, ironic laugh. "Sir Sagramore hated Sir Tristram. Absolutely despised him." To our appalled expressions, Elaine continued with an explanation. "Not at first. At first, he sympathized greatly with Tristram. You see, Sagramore is himself in love with a maiden attached to the court of Cornwall, and thus was happy to become Sir Tristram's messenger and spy in the court, since it gave him an opportunity to see his own beloved, though he feared he would never be free to marry her. And he sympathized with Tristram's banishment from King Mark's court and his hopeless love for Isolde, his uncle's wife, which could never come to fruition. But when

Tristram forsook his lady and married Isolde of the White Hands, simply because she shared a name with his own beloved, even though he did not love her and never consummated the marriage, breaking his wife's heart—Sagramore began to hate him. He would often invent elaborate plans to harm Tristram in a way that would bring him down. Sometimes he obsessed over it. But it never amounted to anything. He would be off the next day to Cornwall to do Sir Tristram's bidding."

I came out of my reverie and focused again on Merlin, who now lay back with a scowl on his face. He had taken off his boots and the dark robe he generally wore, setting aside as well the wooden staff he typically used as a walking stick. His arm resting in its sling, he lay against the wall in a dark gray-green tunic and hose. His wild gray hair, beard, and eyebrows seemed to overbalance the frailty of his body now devoid of its substantial outer garments, so that he looked not unlike a dandelion stem with its snow-white head that a puff of wind might scatter.

But that impression would belie the uncanny vigor of his powerful mind. "I cannot help but think," he began in a low voice, "that Sir Sagramore's hatred of Sir Tristram must somehow play into the overall background to this crime."

"But how?" I asked. "It was Sir Florent, not Sir Tristram, whose ruin seems intended. And we have Bess's own words that her attacker was not Sir Sagramore, so how might he have been involved in this?"

"Remember, Gildas, that there seem to have been two men involved in this crime. There was one, an unknown figure but likely to have been at the Red Fox that night, who rode a great white horse on which he pursued Bess of Caerleon, caught her waiting in the forest for Colgrevaunce, and assaulted her mercilessly. But there was another, an armed figure on a darker horse, who rode Colgrevaunce down, knocking him over and leaving him unconscious for some time in the dark. A figure verified, as you have told me, by Sir Launfal."

"Verified?"

"Sir Launfal identified the rider in the woods as Sir Sagramore, bearing the royal arms of Cornwall. Unless we postulate dozens of riders in those lonely woods that were all unknown to one another, I think we have to assume it was Sir Sagramore who knocked down Colgrevaunce."

I slapped my forehead at my own stupidity. "So you're saying . . . the two riders were working together? Sir Sagramore went out of his way to prevent Colgrevaunce from keeping his tryst with Bess in order to give his accomplice the opportunity to rape her? But why would he do such a thing? He disliked Sir Tristram, but Colegrevaunce had nothing to do with Tristram. Neither did Bess."

"We must discover who actually attacked Bess, and at that point I believe the motive will come clear," Merlin asserted, still apparently deep in thought.

"What do you suppose Sir Sagramore was referring to when he talked to Lady Elaine the afternoon of the king's condemnation of Florent?" I asked, changing the subject in hopes of finding some breakthrough. "She said he seemed distraught, but that he told her he had thought of a way to permanently sever their betrothal, so as to set her free to pursue marriage with the man she loved. What could he have meant?"

"What could break an engagement of such long standing? His getting a bastard upon some noble woman whose father insisted on marriage?"

"His joining a monastery?" I suggested.

"His portending death? Was he ill, perhaps?"

"His public disgrace?"

At that Merlin looked at me with a new respect. "God's

mustache, Gildas, that has to be it! Sagramore had just seen Sir
Florent condemned for a crime he knew full well Florent had
not committed. And he knew who truly *was* guilty! But to reveal
the identity of the culprit, he would have to disclose his own
role in the conspiracy. And he knew that at the very least he
would lose his knighthood for such a crime. He might even be
condemned to death, along with the rapist himself. In either
case, the Lady Elaine and her family would be freed of any
obligation to him or to the Emperor of Constantinople or any
of his kin. She would be free, but he would be lost. No wonder
he was distraught."

"Then it's clear," I concluded. "Find Sagramore, and find
the culprit. We have to find him tomorrow."

"We do," Merlin agreed. "Even if we have not yet caught the
villain, Sagramore can testify to the truth at Florent's retrial,
and it should be enough to save him."

"But where is he? Can he be hiding? Did he change his mind
after he talked to Lady Elaine? Where can we look for him that
Sir Gareth failed to look?" I asked, exasperated.

"We'll cross that drawbridge when we come to it," Merlin
quipped. "And hope we don't fall off into the moat. Come, let
us get some sleep now, so that we can rise all the earlier tomorrow and do an all-out search for Sagramore. We'll enlist the
help of all Gawain's brothers and their squires, and anyone else
the queen can spare."

"I can get Robin and the guards to help out as well. If he's in
Camelot or Caerleon, or anywhere in the vicinity, we must draw
him out tomorrow." I sighed as I sat down on the pallet next to
Merlin's, rubbing my temples with anxiety. In an offhanded effort to distract myself, I snatched at the parchment that Merlin
still held absent-mindedly in his good hand. "A love poem," I
observed, "from the Lady Elaine's secret admirer." I considered
how the queen had plucked the folded scrap from Elaine's sleeve

during our interview, and how Elaine had blushed but conceded that it was from her lover, though refusing to give his name. She was not ready, she said, to reveal him as long as her public engagement to Sir Sagramore was still popularly assumed. The queen had not pressed, but handed the parchment to Merlin in case it could have any relevance to our investigation.

"I wonder," I speculated aloud, "how much Sir Sagramore knew about this secret lover of Lady Elaine's? Could there have been some enmity between them? Might there be some connection to this affair in that way?"

"Enmity?" Merlin repeated, closing his eyes. "I doubt it. Elaine seemed to know all about Sagramore's Cornish lover, and apparently saw nothing in that but a mutual sorrow she shared with him. No reason to think he felt different about hers."

"Hmmph," I answered. Then I blew out a long sigh through puffed cheeks and glanced down at the page in my hand. "So, let's see what kind of a poet our Lady Elaine's lover is." I looked at the carefully constructed stanzas on the page, and began to read them aloud:

> My lady says she loves me not
> She sees Love as a jest.
> But I pursue my love with Love's own bow
> That I may loose upon her the sharp blow
> To pierce her breast
> With Love's most perfect shot.
>
> And when I have her heart in thrall
> I'll not be cruel to her.
> For Love goads me to mark my Lady's will,
> In humble deference to serve her still.
> As if she were
> My God, my sovereign, and my all.

But she makes me to languish deep
In prison's dark stone walls,
And never will I see the light of day:
My Lady's pity is the only way
But to my calls
Her ears are deaf, and I must weep.

Only she can salve Love's wound,
For her eyes have caused this gash.
Her pity is the medicine I crave,
Her grace the only ointment that can save
My trembling flesh.
Oh Love, please let her grace abound.

I considered the poem for a few moments and shrugged. "His verses are fairly well crafted, don't you think? I mean, the rhyme and meter seem rather skillful, I would say."

"Trite, sentimental claptrap. Silly, uninspired rubbish like all these love-struck boys," Merlin grumbled, half under his breath, as he rolled over to try to sleep.

"Well," I said, considering the verses again. "I rather like it."

"That's because you're a silly, love-struck boy yourself, with the taste of a twelve-year-old girl. I'm going to sleep."

I knew it would be useless to berate him about his own love-struckness regarding the Lady Nimue, and so I got up, announcing, "I think I'll go down to the garderobe before I turn in."

"That is news you might have spared me," the old man muttered, barely audible as he drew a thick blanket over his head. "Now close that gaping maw you call a mouth or I'll turn you into something unnatural. An intelligent Cornishman, for instance." At that I heard some hog-like snufflings under the blanket and knew he was having a laugh at his own witticism.

So I left the queen's outer chamber and walked the thirty

paces or so to where the corridor ended, at a corner of the castle's outside wall. As I walked, I could not get the verses to Lady Elaine out of my head. There was something . . . some buried memory in the deep recesses of my brain that I could not quite call to mind. But something about those verses insisted that I disinter that memory and look at it straight. Something important.

Soon I had reached the end of the corridor. Here, hanging balcony-like out over the moat, was the small closet that housed the privy for that floor of the castle. A torch blazed away within the room, providing enough light to allow me to see what I was doing as I stood over the hole in the stone bench that pointed down into the moat. As I did so I looked out of the small window, with its view of the forest to the north of the castle. I was struck for a moment by the natural beauty of the evergreen trees. In the deep silver glow of the full moon, the pines looked like dark silhouettes of themselves. *In the darkness,* I thought, *the green cannot be distinguished from black.*

The green limb is black, Merlin had said in his trance.

And suddenly I knew what had happened.

I ran back to the queen's outer chamber, at risk of falling and breaking my neck in that dark corridor, but there was no time to think of that now. "Merlin! Merlin, listen!" I cried as I screeched to a halt in the chamber.

The old man sat up with one eye closed and the other squinting unwelcomingly at me. "Keep your voice down, boy, or the queen—"

"The queen will love me," I finished. "Listen: I just realized. In the dark, you can't tell black from green!"

Now Merlin sat all the way up and opened both eyes, raising those shaggy brows in mock surprise. "God's anklebones, Gildas, next you'll be revealing the shocking news that daylight is caused by sunshine. Why is this latest breakthrough disturbing my much-needed sleep?"

"The shield!" I cried, barely able to speak the words coherently. "Bess of Caerleon saw a shield with a black tree. But it wasn't Florent's shield. It was the green tree of Cornwall she saw on the shield. It only looked black in the darkness!"

"God's molars," Merlin said and slapped his forehead. "It was Sagramore's shield she saw!"

CHAPTER SIXTEEN:
SIR SAGRAMORE

The next morning Merlin and I met Sir Gareth in the courtyard of the lower bailey at the foot of the staircase leading down from the queen's rooms. It was time to find Sir Sagramore, and we hadn't much time to do it. On the chance that Sagramore had left Camelot, Gareth had stopped at the stables and consulted with Taber, only to learn that Sir Sagramore's horse was still stabled, and that the knight had not been to ride him for several days. That eliminated the possibility that Sagramore had taken this opportunity to make one of his frequent trips to Cornwall on Sir Tristram's business. If he feared exposure, such a trip would have given him the perfect excuse to leave Camelot and still avoid suspicion. But he had not done so.

Now Gareth met us leading Dido and Aeneas, Queen Guinevere's two hunting greyhounds. "If we are on a hunt," Sir Gareth said, "it may be they can help us find our quarry. I had no luck on my own yesterday, though I searched throughout the castle and asked every knight I knew if they had seen Sagramore. No one knew anything. That's why I focused on the Lady Elaine: She was the only one who seems to have spoken with Sagramore in days."

"Sagramore has no squire who might have known something of his whereabouts?"

"Sir Sagramore has always been a loner, and he is not a wealthy knight," Sir Gareth explained. "He was attached to Sir Tristram as something of a subordinate, and spent a good deal of time on secretive trips to Cornwall in Tristram's service. He does not seem ever to have had a squire of his own, though in tournaments and the like Tristram's squire, Kurneval, acted as squire to Sagramore. And Kurneval is not here, having left for Brittany with Sir Tristram. So Sir Sagramore cannot have contacted him, nor can he help us in this search."

"Well, let's see what the dogs can do," Merlin ventured, though his voice did not hold a good deal of optimism. He held a sleeve the Lady Elaine had given us that morning, a token of hers Sagramore had worn in the most recent tournament at Camelot. In the hope that it still retained some of the knight's scent, Merlin let Dido and Aeneas sniff it to their hearts' content. In theory, the dogs might now recognize Sagramore's scent and lead us to him. Or, barring that, at least bark animatedly if they noticed the scent somewhere else in the castle.

We began a slow walk around the castle grounds, passing first the great hall and the kitchen area on the left. Merlin tried to hustle us past the kitchen, since much time spent in that vicinity would cause the dogs to forget about any scents other than the aromas wafting from Roger's cooking.

On the way, I felt the need to let Sir Gareth in on what we now knew or surmised about Sir Sagramore's involvement in the Bess affair. Merlin and I had talked a good deal after I returned from the garderobe last night, but most of what we concluded could be summed up fairly quickly: "We know Bess of Caerleon misidentified her attacker's shield," I began.

Sir Gareth looked at me with some disbelief. "You mean, she lied about the coat of arms? What is this all about, then?"

"No, no," I told him. "She *thought* she saw Florent's shield—the black tree on the silver field—but in fact she saw the royal arms of Cornwall, the green tree on the white. The trees depicted on the shields are almost identical, and in the dark, green looks black. And silver appears white in the moonlight.

223

She identified the wrong man!"

"But the royal arms of Cornwall—that would be the shield of Sir Tristram! Is it possible?"

Merlin stepped in at this point. "Of course not, Beaumains. You know Tristram's courtesy as well as I do. But Sir Sagramore, Tristram's vassal and his liaison with the Cornish court, typically bore a shield with the same markings when on Sir Tristram's business. His own arms, the swan argent on a field purpure, were on the shield he bore on the morning of Bess's accusation. But the night before, the night of the attack, he was riding in the wood bearing the royal Cornish arms. We have that on good authority."

"But he didn't have his shield when he attacked Colgrevaunce!" I added.

"Wait—Sagramore attacked Colgrevaunce?"

I had forgotten that this last was not common knowledge. Merlin closed his eyes, and then began again slowly. "Our young squire is getting ahead of himself a bit. But the facts we can surmise are these: First, Sir Sagramore and one of the squires present at that drinking bout conspired to take Bess of Caerleon's virtue. Second, Sagramore's part of the conspiracy involved loaning his shield with the green tree to his accomplice, and making sure Colgrevaunce never kept his tryst with Bess in the woods. Third, the accomplice stole a white horse intended as a gift to Florent from the Lady of the Lake, and, bearing the arms of Cornwall, rode to the place where Bess was to meet Colgrevaunce and raped her."

"So you're saying the intent was never to frame Florent for the attack at all? What was the point of using that shield? What could Sagramore have had in mind? The only one using that coat of arms in Camelot is . . ."

"Precisely. Sir Tristram," Merlin completed the thought. "The elaborate scheme was simply a plot to disgrace Sir Tristram, and perhaps make him forfeit his life. Bess, Colgrevaunce, Florent, they were all simply collateral damage."

Gareth nodded. "Of course. Lady Elaine told us yesterday how much Sagramore hated Tristram. But she didn't think he would go this far. Obviously she was wrong."

"Obviously," Merlin agreed. "But she is rather insistent that he never told her about the plot. I suspect it hatched that very evening. Sagramore saw the opportunity when he heard Bess making plans to meet Colgrevaunce later. He saw it, and his accomplice saw it."

"But what did he feel when the plot backfired? He told Elaine he was going to do something that would cut off their engagement for good. Was he going to confess what he had done, and take the consequences for it? Or did he plan to sneak out of Camelot and never come back? Live in hiding?"

"Either way it would have meant the end of their betrothal," Gareth agreed. "And it's looking like the plan really was to run away. We haven't seen a sign of him anywhere in Camelot."

Against the east wall of the castle, between the fortified northeast and southeast guard towers, Robin Kempe was drilling a dozen of his archers in target practice. The butts, on mounds raised against the southern wall close by the tower, were made up of six empty wine casks laid side by side, with targets painted on the ends that faced out. Half a dozen archers at a time were lined up directly across from these, against the north wall, about a hundred yards from the targets. At this distance, and with their long bows, Robin expected each marksman to hit his bull's-eye three out of five times.

Robin stood beside the archers and shouted commands. "Ready your bows!" he called, at which each of the six marksmen pulled an arrow from his quiver.

"Nock!" Robin shouted, and the marksmen all notched their

arrows onto their bowstrings.

"Mark!" Robin called again, and the archers brought their bows into position and aimed at the targets.

"Draw!" At this the marksmen pulled their bowstrings back, each as far as his right ear, and tensed to fire.

"Loose!" All six arrows flew at great speed, burying their points in the empty casks with deadly force. I heard five echoing "thwocks" and one barrel that made more of a "thud." Must have been a different kind of wood, I thought absently.

Robin noticed us coming, and told his men to take their ease for a moment. Had I been the only one approaching, no doubt he would have aimed some barbed comment at me, and I would have responded in kind, but the presence of the king's nephew apparently inspired him to a more courtly attitude, and he inclined his head slightly toward Sir Gareth with a nod of welcome.

"My lord Gareth," he began. "Of what service can I and the king's archers be to you this morning? That is, to you and your noble companions," and with that he gave me a quick and barely noticeable raise of his left eyebrow, suggesting a tongue at least partially inserted in his cheek at that description of Merlin and me.

Sir Gareth made no sign of recognizing any irony, but plunged ahead. "Robin, we have reason to believe Sir Sagramore was involved somehow in the unfortunate events of last week that led to the condemnation of Sir Florent . . ."

At that Robin appeared to take a much more serious interest in our visit. "Involved? In what way involved?"

Merlin took over the interview. "We're not at liberty to divulge that right now, because we don't yet know the whole story. But rest assured we'll know it by the end of the day, or I'll know the reason why. Now listen, Robin Kempe, we have not been able to find Sagramore for at least two days. His horse has not left the stables, but what we want to know from you and your men," Merlin looked over at the dozen archers milling about with their weapons, but knew that the king employed dozens more in the castle guard, and he didn't have time to interview every one, "is whether anyone saw Sir Sagramore leave the castle on foot, or by any other means, in the past, oh, four days or so."

Robin considered the question, knitting his brows and frowning while he looked at the ground. "Well . . . I know I haven't seen him in that time, and I am in command of the barbican guard most days." He turned to his archers and posed the question. "Listen, men! Is there anyone here who saw Sir Sagramore leave Camelot in the last four days? Or for that matter, have any of you seen him at all?" There was a certain amount of mumbling, of looking at one another, of shoulder shrugging, all of which essentially ended in the shaking of heads. No one had seen Sagramore, at least not recently. Then Robin did something we hadn't expected, but welcomed. "We will spend another twenty rounds here at the butts," he ordered his men, "and then I want you to begin scouring the castle grounds for Sagramore. When we are done here, I'll be going to the keep to order anyone not currently in the guard towers to help with the search. We'll find this bugger," he said, turning back to us, "you've got my word!"

It was a godsend. With so little time to track the knight down, and so much at stake, the help of the entire castle guard was a welcome relief. It seemed clear Sir Sagramore did not want to be found, and so he would have to be unearthed and chased from his hole like a rat. We nodded to Robin again and thanked him, turning to head off ourselves and begin our search. "I propose we go back to the kitchens," Merlin began, "to get a bite of breakfast, but also to see if anyone there has seen Sagramore. If he is in the castle, he has to eat. If they haven't seen him at the kitchens then his accomplice may be taking him food wherever he may be hiding."

Behind us we heard Robin giving the orders again: "Ready your bows! Nock!"

"His accomplice has got to be one of the three squires, right?" I asserted. "What if we wait and see whether Thomas, Baldwin, or Bertrand takes some food from the kitchen that he doesn't eat, and then follow him to see where he takes it?"

"Mark! Draw!"

"That would be too obvious," Gareth said. "Whoever he was would know he was under surveillance and avoid giving Sagramore away."

"Loose!" And again came the "thwock, thwock, thwock, thwock, thwock, thud," that we had heard before.

I glanced back and muttered, "Odd sound, that last barrel. But Merlin, don't we have enough evidence now to free Florent? We can easily make the case that Sagramore is guilty, and we can find out who his accomplice is later on."

"But without Sagramore himself there, we have little hard evidence. And finding his . . ." Merlin stopped in mid-sentence. He stood still for a moment, blurted out "God's elbows!" and then turned and began to run, or at least move as quickly as a man his age could move, back toward Robin, waving his good hand in the air and calling, "Stop! Hold your fire! We must look at those barrels!"

Robin quickly had his men put up their bows as the old mage rushed into the line of fire toward the barrel targets, shouting back over his shoulder, "Which of the casks was making the odd sound?"

Robin shrugged. From a hundred yards away, and with the nearly simultaneous thump of six arrows into six casks, it was difficult to say which of the targets had failed to echo in the way the others had. By now Sir Gareth and I had caught up with Merlin, Dido and Aeneas leading the charge, racing joyfully ahead of the knight, who still tried to hold onto their leads. We all reached the six barrels together, and almost immediately the dogs focused on the second barrel from the left. They sniffed at it eagerly, eyes wide open and ears flattened back against their heads. The dogs surely thought they had found what they were looking for. Merlin knocked on the cask. The knock was muffled somewhat. There was no echo. Something was definitely inside.

The six casks were each some four feet long and about three feet in diameter at their widest point, and were set upon a mound of earth some three feet high, so that the barrels rose higher than any of us stood. By now, Robin had made his way to us, and with a cry of, "Now what the bloody 'ell is this?" he and I pulled at the barrel to get it off the mound and set it upright. It was quite heavy, and Gareth at last had to come to help us, handing the dog leashes off to Merlin.

When we had stood the barrel up, its target side to the ground, Robin examined the sealed end of the cask, which was now on top. Fingering it along the circular ridge, he shook his head and said, "Yeah, somebody's been tampering with this all right. You can see it's been opened and sealed shut again a couple of times."

"Can we pry it loose with something?" I asked, feeling about me for something to use as a lever.

"Got something quicker than that, my lad," Robin replied, and called out to the tallest of the archers at the other end of the field. "Aleyn! You still got that mace you carry with you?"

At that Aleyn came trotting across, pulling a small war club—a pernach with a six-flanged iron head—from his belt. "Smash that barrel in, quick now!" Robin ordered, and Aleyn cocked his arm, bringing the mace down like a hammer on the top of the barrel. The top collapsed like paper beneath the blow, and all five of us leaned forward to see what was in the cask.

The dogs were right. It was indeed Sagramore. Or what was left of him.

The body had been in the barrel for several days, apparently shoved in after Sagramore was already dead. We found three crossbow darts in his chest that the killer apparently hadn't had time, or hadn't bothered, to retrieve. But most likely the murder and the concealment had been done in haste, and in the dark, here on the archery practice field on the far edge of the castle grounds. Here, only the guards in the two corner towers were likely to be astir in the dark of night, and their attention would almost certainly have been on possible threats from outside the castle. They would not have been looking in, unless they heard strange noises. The killer's crossbow shots would have made no sound, particularly if they were fired at close quarters. As to the smell, this far away from the castle proper, no one had noticed it.

"This was done to conceal the earlier crime," Merlin pronounced. "Do you see?" He looked around, as Gareth and I leaned forward with interest, while Robin and Aleyn looked at each other in puzzlement. "Who would have killed Sagramore so soon after the attack on the girl other than the person responsible for the attack? Especially if Sagramore was the only other person alive who could identify him? It seems clear to me now. When Sir Sagramore told the Lady Elaine he was going to cancel their betrothal for good and all, he intended to confess to aiding in the rape. He arranged a meeting with his accomplice here, in the dead of night, to tell him his plan. But the other had no intention of confessing, and no desire to let Sagramore drag him to the gallows as well. He shot our knight right here, at point-blank range."

"So our rapist is also a murderer. And why not?" Gareth

asked. "The king condemned Florent to death. The true rapist knew the law would hang him if he was caught, and he could only die once. Why not take the chance of killing the only witness and maybe getting off scot-free? Die for murder or die for rape, it's the same thing. He had nothing to lose."

"And if he was going to kill one, he might as well kill three," I added. "Surely Sagramore's killer was the same person who tried to shoot Merlin and me on the road back from Caerleon the other night. Thank God for Nimue! We'd have found ourselves stuck in wine butts and no one the wiser!"

"Pretty clean shots," Robin commented, admiring the killer's marksmanship. "Pierced his heart."

Pierced his heart, I thought. And then, *Or pierce her heart.* Something clicked with loud finality in my brain. "Merlin!" I grabbed him by his good arm. "That poem of Elaine's . . . I just realized . . ."

The old man gave a quick start and then scowled at me. "Never mind that now, boy. This is more important. We need to find the killer, and we need to find him before he finds us!" Now it was my turn to start, for it had never occurred to me that, once thwarted, the murderer might very well try to complete what he had begun, and finish off the two of us, especially if we were getting close to the truth. "Captain Robin," Merlin added. "Do you think you and your men can take care of Sir Sagramore? He should, I suppose, be delivered to the chapel, so that he might be prepared for burial. I don't think his body is likely to give us any more information."

"Right!" Robin said, and called his men. "You lot, come over here and help us get this bloody corpse out of our target! Step lively now . . ." and with wondering looks the other five guards made their way to the target side of the field.

"Well, I'm off to get these dogs back to the queen," Gareth said. "Their job, at least, is done, and I don't fancy keeping them around. They're not very well-behaved." At that, as if to punctuate Sir Gareth's claim, Dido jumped up on him and tried to lick his face.

"Yes," Merlin said, taking me by the shoulder and turning me away. "Greet the queen for us as well, will you? And tell her what's happened with Sagramore? Young Gildas and I are going to take a walk and . . . cogitate."

Gareth rolled his eyes and started off. He, I knew, had a bias for action, and probably saw no point in Merlin's desire to ruminate more on the matter when so much was at stake and so little time remained. Robin and his men began the unsavory task of pulling the bloody corpse from the old wine barrel. Merlin ushered me south from the practice field, toward the middle bailey alongside the castle's great stone keep. "Gildas of Cornwall," he said to me in low tones, his head down. "It is time for you and me to be very secretive. The more who know a thing, the more likely it will spread even further. And not only are you and I in danger right now, but we are perhaps equally in danger of losing our quarry. When word gets out that we have found Sir Sagramore, it will be fight or flight for our culprit. He will either try to kill us or try to run. Or both. Now tell me what you were about to blurt out back there. What of the Lady Elaine's poem?"

"But I thought you said it wasn't pertinent . . ."

"Dunce! I *said* we need to be careful who knows what we know. And who to tell afterwards. Now tell me what you think, and quickly too." At that he looked around, but we were not being followed, and no one passing by paid us any mind.

"I was going to say, I just realized the Lady Elaine's poem was in precisely the same verse form as the song Sir Palomides wrote for our hunt the other day. Same rhyme scheme, same imagery in part, only hers was more direct and serious while the one from the hunt was comic, even ribald. Does it mean Sir

Palomides is the Lady Elaine's lover? Do you think it has a bearing on this case?"

Merlin shook his head. "It doesn't make sense. It is well known that Sir Palomides is in love with Queen Isolde of Cornwall. All his own love poetry is written for her sake, and laments his unrequited love of her."

"And, of course, he was nowhere near the Red Fox the night of the rape. That much we know for certain. He can't have been Sagramore's accomplice," I agreed.

"But it is curious," Merlin continued. "Of all the knights in Camelot with a grudge against Sir Tristram, Palomides must be at the top of the list. Surely he resents, even hates, Tristram for winning the love of his lady Isolde, and for deserting her and marrying his Breton wife. Palomides has made great show of his truth and faithfulness to La Belle Isolde, even in the face of her definitive rejection."

A new thought now struck me, so obvious that I should have seen it immediately. "Palomides's squire," I said. "Bertrand de Toledo! He acts as his master's jongleur. Surely he has memorized the Moorish knight's style and can imitate it at will. He has memorized and sung nearly every verse Palomides ever wrote. And he is close enough to his master to have absorbed his hatred of Sir Tristram."

"God's anklebones, Gildas, of course it's him! He was one of our suspects anyway, and this makes it clear he had the motive. And look you: He and Sagramore had a common interest . . ."

"The Lady Elaine!" I agreed. "She claims Sagramore did not know her lover, but she must have been lying to protect him."

"Of course she was lying. And she was lying—or at least not telling the truth—about her knowledge of the plot as well. She told us just enough to implicate Sir Sagramore, but she knew we were already aware of his part in the plot. She just needed to keep us away from Bertrand."

"No wonder she balked at giving up the poem when the queen found it," I said.

"But she couldn't make her reluctance too obvious," Merlin continued. "Or it would have looked suspicious. So she did ultimately give up the poem."

"But she refused to tell us who gave it to her."

Merlin shrugged. "Ah, *fin amors*. 'When made public, love rarely endures.' It's a tenet of the code, and one that the queen, most certainly, would condone. Elaine relied on the customary secrecy of courtly love to protect her paramour."

"So do we believe Elaine had prior knowledge of the plot that Bertrand hatched with Sagramore?"

"Not of the specific plot," Merlin said. "The three of them could not have known beforehand that Tristram's presence at the inn, along with Colgrevaunce, Florent, and Bess, would give them the perfect opportunity to discredit Tristram and bring him to the dock—that they could use Bess's planned rendezvous with Colgrevaunce as the scene of their deception. That plot had to have been hatched on the spot. And remember," now he smiled grimly. "Sir Dinadan told us Sagramore left with the squire Bertrand. We had that clue from the very beginning."

I put my hand to my forehead and shook my head at my blindness. At *our* blindness, it must be said, for Merlin hadn't taken that fact into consideration either. "So they must have come up with the plan right then, right after they left the inn."

"The shield was the key, and Sagramore already had the shield," Merlin began, replaying events of that night in his head. "That was to identify the attacker as Sir Tristram. Bertrand had to take the part of the rapist, because they couldn't take the chance that Bess would recognize Sagramore, as indeed she could have. Then they had to ensure Bess would not be met by any other knight before Bertrand reached the rendezvous spot. They followed Florent to where he fell asleep in the woods, and must have found him after Nimue brought him the gift of the great white horse. Luck played right into the conspirators' hands at that point, and Bertrand mounted the horse, took Sir Sagramore's shield, and rode off to make his tryst with Bess."

"And so Sagramore, on his own horse, went off in search of Colgrevaunce," I continued, taking my cue from Merlin. "After he knocked Colgrevaunce out, he rode back to Camelot, stabled his horse, and went to sleep. Nobody the wiser. He was just a knight returning from a few drinks at the inn with some of his fellows. But Merlin," I continued, "why, when she had the chance, did Bess not identify Sir Tristram's shield? Why did the plan end up backfiring, and snaring the wrong knight? I mean, she saw Tristram holding that shield . . ."

"Remember, though, Bess told us she knew her attacker was not Tristram because she would have recognized him, even in the dark, by his movements and the way he sat his horse. When she saw that shield in Tristram's hands, she told herself it couldn't be the right shield, because she knew Tristram wasn't the attacker. So when she saw Florent's shield, that had looked so much like Tristram's in the dark, she picked that one out because she told herself it could not possibly be the other."

"And thus a man is condemned to death," I mused. "But what must we do now? Shall we go back to Robin, have him call out the guard and find Bertrand? He must be arrested, and Florent freed."

Merlin took his time thinking. Finally he raised his head and, stroking his wounded arm in its sling, said, "This is a dangerous criminal, and one that cares nothing for human life or dignity, unless it is his own. He assaulted an innocent girl with no purpose other than to blacken the name of a worthy knight. The girl was nothing to him. He killed another knight and stuffed his body into an empty wine cask, as if it was so much garbage. He attacked us under cover of darkness merely because he thought we *might* find out who he was. He is a cold-blooded killer and no one is safe. I begin to fear, in fact, for the life of the Lady Elaine. This is not a man who truly feels love. He is simply one that can put the right code words into verse by imitating his master. No, if we put out the word to have him arrested, I fear what his next move will be. If he knows he is being hunted, neither you, nor I, nor Elaine, nor Florent, nor Bess, no, not even the queen, is safe if he sees a threat to himself."

"Well, what do we do, then? We can't let this killer just have free rein in the castle."

"Carefully and quietly, I think, is the way to go with Bertrand of Toledo." Merlin spoke slowly. "Tomorrow is the retrial of Sir Florent. He is to come before the queen in the great hall at the hour of prime. Everyone in Camelot will be there to see the outcome of this matter. He will give whatever answer he has found to his quest, but in any case we must then step in to demonstrate his innocence. By then, Sir Sagramore's death will be known, and it is essential that we demonstrate convincingly how Sagramore's murder connects to the assault on Bess of Caerleon, and how the trail leads directly to Bertrand."

"The queen will want to know of this plan, Merlin—we cannot catch her unawares with this information."

"No, we cannot," the old necromancer agreed. "But only the queen must know, none of her ladies-in-waiting. And she herself must be aware of the vital need for secrecy. If the Lady Elaine were to know of this, it would mean disaster. It would mean, I suspect, her own death and Bertrand's escape."

"Her death? Why would he—"

"It cannot have escaped your notice, young squire, that the one factor that unites Sir Sagramore and Bertrand of Toledo is the Lady Elaine. Both men may have hated Sir Tristram, but who could have put them together, who could have matched their common interests save the lady herself."

"I still don't understand."

"Think, Gildas!" Merlin furrowed his brow impatiently. "What is the Lady Elaine's background? You told me yourself not long ago."

"Well, she's Irish. Father a big landowner there, cousin to the king. But . . . wait! You mean she sees Tristram as an enemy because of his killing the Marhault?"

"There can be no doubt!" Merlin exclaimed. "Like Isolde's own mother, Lady Elaine wanted Tristram dead. He killed their kinsman, forced Ireland to pay the tribute it owed Cornwall. Her own poisonous tongue may have had a significant part in turning Sagramore against Sir Tristram, and in moving Bertrand's resentment into violence. She may not have committed any assault or murder herself, but she is at the root of this conspiracy, you can bet on it, and none of this would have happened without her urging. Who knows? She may have come to Camelot years ago with this sole purpose in mind: to destroy Sir Tristram."

"But why do you think she's in danger?"

"She's the only person alive now who can bear witness against Bertrand. She's the only one who knows for certain he is the killer, because she was the one who engineered it. She told Bertrand Sagramore was planning to confess to his part in Bess's assault, knowing Bertrand's only move would then be to kill him. That protected Bertrand and protected her. But it also showed Bertrand that the way to get away with a crime is to make sure there are no witnesses."

I scoffed. "Then why not let Bertrand kill her? Doesn't she deserve it?"

"Death is everyone's reward, young Gildas. And it will come for her in time. But it is not our right to decide when that should happen, any more than it was Bertrand's right to snuff out Sagramore's life because it turned out he actually had a conscience, even if a small one. The Lady Elaine, like Bertrand himself, should stand before the king's justice and pay for her crimes according to the law."

I nodded without much certainty. "I guess you're right, old man, but how do we keep anybody else from getting killed if Bertrand is in the crowd at the hall and realizes he's about to be exposed?"

"We tap people we know we can trust in this matter. Sir Gareth. Colgrevaunce. You. All *very* well armed. We watch the great door of the hall closely, to catch Bertrand if he tries to leave before I have given my evidence. We tell Robin to let no one out of the castle during that time, in case he slips away early. Once his name is revealed, he will have no chance to exit the hall, for the knights there will detain him. The important thing is to keep him in sight, where he can be contained and neutralized once his guilt is known."

"What about the king's door, behind his throne?"

"He won't run that way," Merlin said. "He'd only get as far as the king's private solar, which is stoutly guarded, or the battlements. Neither of them good choices for an escape."

"Riiiight . . ." I answered, with a lot less confidence than Merlin seemed to be feeling.

"Right!" he agreed, with gusto. "Now let's you and I go visit the queen, so she knows what's going on tomorrow morning!"

"And so we do as well . . ." I added, knowing the queen would most certainly keep charge of the order of events.

As we turned to our right to walk past the great castle keep and back toward the great hall and the queen's apartments, I had another thought that brought me up short, and I stopped dead in my tracks. "The crossbow!" I blurted out.

Merlin stopped and looked back at me, patiently agreeing: "Yes, the crossbow. The same crossbow that killed Sir Sagramore most certainly did this to my arm." He lifted his injured limb for emphasis. "And Bertrand of Toledo was surely the malevolent force behind it, who tried to put us both into the ground."

"Yes," I said, "that's clear. But what just struck me . . . I should have suspected Bertrand from the beginning. The crossbow—he was the one that brought the deer down on the hunt with Sir Gareth. I knew he was a crack shot with the crossbow, but I never put it together. I should have. You know, your 'vision'? 'The rose's thorns are darts'?"

"It's all right," the old man consoled me, putting his hand on my shoulder and continuing our walk to the queen's chambers. "Sometimes things only make sense when you look back on them."

"Hmmph," I snorted. "I hope that's not going to be the case tomorrow. I hope we've anticipated every eventuality so that everything makes sense while it's happening."

"Of course!" Merlin scoffed. "What could possibly go wrong?"

CHAPTER SEVENTEEN:
THINGS GO WRONG

The queen sat on a modest throne on a raised dais, to the left of the elaborate throne of the king, which stood empty this morning. Arthur had turned over the decision in the case of his grand-nephew to the judgment of Queen Guinevere, as she had requested a week earlier, and in order to underscore the queen's authority in this judgment, had opted not to appear in the great throne room at all during the day's proceedings. Besides, he had the newly revealed murder of Sir Sagramore to deal with. What he didn't know was the connection between the two events, and the fact that we already knew who the murderer was.

The queen wore her hair loose down her back, fastened behind by an ornate golden barrette wrought in the likeness of a dragon. On her brow she wore a relatively simple crown: a circlet of gold with four raised crosses, the one in front decorated with a sapphire stone at the intersection of the crosspieces. Her kirtle was royal purple with long, pointed sleeves, and she wore it beneath a bright blue overskirt. She wore a woven belt with long ties in front, from which hung a finely crafted rosary.

Behind her was the great tapestry depicting the young King Arthur's victory over Sir Florent's grandfather, King Lot. Lot of Orkney was shown kneeling in fealty to Arthur, who held high the sword Excalibur in victory and in salute to the God who put him on his throne—and as a kind of symbol therefore of his responsibility to do justice.

To the queen's left, on the south wall of the throne room, two tapestries hung on either side of the huge double doors that were the chief means into and out of the hall, and at which Gareth, Colgrevaunce, and I stood guard bedecked with chain-mail and broadswords. One of these flanking tapestries depicted Arthur's decisive victory over the Irish King Rience, showing Arthur leading a cavalry charge that would crush the Irish army. On the far side of the door was shown another of Arthur's battles, this one his decisive victory over the Saxon invaders at the Battle of Mount Badon. This tapestry showed a charging Arthur, holding high Excalibur and laying low nine hundred of the enemy in a single attack, the image of the Virgin Mary on his shield. Directly across from the queen, on the west wall, a huge tapestry portrayed Arthur's most spectacular victory, over the Emperor Lucius, which established his claim to the imperial throne of Rome.

To the queen's right was the wall against which the king's throne stood. On this wall were long windows reaching from the floor to the intricately vaulted wooden ceiling. The small door that only the king himself generally used stood directly behind the throne.

The hall was abuzz as nearly the entire court congregated in small groups along all four walls of the throne room. The room was not built to hold more than about three hundred people, and we were certainly nearing that capacity, though a relatively small area directly in front of the queen was kept free so that Sir Florent could appear before the queen's justice seat and make his defense. At Guinevere's left on the dais sat Merlin, looking grim and foreboding. I had no doubt that all but a few of the courtiers present were confused as to why the old man was there. Notably absent from the dais was Sir Gawain. Too distraught to sit calmly through the proceedings that could save or condemn his eldest son, he had chosen to wait elsewhere, in the company of the king, and hear the outcome of the trial after the fact. To Merlin's left was, surprisingly, Mistress Bess of Caerleon. The queen wanted her present and prominent, for Bess herself must agree with the queen's judgment if her verdict was to be generally accepted as justice.

Directly before the queen's throne, Sir Bedivere, acting as bailiff of the queen's court, held a long wooden staff, the bottom end of which he pounded three times on the stone floor of the throne room to quiet the crowd. "Hear ye! Hear ye!" Bedivere cried out. "The queen's court of Camelot is now in session. All those having business before this court are directed to come stand before the dais forthwith."

Sir Gareth, Colgrevaunce, and I stepped back as Sir Florent appeared behind us, just at his appointed hour. He strode with purpose, his head held high, wearing dark blue hose with black shoes, and a rich-looking purple tunic, over which he sported a sleeveless surcoat adorned in front with the same coat of arms that had condemned him through his shield—the black tree emblazoned on a silver background.

As Florent walked through the door, he was followed closely by a figure dressed in a long black robe, with a large hood hiding her face. She leaned heavily on a crooked walking stick, and moved with the slow, unsteady gait of one who was very old. I looked quizzically at Sir Gareth, who shrugged as the figure in black moved through the door. The great throng in the hall parted like the Red Sea to allow Florent and his curious companion to move through, straight into the open space before the queen's throne.

Immediately, Sir Florent knelt and bowed his head in obeisance to Queen Guinevere. "My Sovereign Lady," he began, never lifting his eyes from the floor. "I am supremely thankful for the reprieve Your Grace saw fit to grant me, though it were but a single week. I searched most diligently to find the answer to the question you posed me: What is it that women want most, you asked. I confess I thought at first the task would be simple. Just find every woman in Camelot and Caerleon and all the surrounding villages, and ask them. Surely there would be some consensus."

The queen smirked in her most ironic manner as she asked, "And how did that work out for you, young man?"

Florent shrugged, now looking up into the queen's face, though he remained on his knees. "Well, for the most part, women asked about material things. Shoes and dresses, some women in the court said. Gold or fine jewels, said a lot of the women in the city. Many of the village girls longed for a handsome husband. But I knew even as I listened to them that these were flippant responses. None of these women thought I was taking them seriously, and none of them felt comfortable talking to me, a complete stranger to some of them, and a relative stranger even to the ones I knew. It occurred to me then to talk to the nuns at Saint Mary Magdalene's convent, and I received permission from Mother Hildegard to speak to the sisters in her presence, thinking perhaps they would take my quest more seriously or would open up to me more honestly. But perhaps it was the presence of the Mother Superior—in any case I was dissatisfied with their answers, all of which involved their spiritual health and eventual salvation. It may in fact be that women desire such things, but no more so than men and, in any case, for those outside convent walls it seems a desire most likely put off until very late in life."

Guinevere smiled again, but less ironically this time. "It seems you have had a good deal of disappointment on this quest."

Sir Florent gazed down at the floor again. "Disappointment, yes," he agreed. "But some success. I did realize that one thing women do not want is to reveal their most intimate thoughts to someone they do not particularly trust. And here was I, a convicted rapist, asking them to open up to me. It's most certainly relationships that mean much to women. And thus finally I approached the one woman that I could be said to have some sort of relationship with, the Lady Rosemounde." At this he raised his eyes to Rosemounde's and I cringed as she looked back at him and blushed prettily. "But even she was no great help, I'm afraid," Florent continued. "She could only say that her greatest desire was to see me freed and safe. But from that I concluded it is of great importance to women to ensure the safety of their loved ones. And in this I felt I was very close to truth."

Now the queen gave a grudging nod, and Florent went on, returning his gaze to her. "But again, this is not exclusively the desire of women. Though men may occasionally put other things—honor, justice, the good of the state—above that desire. And so I was not confident that I had found the true answer."

It seemed now that Sir Florent was coming to his final answer, and a profound anticipatory silence fell over the assembled crowd. "Yesterday, at my lowest ebb, when I was near to despairing over the question I sat under a tree in the wood—actually in the very spot where I awakened the morning after this vile deed of which I am accused. It was there that I met this most reverend old woman who accompanies me here," and now for the first time Florent gestured toward the dark-robed figure he had escorted into the throne room. "We talked for several hours, until she knew all the secrets of my life."

To the queen's puzzled look he spread his arms and blurted, "She's a very good listener! But to the point, after some time in this close conference, she had become familiar with my dilemma, and offered to give me the true answer to your question, so long as I granted her the first boon she asked of me, if her answer contributed to my pardon. In that hope, my lady, I shall now offer you the answer to your challenge."

The queen drew herself up and prepared to listen attentively. "Proceed," she encouraged the kneeling knight.

"What women want most," Florent declared, "is sovereignty."

When the queen started back and scowled at him, tilting her head in preparation for a stinging reply, Sir Florent expanded his statement. "Not, Your Majesty, sovereignty in the sense that you possess it—that is, not supreme power over the body politic. I'm talking about sovereignty over herself, that is what a woman desires. A woman wants to be admired by men, certainly, but has no wish to be controlled by any man. Neither father nor husband, nor guardian, nor lord, should have authority to force a woman against her will. I'm not simply talking about rape—a crime, I protest again, of which I maintain my innocence. I'm talking about marriage, I'm talking about vocation in the church, I'm talking about childbearing. These are things that women want to be in control of themselves, not leave to any man to control. A woman wants the ability to choose. A woman wants to be able to make her own decisions about her life. A woman wants sovereignty, Your Grace, over herself."

Now Queen Guinevere raised her chin and a look of triumph crossed her face. She glanced at the ladies-in-waiting sitting beside her on the dais, but not one of them could contradict Sir Florent's assertion. Florent continued: "I admit, Your Majesty, that though I am innocent of the crime I have been convicted of, I am in some manner grateful for the opportunity I have had over the past week to pursue this quest. My eyes have been opened in a way I had not expected. But I also say this: As with my earlier tentative answers to your question, my Queen, this final answer is once again a desire not limited to women but is just as true of men as well. Service is an ideal of chivalry, but for men that service is self-chosen. What all men desire is the same as what all women desire: the freedom to choose to live their lives as they most wish."

"You have done well, Sir Florent," the queen responded. Then, with a glance at Bess of Caerleon, who seemed to grow more and more agitated as Florent's monologue continued, Guinevere added, "But you will recall, there was a second part to the charge I gave you."

"I have not forgotten it," Sir Florent answered, and now finally rose to his feet. With a nod to Bess, he continued: "You directed me, as well, to find a way to make women's deepest desire come true for Bess of Caerleon, in reparation for the great harm done to her. This, I fear, may be more difficult, but let me make an attempt. My lady Bess," he inclined his head as he faced her on the dais, "although I still maintain that I never harmed you, I am aware that you are convinced I have violated your person. One result of your violation, I think, must be a reduction in the likelihood of your finding a suitable husband. If you believe it will in any way alleviate your pain, I would be prepared to offer myself in marriage to you right now." At that an excited murmur ran through the assembled crowd, but from the doorway I could see the old woman in the black robe visibly flinch. On the dais, the Lady Rosemounde stood up, crossing her arms in indignation. Bess, however, did not look pleased.

Florent continued, "Or, if that is not to your liking, let me propose this. My family is among the wealthiest in Arthur's kingdom. I and my family would be willing to provide you with a dowry that would enable you to attract any husband you desire. In this way, at least, I believe I can give Bess complete control over at least one decision that will significantly affect her life. My lady Bess, how do you answer?"

It was just at that point that all hell broke loose.

The queen was the first to speak, raising her voice and declaring, "Sir Florent of Orkney, I find you have grown so in this quest that your sentence may be mitigated . . ."

Before the queen could finish her sentence an angry Bess sprang to her feet. Pointing straight at Florent, she cried "I wouldn't marry you if you begged me on your knees. And I spit on your money. You think because you're rich you can buy your way out of this! This is not justice, my Queen, this is a whitewash . . ."

To prevent Bess from carrying on her tirade, and in the hope of bringing calm after this outburst, Merlin arose and addressed the assembled principals in the case: "And I say Florent shall not be condemned, because I have new evidence of his innocence! This knight is not the one who assaulted you, Bess—"

"I saw the shield with my own eyes!" she argued. "He must die!"

"No! My lady queen, hear me," came a voice from the black-robed woman at Florent's back. "He promised me a boon if my answer spared his life, and I claim that boon now! Sir Florent must marry me, and no other!" With that the crone seemed to throw off scores of years as she threw off her hood and stood erect.

"Nimue!" cried Merlin. For it was indeed the damsel of the lake.

Bess and the queen continued to wrangle with Nimue, each woman's voice rising to outshout the other, but Merlin suddenly sagged back into his chair as if the wind had gone out of his sails. I stared at him, feeling as if a brick had just dropped through my stomach. Hearing his beloved Nimue say before the entire assembled court that she desired Sir Florent for her husband was more than the old necromancer could bear. I knew the feeling all too well.

At last the queen quieted the other ladies down, ultimately resorting to pulling rank on them. "Is it I who am queen here, or do you imagine it is you? Silence, I say, or my guards will be dragging off a pair of unruly young women to do some unanticipated time in the royal dungeons." At that Bess ceased, but stood defiantly with arms crossed and a look of wounded intensity on her face. Nimue ceased as well, but her look was haughtier, as if to say *you may be queen here, Guinevere, but I represent the Lady of the Lake, who transcends all worldly hegemony.*

"Now Merlin," Guinevere continued, looking down where the old man slumped in his chair. "You began to say you have evidence of Sir Florent's innocence, I believe?"

"Innocence? Yes," Merlin mumbled, trying to rouse himself to the occasion. "It was not Florent. The shield . . . was not Florent's . . ." he gazed around desperately, his eyes finally catching mine in a kind of pleading look. I had just begun to move forward when Nimue broke her silence.

"Your Majesty, if I may speak?" The queen nodded to her. "I believe I can shed light on Lord Merlin's announcement. It is true that he and young Gildas of Cornwall have looked into the events of the night Bess was raped, and have found convincing evidence of a conspiracy—a conspiracy involving Sir Sagramore, who was just found slain by his own accomplice. It was Sir Sagramore who provided the shield that Bess here mistook for that of Sir Florent."

"How could that have happened?" the queen wanted to know.

"Sir Sagramore had access to a shield bearing the royal arms of Cornwall, a green tree on a white background. Very similar in design to the black tree on a silver background that Sir Florent bears. But the royal arms of Cornwall are borne by only one knight of Camelot: Sir Tristram. This conspiracy was intended to bring Sir Tristram down. Sir Florent was an accidental victim of the conspiracy. Like Bess herself."

Bess turned pale and shook her head in disbelief. But Nimue continued: "The mastermind of this scheme was the one person in Camelot who most hated Sir Tristram, the one person with the blood of the Irish king in her veins, and who therefore sought revenge on Sir Tristram for killing the Marhault in single combat and ending Ireland's rebellion against Cornwall. The Lady Elaine."

Before Nimue reached the end of her accusation, the Lady Elaine rose from her seat and tried to rush off the dais. How exactly she thought she could get away in that crowded throne room, or slip away unnoticed when she was sitting in front of three hundred people—or, for that matter, where she thought she could possibly go—was a mystery to me. I suppose it was an instinctive desire to run from the danger she was in, and involved no thinking at all, but she did not get far. My Lady Rosemounde, who was already standing, stepped quickly and purposefully into Lady Elaine's path. Rosemounde's jaw was set and her eyes were burning, and she had the determined look of one who had escaped once from disaster and was not about to be put back into it. When she came face to face with Rosemounde, Lady Elaine tried to duck around to Rosemounde's right, whereupon my lady reared her right arm back and brought her open palm around at full speed, catching the Lady Elaine full force in the face. Elaine's head snapped back and she fell, shaken, to the floor of the dais. Two knights present dragged Elaine to her feet. Demurely, the Lady Rosemounde smoothed out her skirts and primly reseated herself to hear the rest of Nimue's revelations.

"But the chief villain here," Nimue continued, "whose principal motivation was to impress his lover and, in part, to hurt a knight he perceived as an enemy of his master, is the squire who murdered his accomplice, Sir Sagramore. The same squire who actually raped Bess of Caerleon: Bertrand of Toledo!"

Many in the throne room gasped. Heads swung around to where people had seen Bertrand standing only moments earlier.

Nimue turned her eyes to the same spot. It was empty.

I let out a little gasp myself. I had kept my eye on the figure in the crowd during the entire proceedings, only glancing at the dais on occasion to watch the more interesting developments, but I admit that when my Lady Rosemounde took that wide swing and flattened Lady Elaine, I focused all my attentions on that brief melee. When I turned back to the object of my watch, like Nimue, I was startled into action.

"Where is Bertrand of Toledo?" Nimue cried. "He must be caught!"

"Find him!" the queen commanded as she stood up. "He's a killer and a rapist! Bring him to this court!" She was not about to forget that, according to the king's own word, it was she and she alone who had jurisdiction in this case.

It took me only a moment to notice that the small door behind the king's throne was slightly ajar. Clearly Bertrand, once he saw the direction Nimue's testimony was about to take, had made his way unnoticed to the door, and bolted when the opportunity presented itself.

"He's gone out the king's door!" I cried, pointing to the exit, and several knights went dashing out of it to follow him.

Sir Gareth was quick to move. "With me!" he ordered, and Colgrevaunce and I were on his heels as he sprinted out of the hall and outside. He didn't have to tell me his concern. It was unlikely Robin and the guard would have watched the king's door closely. It led only in two directions, one of them for about forty meters along a narrow path between the great hall and the outer wall of the castle and from there into the king's private solar. That door would be under heavy guard and was almost certainly locked. The only other choice of exit was a narrow stair leading up to the battlements. Bertrand had surely gone that way, but to what end? He couldn't hide up there on the castle wall itself.

We dashed out the door and I looked to the wall. I saw no one along it, but Gareth shouted to Robin, "Train your arrows on the wall! Bertrand of Toledo has escaped along the battlements."

"He must have headed for the barbican!" Colgrevaunce called out, and we ran in that direction, with Robin and several of his men at our heels. A shout from the guard tower above the gate made it clear Colgrevaunce was right. In our revelation of the truth of Bess's assault and Sir Sagramore's murder, we had counted on the element of surprise: We expected to catch Bertrand off guard, surround him, and disarm him in the throne room, keeping the archers outside just in case he forced his way to the door. We hadn't counted on someone with a well-organized escape plan. In retrospect, maybe we should have. This was a calculating rapist who was ready to let an innocent man be hanged for his offense, a cold-blooded killer who had lured a doughty knight to a secret place and murdered him, hiding his body in an archery butt. How could we think he would not have an escape route well thought out in advance of his accusation?

Before we knew he was gone, Bertrand had been out the king's door and up the steps, running at top speed along the wall while the rest of us were still trying to figure out which way he went. By the time Sir Gareth, Colgrevaunce, and I were shouting to Robin to watch the battlements, Bertrand had already surprised the guard in the gate tower and, as we discovered, had rushed past them and leaped from the tower's opening onto the drawbridge, which he somehow knew—or guessed—would be open.

"Stop that man!" Robin shouted to the guard in the tower, who was knocked over by Bertrand's well-aimed thrust as he ran through. By the time the four of us arrived at the gate, Bertrand had whistled for his horse, which he had left just on the other side of the moat to facilitate his escape, and was riding off at a reckless gallop.

By now the guard in the tower and two of Robin's archers on the ground had notched their arrows and let fly, but Bertrand's speed and the shelter of the trees through which he was riding made it nearly impossible to hit his retreating back.

"He will not get away!" I heard Colgrevaunce growl on my left. In a kind of berserk madness, he began to chase after the fleeing horse, his sword held high. "Not after what he did to Bess!" I shook my head for a moment, and then I noticed, standing in a clearing on top of the hill toward which Bertrand was galloping, a knight in full armor riding a powerful black destrier.

By now I could see that Bertrand, too, had noticed the armored knight on top of the hill. The knight watched Bertrand ascend the slope, then turned his horse toward the squire, proffered his lance, and moved slowly but steadily toward Bertrand's horse. Bertrand pulled on his reins, looking back over his shoulder as his horse reared up. Behind him he could see Colgrevaunce, closing the gap between them and waving his sword in the air, still crying out, "Stand and fight, you coward! Recreant! Rapist! Fight me or admit yourself a loathsome craven!"

Bertrand could not bring himself to face the knight on the black horse, and was unwilling to stand up to Colgrevaunce, who seemed to be in a kind of battle frenzy. After a split second's thought, Bertrand broke to his right, thinking to outrun the black destrier and make his escape that way. Suddenly, a bright flash burst directly in Bertrand's path, followed by a loud explosion. Bertrand's horse reared and bolted, throwing Bertrand from his back and galloping off at full speed.

I turned around. Gareth, Robin, and I had been joined on the drawbridge by Guinevere, Florent, Nimue, Rosemounde, Bess, and about a dozen other knights and ladies, including—his arm extended in the direction of the explosion—my lord

Merlin. "I did mention that I was a magician, did I not?" he said.

"About time you showed up, old man," I chided him. "I thought I was going to have to do everything myself!"

"Well, if that were the case," Merlin replied, "I'd simply have to do everything over again, to fix your blunders, you dolt of a Cornishman. Now, what does your friend think he's doing out there?"

"I think he thinks he's saving the day," I replied.

"Ah," Merlin said. "A romantic."

Chapter Eighteen:
Triumph and Tragedy

The knight on the black horse put up his lance, watching what was occurring a hundred yards in front of him. Several of Robin's archers knelt and notched their arrows, but Robin held up his hand, saying, "Hold your fire! But keep him in your sights."

By now Bertrand of Toledo had picked himself up and shaken off his fall, only to find Colgrevaunce advancing on him at full speed brandishing his short sword. With a grim smile Bertrand raised his own weapon of choice, his crossbow, armed it quickly but efficiently with a bolt, and took aim. Colgrevaunce was now within twenty yards of his quarry and closing fast, forcing Bertrand to rush his shot. Colgrevaunce, facing that bolt, feinted to his left and then dived to his right. Bertrand's bolt sailed over Colgrevaunce's lunging body, missing him by inches. Colgrevaunce rolled and bounded up, continuing his onslaught while Bertrand fumbled to load another bolt. He had no time to take careful aim before Colgrevaunce was upon him, cursing him for a coward and a murderer. But Bertrand did have time to loose his shot, and by some stroke of luck it lodged firmly in Colgrevaunce's left thigh. With a cry of pain, Colgrevaunce went down, but not before he swung his short sword in a mighty upward arch, sending the crossbow flying into the air in several pieces.

As Colgrevaunce fell to the ground Bertrand drew a rapier from the sheath on his belt. He thrust at Colgrevaunce, but from the ground Colgrevaunce rolled and parried. As he struggled to his feet, Colgrevaunce managed to ward off another of Bertrand's thrusts, and set himself as best he could, though he was clearly favoring his injured leg. Now Colgrevaunce had some stability to parry the mad thrusts of his enemy, but he had no mobility at all, and Bertrand could dance around him all day, looking for an opening on Colgrevaunce's flank or back.

Or, of course, Bertrand could have run. His horse had bolted but he still might be able to dash off into the woods, though Robin's archers might well have felled him as he ran, and the knight on the black warhorse stood ready to ride him down. Indeed, it was hard to imagine what Bertrand thought he would do once he defeated Colgrevaunce. For all the time this mortal combat was taking place, Merlin, Gareth, and I, with Robin and his archers, and the queen and her party (including her knights, several of whom were armed), had been making our way toward the battle, and by now were encircling the combatants.

"Yield while you can, Bertrand of Toledo!" the queen commanded.

"Throw yourself on the queen's mercy!" Merlin called out.

Bertrand laughed as he circled Colgrevaunce, toying with him, making little thrusts from behind and from the side. "Ha! That's rich. The king has already condemned the rapist to death. But they can only hang me once, so I'm taking this fool of a squire with me. Clumsy fool." He spat his venom at Colgrevaunce. "Before they all have at me, I'm going to pierce you just like I pierced that little serving wench of yours!"

Bertrand had reared back to thrust again, but an inarticulate roar escaped from Colgrevaunce at that last taunt, and he knocked Bertrand's rapier away with an upward sweep of his sword. Then, straightening himself, he swung the sword from the greatest height he could reach, straight down on Bertrand's shoulder with all the force of his burning rage. A soft sigh escaped Bertrand's lips as the crunch of shattering bone accompanied the sound of his left arm dropping in a bloody pool at Colgrevance's feet.

It was probably a mercy Bertrand was unconscious before he hit the ground. As he lay on his back, blood spewing from his shoulder, Colgrevaunce put the heel of his boot on Bertrand's face and held the point of his sword against the fallen squire's neck, ready to end what remained of Bertrand's life. But Colgrevaunce remembered his chivalry. His sword poised over the vanquished squire's throat, Colgrevaunce raised his head and found among the bystanders the one face he sought.

"My lady Bess," he called out. "What is your will? Shall this beast die on my sword, or do you want him spared?"

Bess was taken completely aback. She turned red and looked around, realizing that all eyes in that great circle were on her. Her face betrayed inner turmoil as she thought about all that had happened to her and all that had transpired this day. She looked back into Colgrevaunce's eyes, glanced down at Bertrand's quivering body, and shook her head slowly. "No," she said in a voice barely above a whisper. "Let him live, if he can."

Colgrevaunce put up his sword and sheathed it, stepped off Bertrand and toward Bess, falling down on one knee before her, the grimace on his face revealing the pain his wounded leg was causing him. "At your command, my lady," he said. Several of the other assembled knights looked at one another and smirked or rolled their eyes at Colgrevaunce's treating the lowborn Bess as if she were a lady-in-waiting to the queen. While four of the knights picked up Bertrand's bleeding husk and carried him back toward the castle, Colgrevaunce went on speaking to Bess, his head down. "I beg your forgiveness, my lady Bess. This outrage never would have happened to you if I had been with you on that terrible night in the forest. I hold myself a craven and recreant, for my duty and service should have been yours from the first. I do not ask your thanks or even your forgiveness, but only your mercy." At this he drew his sword again and placed it before him like a cross.

Bess, clearly bewildered by this language, and turning redder with mortification as all eyes focused on her again, shook her head, not knowing how to respond. Then she turned to the queen, who stood directly beside her. "Y . . . Your Grace," she stammered in a low voice. "May I speak?"

"By all means, Bess, you are the chief plaintiff here. Your wrongs have been righted now, I presume?"

Bess looked up, puzzled, into Guinevere's eyes. She said nothing for a moment, searching for the words that would make her feelings clear to the nobles who stood around her. "Oh no, my lady. How could such wrongs ever be made right? Will I have my maidenhood back? Will I live again without fear and find joy in a walk in the woods? There is some justice in this squire's punishment for his crimes, I suppose. But beggin' your pardon ma'am—sorry, I mean Your Grace—what is marred shall always remain marred.

"But what I want, my lady, is to speak of what Sir Florent said in the throne room . . ." At that, she looked across the circle to where Florent stood, and gave him a sad, twisted smile. "I beg your pardon, your honor, for the grief I caused you by charging you falsely. It was an honest mistake." Sir Florent nodded to her in charity, and she continued. "What my lord Florent said was that women want only to have control of their own person. That they want to be able to choose for themselves. Well, that's true, and you know it just as well as I do if you'll admit the truth of it, beggin' your pardon again if I've said amiss. I may not be noble-born like the rest of you ladies here, but I want to claim that same right. I want to choose. If I'm what you call the chief plaintiff here, as you say, Your Grace, then what I demand is the choice of my own way. And my choice is this: This man risked his life for my sake. He comes from some high lineage, I'm sure, and I know I'm just the daughter of a carpenter from Caerleon, and so nobody as far as some of your court minions is concerned," and with that she glanced toward the knight who had smirked at Colgrevaunce earlier. "But I've never been a liar or a cheat. I've never stole from anybody. I've never hurt anybody. And until the night I was raped, I ain't never been with any man. I go to church and I pay my tithes. I know a lot of you gentles, begging your pardons, my fine lords and ladies, can't say the same. About any of it. So what I'm wondering is, what is it makes you so noble, eh? I reckon I'm as noble as the next one, and I reckon I've got a right to what Sir Florent said. I've got a right to my own choice. And my own choice is Colgrevaunce. I want to marry him. Beggin' your pardon, Your Grace."

Colgrevaunce looked stunned, and the highborn knights and ladies, as well as Robin and his archers, stared at one another in surprised silence. By now Colgrevaunce had regained his composure and responded—but to the queen. "Your Majesty, I desire what Bess desires. If she will have me, no man in Camelot, noble or commoner, could be happier. But I fear my father may not approve this match . . ."

"*My* father can go whistle up a well if he thinks he's going to stand in my way," Bess stated matter-of-factly.

"Your parents will both give their consent," the queen responded. "I will see to it. And if either of them makes any difficulty for me, the king shall know of it. For know this, all of you: Sir Florent has shown us what women most desire, and that desire stems from what they do not have: the freedom of choice God gave to all. If women are wed to those they cannot love, how does that help the commonwealth? Is it not simply a recipe for adultery?" With that she turned red, and I knew it was not Bess she was thinking of. But she concluded, "This marriage shall occur at my command, for it grows from the findings in my court of justice, the court the king granted me."

"Thank you, Your Grace," Bess whispered. Colgrevaunce took her hand and held it to his lips, and then two other knights helped him to his feet. With their aid, he limped back toward the castle to have his wound attended to. Bess followed close behind.

When I looked up, I saw that the knight on the black destrier had ambled in and stopped directly outside the circle, near Nimue. He led a great white horse with him, and said—not surprisingly, in Sir Launfal's voice—"Here is the stallion, my Lady Nimue." For indeed, it was Snowfax.

Guinevere looked at Nimue, who stood directly to her left, then followed Nimue's blue eyes as they focused on Sir Florent, standing on the right side of the circle next to his uncle Gareth. "This horse was meant for you, Sir Florent. It was my gift to you, stolen by Bertrand of Toledo," Nimue said. "It is now restored to you."

Florent seemed bewildered, but stammered his response, "I . . . I thank you my lady. But . . . I don't understand. It is a marvelous destrier, but why are you giving it to me?"

Nimue pursed her lips and looked down. It was Sir Launfal, putting up the visor of his helmet the better to be clearly heard, who answered. "When the Lady of the Lake chose me," he said, "she gave me a bottomless purse. Nimue knows you have plenty of wealth, as the heir to Sir Gawain and ultimately King Lot. But there are only a few of these pure white stallions in Logres, and all of them are owned by my Lady, the Lady of the Lake. That is why Nimue chose this gift."

"Chose *you*? Then Nimue . . . ?"

It was the queen Nimue now addressed, not looking at Sir Florent at all. "Your majesty," she pleaded. "I taught Sir Florent the answer to your quest, and in return he promised on his honor as a knight that he would give me whatever I asked him. Of course, he did not know I was Damsel of the Lake under my hood and cloak, but that should make no difference. Following the lead of the bold Mistress Bess of Caerleon, let me here declare that my desire is for Sir Florent."

"It means leaving the court," Sir Launfal interjected. "It means living in a palace under woman's sovereignty. It means defending that castle against any outside threat. And it means, essentially, living away from the world. Almost like a monk."

"Well," Sir Gareth called out, as Sir Florent seemed too tongue-tied to speak. "You make it sound so appealing! How could my nephew possibly turn down such an offer?"

"He must know what he is getting himself into if he agrees to this," Sir Launfal stated with emphasis.

"Then tell us," Gareth continued, "what is in it for him?"

"Me," said Nimue.

"Bliss," said Sir Launfal.

The queen was quick to intervene. "Our nephew is previously betrothed to the Lady Rosemounde of Brittany. His father, the heir of King Lot of Orkney, arranged this marriage with Duke Hoel of Brittany, and my lord the king has given the match his blessing. I cannot allow this proposal to break an engagement already settled on."

"I beg your pardon, Your Grace," Nimue answered, with confidence and restrained politeness. She raised her brown eyes to the queen and declared with self-assurance, "My Lady of the Lake makes a special effort to assist and protect my Lord Arthur's realm. This she does because she recognizes that in the everyday world of men, Camelot and its code of chivalry represent the highest aspirations of human beings. But my Lady is not a subject of your king. The Lady governs her own world of Faerie. She weaves her enchantments in ways no mortal can equal, and her realm does not strive for perfection, as Arthur's does; it *is* perfection. She does not follow the king's commands. I am of her realm, Your Grace, and I do not recognize this betrothal. My own interest in Sir Florent goes back years. I have observed him at his prayers, at his lessons, at his practice with the sword and the lance. I know his purity of heart, his devotion to chivalry, his striving for the ideal. That is why I have loved him. That is why I want him with me in Avalon, and that is why I believe he will choose to come with me."

Listening to that, I hung my head. Many a time I had ridiculed Sir Florent for his priggishness, for his being little mister perfect, but I could admit to myself now that all that was mainly envy. I looked at the queen and saw that she was not a little put out by Nimue's tone.

"My husband," she said coolly, "may have a different interpretation of the Lady's relationship."

"Be that as it may," Nimue tossed back, "there is little he can do but bluff and bluster. But I do not think he will do so. What the Lady does, she does. What the Lady knows, she knows. Who the Lady protects, no man may harm. The Lady now, through me, offers that protection to Sir Florent, if he will accept it. The choice, as he himself indicated in his earlier judgment, is his and mine alone."

Sir Florent had drunk all of this in. He remained silent and pensive for a few more moments, then looked at Sir Gareth. "My father and my uncles, my cousin the king, no one could feel more loyalty to them than I. But I know they are human, and have human flaws. And as Nimue has said, I strive for perfection. To live the ideal—that would be a joy beyond my dearest wish. Only one tie of honor binds me: my promise to the Lady Rosemounde. I could not now break that promise without feeling myself dishonored, and that I could never bear."

Rosemounde, whose head had hung low since this entire conversation began (whether out of embarrassment or anger or jealousy, I couldn't say), now looked up toward Sir Florent with something like appreciation in her eyes. But Nimue was not so easily put off.

"Ask her."

Florent gazed toward Rosemounde. Rosemounde waited expectantly. In the hushed silence that followed, Sir Florent probed his betrothed with a simple phrase: "My lady?"

The sun had crept to a height in the heavens that cast shadows of the surrounding trees over some of the figures in the circle, and Rosemounde stood directly in the center of the darkest of these. In the gloom her face remained impassive, but it was not her face. Gone were the playful crinkles in the corners of her eyes, gone the sly upturned corner of her teasing mouth. There was nothing of my own Lady Rosemounde in that visage. "Go," she responded. "I will not be a second choice. If you want to go with this woman, do so. I release you from any promise you ever made to me. Follow your inclinations. Follow them with your honor intact. And I will forget any bond ever existed between us."

I have to say, if I were Florent, I couldn't have felt very good about that send-off. But I guess he was too enamored of the Damsel Nimue to take much note of Rosemounde's tone.

Without another word, Sir Florent swung himself up into the saddle of the great white charger. Once astride the horse, he turned to Sir Gareth and nodded courteously. "Uncle," he began, "you are the best of my kin. Keep my father and your brothers from any further outrage. I believe you can. And Your Grace," he turned now toward Guinevere. "I thank you for your generosity in my trial. I appreciate the faith you had in my innocence. But I can no longer live in a court where my virtue is given the lie in this way. Give my best to King Arthur, and please tell him there is no other earthly king I would follow. But I have gone to seek higher things." With that he turned his horse, and the Damsel Nimue mounted behind him. On their pure black and white destriers, Sharka and Snowfax, Sir Launfal and Sir Florent trotted off up the hill and disappeared over the ridge, moving on toward the palace of the Lady of the Lake.

There was nothing left to see, and we all began to make our way, by twos and threes, back toward the castle. As Sir Gareth brushed by me, he muttered, "How the blazes I'm going to explain *this* to Gawain, I haven't got a clue." He stopped to look down at me for half a moment, and then said, "Well, the case is over now, I guess. At least I'll be able to have my squire back. Catch up with me tomorrow morning. We need to go hunting. Or hawking. Or something. Just get me out of here for a while." And with that Gareth passed by toward the castle.

The queen, too, was resigned. "Gawain?" she muttered. "What on earth am I going to tell the king? Oh Gildas, you're the only person I can stand."

I rolled my eyes. "You always say that, Your Majesty. But you know it's not true."

"Some days it is, my boy," Guinevere countered. "This is one of those days. Why doesn't everyone just do what I say? They'd be so much happier."

"Their own choice, remember, Your Grace?" I answered.

"Yes, yes," she sighed. "Well it appears you and your friend, the old necromancer, have bailed out the crown once more. Give him my thanks, won't you? Right now he doesn't seem in the mood to talk."

I looked over to where Merlin stood alone, gazing in the direction in which Nimue had disappeared. I saw only his back from where I stood, but it was bent with the weight of the world on it, and the old man did not appear desirous of company.

"But your Lady Rosemounde," the queen continued. "It appears she is free again. I don't know what guardian angel watches over you, young Gildas of Cornwall, but he seems to have preserved your Rosemounde for you once more. I advise you to take this chance and do something with it, or you're a complete idiot." And with that, Queen Guinevere went on her way back to Camelot, joined by the few remaining knights that had helped form our circle.

Like Merlin, Rosemounde stood looking after the vanished figures of Sir Florent and the Damsel Nimue. Her stony face had not changed, but I screwed up my courage and approached her. She seemed to feel my presence even as I came toward her from behind. "Did you ever imagine, Gildas, that this would be the outcome when I asked you to look into the rape of Bess of Caerleon?"

"My lady, no one could have imagined how this all turned out."

"Have I lost my honor, Gildas? For a girl to be put aside as I have been—will there not be questions from future suitors? Why should Sir Florent have cast me off, they'll all want to know."

"My Lady Rosemounde, anyone who knows the story will have no such questions. But my lady, you will never have any shortage of suitors." I looked into her bottomless dark eyes and was near to losing myself in them. "There is one in particular who would never give up his suit for any reason."

Rosemounde turned her stony features to me and said, without apparent emotion, "Your feelings for me will not make any difference, Gildas." After a short pause, she lowered her eyes and added, "Nor mine for you."

"But why, my lady?" I pleaded. "If Bess of Caerleon can choose her own husband . . . if Nimue can defy the queen and make her own choice . . . why should you not make your own choice too? I love you, you know I do, and I feel certain that . . . that you . . ."

She closed her eyes with some impatience. "Neither Bess nor

Nimue is the daughter of the Duke of Brittany. Duke Hoel will arrange my marriage with the next most eligible bachelor in King Arthur's family, now that Florent is out of reach. And I'll have to do it. Because I'm special. I'm a princess."

"My lady, my lady, my lady . . ." I begged her again. "I'm learning chivalry. I'm sure to be knighted soon. Can your father truly stand in the way, if you want it? If the queen intervenes?"

"The queen will not intervene, Gildas. I'm sorry. It's naïve. The queen will do—must do—what is politically advantageous to the realm. She will not step in if my father opposes the match."

I had already resigned myself to the fact that Rosemounde was betrothed to Florent. For an instant I had allowed myself the slim hope that maybe . . . just maybe . . . I could still win her. But whatever hope I thought I had, she was murdering now with that face of stone.

"Run away with me," I begged her, only half-joking. "We can go . . . somewhere. Cornwall? Even Ireland? Love is all that truly matters, isn't it?"

I'm glad I said it. For one thing, I meant it. But more important, I actually put a crack in Rosemounde's flinty demeanor. She focused her dark eyes on me, actually seeing me, I think, for the first time today. "Yes," she answered. "It's nice to tell ourselves that, isn't it?" And the corner of her mouth turned up in a half-hearted smirk, enough to make me believe that the Rosemounde I knew was still in there, somewhere.

With that she slowly moved toward the drawbridge, leaving me standing in that clearing with the only figure still left.

Merlin.

He looked like a boulder beaten by the tides off the Cornwall coast: bare, bleak, alone. His long gray hair lay disheveled about his shoulders and his shaggy eyebrows quivered as his blinking eyes fought back tears. His chin rested on his chest, which heaved with slow sighs, making his long beard rise and fall like a wounded animal.

I stepped to him and took his arm. "Come on, old man," I said to him softly. "Lean on me and I'll help you to your cave."

As one in a trance, Merlin did as he was told. We walked in silence for a few moments before he finally spoke. "I knew she was not mine," he rasped. "And I could live with that. As long as she was no one else's."

"Tell me about it," I murmured.

"It makes it final. It makes it real."

"Does this mean you're feeling one of your moods coming on?"

"One of my moods?" the old necromancer responded. "No, not just another of those. One, I think, that may last for quite a long time."

I hated to think of him sunk in depression, buried in his cave, for weeks, or months. Or maybe, in this case, years. "You're needed around the castle, though. Don't you realize that? How would this murder and rape ever have been solved if you hadn't been there to figure it out?"

"You'd have done it yourself, dunce," Merlin told me. "From the beginning you did more in this case than I did. No, I'll not leave my cave again."

"What will you have there? Your books? You know them all by heart. Nimue will not be stopping by to play chess with you now . . ."

"God's aching heart, Gildas, you propose to cure the disease by killing the patient? I know she won't be coming. But you will. You will come and pester me, and play chess with me, and bring me any new books that you can, and you'll try to rouse me out of myself. And maybe you'll succeed once in a while. But leave me alone now. I want to be left alone."

With that he stopped leaning on my shoulder and shook his

cloak as if he was shaking years of dust from it as he shook off my touch. "Get away now. Get back to your silly castle and play at being one of them. I know better."

Leaning on his staff, he stalked toward the brook that ran by his cave, determined, I knew, to hole up there for the foreseeable future. I couldn't blame him. For all the hope that Rosemounde had given me, I saw little purpose in pursuing my course toward knighthood. But I still had some hope in spite of all that. Merlin was a lot older. Maybe he'd outgrown hope. But I hadn't. At least not yet.

EPILOGUE

The old monk's last words echoed softly in the cloisters as he finished his story just as he finished his walk. The late afternoon sun cast long shadows from the trees as he looked out over the grove within the cloister walls. Five of the younger monks trailed after him, hanging on his words. Brother Gildas, forty years a monk here at Saint Dunstan's Abbey, was a favorite of the order's newest members, for they all loved hearing him spin his fantastic yarns about the legendary King Arthur, dead at least two decades before any of them was born. Maybe it wasn't the prescribed lesson for this particular saint's day, but the abbott and the prior turned a blind eye toward Gildas's entertainment of the young brothers, first because he had been in the abbey longer than they or anyone else, and second because he was a popular mentor for the new pledges, and his tales were not, after all, irreligious or provocative. Besides, they remembered him telling them the same stories years ago when they themselves were new postulants.

But Brother Gildas's audience noted how subdued he was at the end of this particular tale. He looked pensive, and each of the young monks knew this story had taken a good deal out of their aged brother.

"But Brother Gildas," the youngest of them began, scratching his newly tonsured head beneath his golden blond curls. "What happened to Bertrand of Toledo? Did the king condemn him?"

Brother Gildas gave him a half-smile. "It never did come to

that," he explained. "The king may actually have been in a mood to pardon him for the rape, since Bess herself had asked that he not be killed. But the blood of Sir Sagramore was a different matter altogether. It cried for justice. But Colgrevaunce had done enough damage to make that sentence unnecessary. Though he withheld the final blow, Bertrand died three days later of his wounds."

"And Colgrevaunce?" the blond boy pursued. "Did he marry Bess? Did they live happily ever after?" And with that he blushed, as the other young monks snickered at the childish expression.

"They married and they were happy," Brother Gildas said, his smile broadening. "As happy as married people ever are. He doted on her, and she remained always grateful that he loved her, and that he had taken her out of her father's house. Colgrevaunce was knighted the next year, but he was never rich. And, of course, he always limped after that battle with Bertrand. Still, they were happy together and they had enough. But ever after? That can never be. We lost Colgrevaunce in the Quest of the Grail. But that's another story. Bess mourned until the day she died—and that was many years."

The oldest of the youths at eighteen, the red-headed monk with the thin beginning of a beard, chimed in: "What of Sir Tristram? Did his enemies ever succeed in ruining him?"

Brother Gildas winced at that memory. "Indeed, Sir Tristram could not dodge his fate forever. He died in the arms of his wife, the second Isolde, but at the hands of his enemies. But that too is another story."

"The L-lady El-l-laine," asked the dark-eyed monk with the stammer. "What b-became of her?"

"Ah," Brother Gildas said authoritatively. "Now her case did come before the king. And she was found guilty of conspiracy and of aiding and abetting a murder and an assault. It may come as no surprise to you that the Lady Elaine, as it turned out, was the agent of King Mark sent to Camelot to assassinate Sir Tristram. That she was a woman saved her, though. The king exiled her, casting her out of the kingdom, never to return on pain of death. She returned to Ireland, where I believe she finally married a minor landholder loosely related to the Irish royal house, who lived in the middle of nowhere, and, I think, used to beat her. I remember I felt no sympathy for her when I heard that. May God forgive me for my lack of charity," and Brother Gildas crossed himself, briefly remembering that he was, after all, in a house of God.

The young monk with the large ears that made him look like a frightened hare asked timidly, "And Nimue and Sir Florent? Were they together for good? Did Sir Florent never regret his decision?"

Brother Gildas looked down and knit his brows together. "Sir Florent never returned to Camelot. At least not permanently. He came to the court after his father's death, in order to attend the funeral, but that was in the middle of Arthur's last great war, and Florent would not take part in that. He could sometimes be seen hunting in the forest around Caerleon, or riding with Sir Launfal through the woods at night, keeping watch over the castle as part of the Lady of the Lake's protection of Arthur and his kingdom. But Nimue never again came to visit Merlin. The old man pined for her the rest of his life. And as he asked, I did visit him regularly to play chess with him, and occasionally to bring him new books. I remember the queen giving me the manuscript of the *Tale of Sir Orfeo* to bring him, but he was depressed by its depiction of the land of Faerie. But he did sometimes help out in Camelot when he was needed. I worked with him again on cases at the queen's request."

"So . . ." the redheaded youth asked, "Merlin did not die of grief, then?"

"No one dies of grief," Gildas told him patiently. "Men have killed themselves because of their grief. But death comes at their own hand. And Merlin did die. They are all dead now. Guinevere. Gareth. Tristram. The king himself. All gone. Gone before I entered Saint Dunstan's. Gone more than forty years."

"And Rosemounde? Is she dead too?" the young blond asked, flinching when Big Ears elbowed him for his lack of sensitivity.

"Rosemounde?" Brother Gildas answered, his eyes glazing over. "No. Not Rosemounde. She still lives."

The five younger monks looked surprised, and murmured among themselves. No one dared ask for more information. It was certainly believable—likely, in fact—that if Gildas had survived the downfall of the Round Table and had lived here at Saint Dunstan's for four decades, certainly Rosemounde, who was his own age, could have done the same. Who knew? Perhaps she was married. Perhaps she had entered the convent of Saint Mary Magdalene outside of Caerleon. Perhaps she had followed Florent to live with the Lady of the Lake. But this did not seem to be the time to pester Brother Gildas for details.

The bells of the abbey began to chime, calling the monks to the holy office of none. In silence the five youngsters walked off briskly toward the church. Brother Gildas followed far more slowly, and took the time to be with his own thoughts while he walked. Those thoughts, most naturally, were with the Lady Rosemounde. Rosemounde, whose body had long ago turned to dust in her tiny grave outside of Camelot, had never really died. As long as Brother Gildas was alive to keep her memory fresh, she still lived through him. That was, after all, the reason for these stories he told all the new monks year after year. She was as vivid in his mind and his heart as she had been in the old days. And somehow he thought, or he hoped, that he could resurrect her in the imaginations of those young brothers whose minds he filled with her image.

"Good day, my Lady Rosemounde," Brother Gildas whispered to himself as he walked somberly through the church door. "I must sing for my supper now." And with that he saw, as vividly as if she were standing there with him, the corner of her mouth twist upward in a little smirk. "Until tomorrow, then," he heard the answering whisper.

AUTHOR'S NOTE

Readers of Chaucer will immediately recognize the basic plot of this novel as the Wife of Bath's Tale. While the motif of the Loathly Lady and the quest to find what women want most is widespread in the late Middle Ages, Chaucer's is the only version in which the protagonist is an accused rapist. In John Gower's analog of the tale, the knight on the quest is in fact Sir Florent. In two later fifteenth-century versions, the hero is Sir Gawain himself, rather than his son.

The tale as Chaucer tells it may have originally been a Breton lay—a type of short romance, often with magical or faery elements, believed to be based on earlier Celtic legends and spread by minstrels from Brittany. Two other tales related within the novel—the story of Launfal (or Lanval), which originates as a twelfth-century lay told by Marie de France, and the story of Sir Orfeo—also seem to have begun as Breton lays.

Gildas, the name of the novel's narrator, is actually the name of a sixth-century monk famous for composing a history called *De Excidio et Conquestu Britanniae* ("On the Ruin and Conquest of Britain"), which is the first text alluding to battles between the Celtic Britons and the Saxons usually associated with the figure of Arthur. Other aspects of the novel—Tristram's love for Isolde and his rivalry with Sir Palomides, the background of Gawain and his brothers' feud with Sir Lamorak, Merlin's love for the nymph Nimue—all stem chiefly from Thomas Malory's authoritative fifteenth-century compendium of Arthurian legend known as *Le Morte Darthur.*

Modern readers may be a bit confused by the use of canonical hours to report time in the novel. At the time in which the story is set, most people thought of the day as divided by the hours of divine office which they could hear announced by church bells. There were eight of these hours or offices: Assuming a day in spring or fall, with approximately equal twelve-hour periods of day and night, the office of *prime* would occur around sunrise, about six a.m. according to modern notions of time. The next office, *terce,* would be sung around nine a.m., *sext* would be around noon, *none* at about three p.m., *vespers* at six p.m., *compline* about nine p.m., *matins* at midnight, and *lauds* around three a.m. These are the approximate times for events in the novel.

Though I have kept heraldic terms to a minimum, I should explain briefly some of the terms I do use. Two aspects of a coat of arms are *tincture* (the colors used in the crest) and *attitude* (the stance taken by a heraldic animal). In describing the shields in Chapter Three, I use the heraldic tinctures *gules* (red), *sable* (black), *or* (gold), *azure* (blue), *argent* (silver), and *purpure* (purple). I also describe the animals in the attitudes *rampant* (when the animal is standing erect in profile, raising its forepaws), *sejant* (when the animal is sitting on its haunches with its forepaws on the ground), and *regardant* (when the animal's head is turned backward, as if looking over its shoulder).

ABOUT THE AUTHOR

Jay Ruud is Chair of the English Department at the University of Central Arkansas. In addition to *Fatal Feast*, the first book in this series of Merlin mysteries, he is the author of *"Many a Song and Many a Leccherous Lay": Tradition and Individuality in Chaucer's Lyric Poetry* (1992), the *Encyclopedia of Medieval Literature* (2006), *A Critical Companion to Dante* (2008), and *A Critical Companion to Tolkien* (2011). He has taught at UCA for twelve years, prior to which he was Dean of the College of Arts and Sciences at Northern State University in South Dakota. He has a PhD in Medieval Literature from the University of Wisconsin-Milwaukee, has newly sprouted twin grandsons and two other grandchildren, in addition to three dogs and a cat who resents them. Further, he is a long-suffering Chicago Cubs fan who believes that the Cubs will win a World Series in his lifetime.